A TWIST OF DREAMS

The Marked Chronicles: Book 1

REMY STEROSS

Paperback ISBN: 979-8-9986209-0-4

Hardcover ISBN: 979-8-9986209-1-1

Ebook ASIN: B0F4Q55754

Book Cover by Peter Ahern

Illustrations by @chocological.art

Developmental Edits and Line Edits: Kelly Hammond from Pickles Literary LLC

Copy Edits: Tabitha Chandler from Tabitha Does Editing

Contents

Content Warning

Your mental health is important to us. Although we would not call this book a dark fantasy, it does touch on some sensitive topics, including:

-Violence and gore

-Death

-Parental death

-Talk of child death

-Graphic description of physical trauma and pain

-Consensual explicit sex

-Consensual explicit sex with multiple partners

-Voyeurism

If you feel that any of these topics may be triggering for you, then we would encourage you read with caution or to hold off on reading this book.

~Remy Steross

For the friends who become our found family.
This story's for you.

Prologue

Sometimes, all the hiding makes it impossible not to think of her.

My mind floods with all of our lasts in the long, cold silence of solitude. The last time the softness of her palm slid against mine. The last time I saw the delight in her smile when she didn't even know I'd been staring at her. The last time I felt her heartbeat. It was a love that fuses souls. I knew I couldn't keep it—a life on the run is no life for an elven woman—but knowing doesn't ease the loss. A searing pain that burns as fresh as the day she was severed from me, twenty-seven years ago.

Still, I'd rather hide than endure one more second in the godforsaken cell I called home for so many years. I'm not sure my sanity would have survived it.

How much this world has changed since I walked its land freely. How much hate has taken over the very soil of our magick.

Once, the gods walked among us, their every touch imbued with magick. With the brush of their fingers, they shaped the world—flora, fauna, and elven kind. They spent many years crafting the perfect balance to ensure their creations thrived. And thrive we did. The world was full of such peace and prosperity that the gods were confident we could flourish without them. So they departed, seeking a new canvas for more divine creation. They stayed connected, offering guidance for a time. But guidance became prayer, and then prayer became myth. They did, however, leave behind a legacy, the tool to tap into their power. To each kingdom, they gifted a sapling. A small, unassuming tree destined to grow not just in stature but also in strength. Slowly, steadily, these trees flourished, enchanting our entire land with wondrous magick. Their essence fed the soil, the air, and the hearts of the people. The land still pulses with it, some of us wielding it powerfully, like soldiers of the gods themselves, and some happily dancing with the lighter sparkling *wifts*. Even those without magick are charmed with the land's favor—blessed with vitality and physical resilience.

It's the trees who choose *the* child. Crafted from the deepest roots, hundreds of centuries old, a gifted child is created for each of the realms. Born from their mother's womb, but connected to the gods by the essence of the tree. They carry a twist of both divine magick and elven blood. Unlike the other people of this world, this child's gift is attuned to the energy that courses throughout the land. As they grow, so too does their magick. Giving them the ability to nourish the sacred trees, keeping their energy and our lands brimming with magick, protecting the sacred balance.

Once that person was me.

How far I have fallen.

I shake my head before I lose any more time to my thoughts.

No matter how much time has passed, I've only ever been a half a step ahead of my captors. It's a wonder that I haven't been found again.

I can't help but think that the same gods—whose essence runs through my very veins—have shunned me. No matter the desperation of my plea, I'm met with silence. If only they would listen, they would forgive me for how I left.

I should have fought harder. I could have, but I let the Souls tear me apart—I wanted them to. As long as I was suffering, they still focused on me, and my people had a chance. It was my captors that destroyed me, not only my body, but my spirit and the connection to my magick. My once boundless power is now only an inkling of what it once was.

The pale yellows and oranges of the sun barely crest the horizon, the air already cooling against the wet stone walls of my current hideout—such a drab, cold dwelling. Nothing here anchors me, so I shouldn't feel any loss when I leave. But it weighs on me a little; it always does. A reminder that this is just one more corner of the realm I can't call home.

The cover of darkness beyond and the scent of fresh air pull me towards the mouth of the cave. My raven's talons descend upon my shoulder, pecking at the worn leather bag slung across my chest, looking for bread crumbs. I sift through my meager belongings and pull out my scraps. A caw echoes across the vast forest, cloaked in dark blues and deep browns, details fading by the moment. This gray dusk might as well be dawn to me now. I've turned into a nocturnal creature, only crawling from my hideout when the sun dips low, the shadows able to conceal me. I've grown accustomed to the sounds of the night, the chirping of crickets and hooting of owls. There's a notion that the night is eerie, quiet. But if you listen closely, the night sings its own song—a melody just for a lonely, hidden traveler like me.

Over the past few days, I've felt an overwhelming sense of restlessness. I've tried to excuse it with exhaustion or hunger, but this feels unnatural. A feeling that I need to *do* something, that someone is praying for my help. Could it be that my powers are returning? Or am I just so desperate that my mind is tricking itself?

I can't be of help to anyone in this state: older, magickless, forgotten.

The woods and I are so well acquainted that I swear it feels as though we move as one. Even in total darkness, I travel silently and unseen for hours. It's only when I start to notice the sun painting the forest awake that I decide to make my camp for the day. The woods offer me the perfect clearing; a tree with a massive trunk to rest against, its branches framing the swiftly brightening sky, covering me.

I pull out my tattered brown cloak and nestle into the roots' welcome embrace, my raven perched alongside me.

Sleep pulls me in faster than usual, but before I have completely drifted off, I hear a sound. It's loud, unmistakable, and one I haven't heard in nearly three hundred years: the desperate plea of a dying soul.

Chapter 1 Evelyn

"Fate weaves the story of every living soul, except yours, child. How you write your story will change even the gods."

I sense these words amidst utter nothingness, a void that lacks all sensation. I hear the words again, a remnant of a voice I swear I have heard before. I try to hold on to it, but it slips away like I'm waking from a dream.

At the edges of those words, something tangible and swirling is born before me, drawing me out of this strange emptiness. Before I can detect any recognizable form, I notice my own strained breathing. It feels like I've been running for hours. My lungs are imploding, my throat shredding with each heavy intake of breath, and yet, all sound is lost in this darkness. My lips split open, as frail as paper, and blood trickles into my mouth. As if sensation follows the trickling blood, I'm suddenly aware that my tongue is as rough as sand and tastes like metal, bile, and salt.

Everything is dulled, my mind surrounded by fog. I don't need total sensation to know that I'm naked and my whole body is trembling. *Convulsing*. With each shaky jerk, I'm yanked backwards, unable to move beyond my spasms.

"Oh, gods." I know I say this out loud. I can feel my torn and cracked lips make the words, but no sound reaches my ears.

Am I floating? Hanging? Am I restrained? Each new question is worse than the last. There is a ferocious wind whipping like arrows of ice piercing my taut skin, and still I hear nothing more than a muted hum. A metallic smell creeps into my growing pool of awareness. The scent of blood is rich and deep, bringing with it a brief glimpse of a memory. A room. A place entirely coated in the sticky crimson liquid. But just as quickly as it came, it's ripped away by these angry winds.

Despite the bitter chill, sweat pours down my neck, and a clammy wetness coats my body. My wrists and ankles are shackled, and there is a bar across my waist holding me to a black stone wall. I stretch my limbs for the ground beneath me, but I'm met with only air and the constant onslaught of the harsh, quiet wind. I pull on my bindings, my shackles tightening to the point of pain.

Screams tear from my lips, over and over, but only muffled echoes sing from my parched mouth. *Where in the Underworld is my voice?*

I blink. Blink. Blink. Blink.

With each flutter of my eyelids, the stinging wanes, and my vision begins to clear. The colors are all wrong; everything is muted gray. I strain to make out anything that will help me understand where I am. I can see my hands above me, raw and dripping with blood, like wax melting from a candle. I tilt my head down—my matted, golden hair spilling around my face—and track a fresh droplet of blood as it falls to my bare thigh. It slows just above a small heart-shaped, silver scar on the inside of my leg. It looks like it has been there for years, but I can't recall when it happened or how. Maybe it's just a trick of the light.

My eyes have adjusted enough that I notice just how badly the cold has leeched away all color from my complexion.

I'm surprised my nipples aren't black with frostbite.

A tangible scene begins to unfold around me, and what I see is far worse than hazy darkness. There are countless other elven people chained up and dangling from this obsidian wall. A wall that seems to stretch on until it fades into pulsing dark shadows that ebb and flow like waves, as if they are alive. Every time I look at them, they seem to be getting closer. If there's anything in front of me, I can't tell. It's like I'm trapped in a cocoon that only encompasses this damned wall.

Well, that's not terrifying at all.

Despair grows within me like a smoky black web. I thrash my head from side to side, willing my cries to get louder, to no avail. The jagged surface of the wall shreds my shoulders, my back, my thighs. My entire body feels bruised, torn, bloody, or burning. With one last strangled sob, I squeeze my eyes shut and take a deep breath.

Then, as if brought on by my deep exhale, it dawns on me.

No, no, no. I can't be there.

I've seen a wall just like this separating the Kingdoms. The darkness, the strange atmosphere, the undeniable terror. The whole thing is both hauntingly familiar and completely unknown.

This is the Grimm Lodge, in the Kingdom of Nightmare. Nightmare's prison. It's the residence of evil. It's the focus of countless scary stories and parents' empty threats to mischievous children. "No one goes near the kingdom's borders, no one! Lest they snatch you up and throw you in the Lodge." There is only death in the Lodge, or an eternity of gods know what. There is no escape.

I shouldn't be *here*. I should be in Daydream, far from anything like this.

I close my eyes and try to remember what brought me here. But I see nothing. It's like there are all these holes in my memories, and I can't trace one thought back to who I am or why I'm here. Surely I'd recall being thrown into a place worse than death.

"There's been a mistake!" Another shout reaching into the darkness like it's trapped under water—muted, wrong.

I keep tugging at my memories, but the more I try, the more a fog surrounds them. I see pieces, but I can't grasp a meaningful picture of who I am. My mind is a flurry of pointless stories, but not one purposeful thought about *me.*

I would never go beyond the Nightmare wall willingly. *Would I?*

The wall is menacing, with obsidian stones as black as a bottomless abyss. It has jagged edges that erupt from the earth, marring the pristine Daydream landscape. The magick is ravenous, constantly threatening to suck you into its void. It's said that anyone who has ever crossed over into the Kingdom of Nightmare has never been seen again.

That wall is built of stone identical to the stone I'm shackled to.

None of this leads to an answer for the burning question festering in my brain: *Why. Am. I. Here?* I try to suppress the surrounding elements and truly clear my mind.

Think. THINK.

The only thing that I can say for sure is that my name is Evelyn and I live in Daydream. But I can't follow a story beyond that. It's just gray. The feeling that the answers are just out of reach is almost as infuriating as this freezing cold.

If I could stop shaking for two seconds, I could figure out how to get out of here.

My neck nearly snaps as I look around. The mass of people chained to the wall are in the same predicament. Below me, the jagged peaks of the wall begin to soften. The crashing of waves wearing them down.

Water? Was it always there?

I'm suspended above a shoreline, the current an angry force pounding into the wall. So strange, both that these furious waves seem to have appeared from nothing, and that they make no sounds above a faint trickling whisper. There could be anything beneath those dark waves, endless depths, barnacles to shred my skin like a serpent's teeth, monsters.

I cannot fall.

The spray of the abyssal tempest coats my shredded flesh with a sting as harsh as amber coals. A sting without pause that only adds to the shake of my quickly tiring muscles.

There is still impending, black darkness taunting my periphery. It doesn't make sense; it's like a bizarre tunnel of vision, changing and evolving as I take it all in. Exactly like a dream, but slower.

I'd give anything for even a *wift* of magick right now—just a little light to broaden my vision, a small dance of flames to warm my skin. In Daydream, children can make anything with a puffy cloud of magick—a *wift*—anything from flowers to frogs. More powerful elves can alter realities and dream-walk. How is it that I ended up with nothing?

The unrelenting mist of saltwater feeds the chill that threatens to bring my life to its frigid end. *How embarrassing that I'm in the most terrifying hellish death trap in the entire realm, and hypothermia is what's going to take me out.*

I position myself to see the top of the wall. A daunting destination, but seemingly the best one. The darkness to my left and right is undeniably closer now, closing in on me. And now it sounds like someone is actively screaming into a pillow.

Terror's cruel fire burns through my veins once more.

Some of the other people look like they're screaming in pain, or maybe fear, their nude bodies writhing. A wave of nausea threatens to take over as the cacophony of muffled sounds, the grating of my skin against the rock, and the smell of seawater, sweat, and metal fills my nostrils.

I need a moment just to endure this. To catch up. I need to let my body adjust to it so I can control myself instead of panicking. *How long will that take?* I let out a long, exaggerated sigh.

As soon as I commit to calming myself, a clear scream pierces the dull silence. Raw and coated in pain.

So much for calming down.

Chapter 2 Evelyn

EACH NEW SCREAM IS a blade, carving fear into my very bones as agony coils through every aching limb. My stomach twists into a vicious spasm that would double me over if I weren't chained.

The disjointed darkness in my periphery pulls closer, as if summoned by my fear. The shadow seems to be creeping in faster, and now hardly any elves remain between me and it. There's something within that void.

Something giant.

I gasp as the metal across my waist constricts and causes each painful breath to become shallower, pain shooting up my ribs. It feels like the bar is tightening, but how is that possible? But the pain is nothing compared to the horror unfolding before me.

An amalgamation of death and decay emerges from the shadowy depths. The details unravel like a bruise blooming beneath skin. A massive skeletal body with dark gray skin stretched thin over bones clambers up the wall like a broken marionette. Its long arms are tipped with shadows. The creature's massive head has empty eye sockets, and pieces of stringy black hair still cling to its scalp, draping down and sticking to its cheeks. The *thing* is covered in ribbons of flesh—some rotting, some fresh, all sticky with blood. And I can *hear* it. An obscene sloshing sound accompanies its movements. It slams against the wall, causing my back to grate against the stone with the vibration.

The world has gone entirely silent. The only exception is when the creature opens its haggard, rotting mouth, and I'm met with the source of the screaming that pierced the sound barrier. It starts recognizable, a young elven voice, then turns into a high-pitched wail only barely reminiscent of anything living. Another person chained just above the beast has begun to scream. The frantic wailing is faint at first, but each cry becomes louder. The creature cocks its head to the side and slinks closer. Its mouth is full of hundreds of yellow, sharpened teeth held in by rotting, gray gums. With its gaping maw, that awful, blaring scream intensifies. The insatiable beast looks as though it's about to inhale the thrashing elven whole.

The poor person is trying desperately to get out, the chains around them so tight it looks as though their hands and feet are going to pop off like the cork from a fresh bottle of mead.

"Move! Get Out!" I scream at the person, but they don't so much as flinch at my words.

A hoarse, desperate shriek laden with dread and despair slices through the air like a roaring storm. The thing bends the top of its mouth back, practically splitting its head in half, and promptly snaps it shut over the person, chains and all.

The echoing sound of their skin ripping. The crunch of their spine snapping in two. The pop of the spinal cord as it's severed in half. These sounds will live with me for the rest of my life.

I let out sobbing cries, and the beast flashes its face towards me, the fastest movement it has made yet. It opens its mouth again, unnaturally wide, and the scream that comes out is a replica of the person's scream whose spleen is still dangling from its open mouth.

I force my eyes shut and focus my attention away from the lurking beast and the pain scraping my flesh. If moving makes the chains tighter, will relaxing my muscles loosen them?

Deep breath. I start at the bottom—a flimsy plan forming as I go—and pull all my attention to my frostbitten toes, willing my body to relax.

Another scream. A clear beacon of sound through the ever-growing muffled darkness.

"I can do this, I can do this, I can do this," I whisper over and over. To my surprise, the shaking in my voice evens out.

I have to do this. And it has to be now. I force my hands to stop trembling.

Another scream. This time, it's deeper, bloodcurdling.

Closer.

"Relax, Evelyn," I whisper to myself.

My feet are warming and have a light tingle to them. With each breath, I repeat: *warm, safe, gentle.* The shackles loosen. *It works!*

As it gets closer, I'm unable to see the creature in its entirety, just the dripping ribbons of skin and disjointed movements of its limbs. The rocks dent inward under the invisible force holding them to the wall. Each movement wafts a putrid stench. I almost vomit, but swallow hard enough to keep it down, knowing the movement would tighten the shackles.

I continue my mantra. I think it even as darkness touches my body. The restraints keep loosening. In one fluid movement—before I'm even sure it will work—I grasp the loosened cuffs on my wrists and pull upwards, straining my abdominal muscles and pulling myself free all the way past the bar at my waist. My toes curl around the edges of the bar, and I keep myself as upright as I can. All I need now is to free my wrists.

I ease the strain, relax my muscles, and ignore the pain. One arm falls free before the other, sending me swaying across the stones. I cry out again, my shoulder stretching beyond what is natural, dangling above the wet darkness below. I flip my body to face the wall. It'll be a miracle if I don't lose my arm.

I can feel the remaining cuff easing its grasp as I relax my wrist. Just before it loosens enough to send me tumbling to my death, I grab hold of the chain with my other hand. My weak grip on the wet links and my deteriorating strength are the only things keeping me from falling.

But I'm not restrained anymore, and I'm still alive.

The small moment of relief is cut short as the dead, empty silence engulfs the air once again, and the smell of rotting flesh fills my nostrils. Darkness swallows me, and my senses fail me again as I listen, clinging to the chain and waiting for any sign of the beast's next move. And then it screams. I think I'm screaming too, but no other sounds breach the shrill screeching coming from within the beast. The smell is unfathomable, bile burning my throat. The monster slams into the wall just below me so hard I almost slip into the depths of its teeth and the darkness below. My arms are screaming, burning, throbbing, but I pull. I pull and pull and pull because it's that or death. The monster exhales, its cold breath spreading like the first coat of ice on a pond across my legs.

I start swinging with intention, praying to any gods that may be listening for something on the wall to cling to. Its breath moves closer, and I jump onto the wall at the height of a swing, my body slamming into jagged rocks. My nails peel back from my fingers, and it feels like the tips of my toes are filed down almost to the bone. Then, my hand catches the slightest ledge.

"Do not let go," The words wrench out of me. Encouraging me to continue.

The beast's gnarled, fleshy hand swipes for me but pounds into the stone instead, missing by just an inch. Its mouth opens, like a vacuum, trying to suck the life from me.

No, to inhale my tormented scream.

I keep my mouth shut despite the chaos. I desperately try to claw myself upwards, but I keep slipping. My skin is so raw, muscle and bone exposed. The creature is inhaling with no satisfaction, hungry and livid. Dejected by my lack of sounds, it starts moving faster, the fog of icy death right on my heels as I push and push. A tiny ledge here, a jut of stone there, barely enough to cling to, let alone climb. Every movement is a prayer made of pain and will. But then, my fingers brush something solid, a full ledge. I'm finally holding on not just to survive, but to rise. My left hand, then my right. I've never clung to anything so tightly in all my life, and I have no idea how I have any strength left at this point. One last agonizing pull, and my elbows crash into a landing. *The top of the wall. I made it!*

The creature's mouth is widening still, its pained, desperate intakes of breath echoing throughout. I heave my chest up just as the jaws of death latch onto both of my legs. The aching, frostbitten blackness of the creature's shadowy breath spans almost all the way to my chest, the weight of it pulling me down.

No, no, no gods no!

"Someone—anyone—please help me! Don't let me die like this!"

Rock bites into my torso, blood trailing down the stones as the creature inhales, preparing to feed. My mouth had been shut tight, swallowing my urge to scream. This is different, hopeless. I can't remember my childhood, my home, or laughter shared with a loved one. What can I hold onto as I leave this world aside from these cold black rocks?

My calf burns with a fire from the Underworld itself, teeth sink into me, and I let out a thunderous, savage wail.

My own screams will be the last thing I hear.

My voice is clear through the muffled density of the air, just like the others, the sound full of terror and pain. And just as I'm about to sink into some other worldly oblivion, a hand clasps my wrist. And I swear I hear the whisper of a deep voice, "got you."

I don't just feel pain, I become pain itself—so sharp and so searing hot. And yet, I'm grateful for every inch of burning agony. I was just in a place beyond pain. Everything was gone. And yet here I sit breathing. I remember the phantom fingers squeezing my wrist, strong enough to pull me from the beast.

The beast. I scramble to the edge of the wall and peer over, but all I see is black—no sea, no beast, no elves on the wall, just an endless darkness.

As I try to stand, the pain blurs into my senses, and I'm suddenly aware of the state of my body. My feet are no longer recognizable, and nails are missing on most of my fingers and toes. There are more gashes and lacerations than I can count, with fresh blood oozing onto the cold stone. My left leg has a gaping wound down the back of my calf, like fabric splitting at the seams. Blood, sweat, and seawater are seeping into my eyes and mouth, and I can feel my hair plastered to my face.

But I'm alive.

I chuckle. And then a manic laughter takes hold of my body and echoes through the air. A sound I can hear, gloriously loud and clear. Every wondrously loud roar fills my ragged body with so much gratitude. I can't get enough. I can't believe this. The sound turns into a prolonged guttural shouting—a release. And as my manic state wanes, the sobbing begins. *I may be alive, but I have quite possibly lost my mind.*

The wall stretches in both directions, into forever. Not a trace of any other being. It's the width of a full-grown person and crafted by the same obsidian. I could swim in its glass-smooth surface, so unlike the serrated rock that dug into my back.

I crawl, the entire world a blur. I need to lie down, just for one moment. The cool stone feels like ecstasy beneath my hands, soothing my raw skin. I lean in to touch my cheek to the cold bite of obsidian, but I never reach it. The cold surface seemingly evaporates, and I'm falling.

Chapter 3 Evelyn

"GET UP, SILLY," I hear a familiar voice say. Her soft, calm tenor stirring up memories of a middle-aged woman wearing a simple yellow dress and apron, spotted with muddy handprints and grass stains.

"Mother?" I swear I say this out loud, but I hear no response.

A warm hand envelops mine, "up you go." The voice says as I'm pulled to stand.

My body is twirling, and I'm unable to control the movement myself. My mind stalls, focused solely on the swishing of my worn light blue dress. It's like I'm looking at a painting and standing in it at the same time.

"Evelyn! Hurry over and help me with this batch of soap."

"Coming, Mama!" I say and run to the kitchen, where my mother sits organizing the ingredients.

There is a haze around everything, a deep, groggy mist that muddles the scene and bogs me down. On a visceral level, I *know* I'm dreaming. But not just dreaming, remembering.

I've never felt anything so odd before.

My thoughts are mine, but my words and actions have a mind of their own. I can *feel* my childhood again.

"Let's get that hair out of your face first, my little flower." Mother takes my honey-colored hair into her hands and ties it up with a strap of fabric, then does the same with hers. Her hair has the same smooth golden glow as butterscotch. Rays of sunshine can't help but dance from each sparkling strand and around the tips of her slight, pointed ears. I smile up at her, and she grins back, small lines like roots crinkling on her skin, leading to her rich, slate-blue eyes, like the color of the sky just before a rainstorm, saturated with joy.

The soap we're making smells of lavender and honey. It seeps into the air from the open containers on the old wooden table in front of us. *This,* this is the smell of home, of Mama, of happiness.

Skipping around the kitchen, I impatiently wait for my next instruction. The pasture and surrounding forest glisten in the morning sun through the giant window at the back of the house. Bleating goats reside next to our large barn, and the hum of bees ventures through our fruit and vegetable garden.

Mama hums like one of those bees as she works. She is contentment in its finest form.

Oh gods, the sweet comfort that comes from remembering her. I want to hold onto this for eternity.

A few wisps of hair dance across my face, and the lush scent of drying herbs in the window fills the room. I reach my hands up—

"Don't you dare touch that rosemary, Evelyn Aria Stone. You know we don't have much left."

I giggle as I skip through the kitchen and hop through the sitting room. I know this place so well that I could do this with my eyes closed. My hands graze the barnwood walls as I continue down the hall, into Mother and

Father's small room, then back out again. Just as I'm about to reach the ladder leading up to my sleeping loft, Mama calls me back. "We're ready, rinse off your hands in the bucket by the door, and come sit with me."

A deep sense of woe floods my mind. *I miss her so much.* But my small six-year-old body keeps dancing around the kitchen, joyfully ignoring Mama's amused efforts to make me focus.

Suddenly, we're out in the garden, picking fruits and vegetables. Even as I stand in the vibrant flowers and juicy fruits, all I notice is Papa meticulously carving our new barn door. My father wanted to give us something different than the usual slabs of wood. He insisted that art is important even though most people in this kingdom think it's a waste of time. I love watching his hands whittle away at the tiny details. I've seen him split wood like paper. He can swing an axe as fast as lightning and shatter a tree stump larger than a sheep. But those same strong hands at the end of his tanned, muscled limbs are so careful with this. The fresh cedar reveals tiny petals and veined leaves beneath his palms like gifts from the trees themselves.

"You see this sweetie, this is going to be our forever garden." Papa's large callused hands continue to carve into the wood, his dark hair falling over slate blue eyes specked with brown.

"It's getting late, my little flower. Why don't you go collect the eggs and help your mother wash the vegetables for supper?"

From seed to flower to table. We bake bread, plant beautiful and fruitful gardens, and care for our animals. My favorite chore is collecting the eggs from the barn. I giggle and twirl all the way over to the coup as Mama brings her harvest basket back into the kitchen.

"Thomas!" Mama calls from the kitchen window, "Don't keep Evelyn out there too late!"

"Ah, Sera, she's just getting the eggs. She'll be right in." He says back, looking over at me and giving a wink.

The dream shifts again, and we're in our sitting area, the flames from our small hearth dance across the walls, and the warmth envelops me.

"Listen up, Evelyn, this one's important," Papa says as he throws a small pillow at me to get my attention.

"This one is about a great and powerful being. Though he has fought and won many battles, his goal is always peace."

"I know this one!" I shout. "Istvan the Great has saved many lives from the threats of dragons and monsters."

My father smiles his knowing smile and continues the tale I know so well. "It was only with his fatal end, in which he tried to save us all, that our realm divided. The grief of his loss was so great that the realm split in two. Our people remained good, prosperous, and peaceful in the Kingdom of Daydream. But the Kingdom of Nightmare became unraveled. They gave in to fear, violence, and darkness. Their land is full of shadow monsters, murderers, and a treacherous king."

My little body leans into his every word. I can feel the fear and excitement bubbling up in my belly. My idle hands play with my rag doll as I listen to Papa's story. Mama listens too, even though it looks like she is intent on whatever she is quietly knitting in her rocking chair.

"Alright, my little flower, time for bed." My father says as he finishes his tale.

"No!" I whine. "One more story, please."

"We have to be up with the sun; the farm won't take care of itself." Papa hoists me up off the floor and guides me to the ladder.

Before my little foot steps onto the first rung, I spin around. "But wait, what *happened* to Istvan?" I say as a big yawn muffles my last words. I hear the creaking of Mother's rocking chair stop, and she turns to Papa with an expression I didn't recognize, sorrow. It's gone in an instant.

"That's enough for tonight, my little one," Mama says as she always does. She stands and pads over to me before sweeping me up in a tight hug and kissing the top of my head.

"But, Mama, I want to know what happened to him, where is Istavn now?"

"That is a story for another day when you're taller. Up you go."

I climb my rickety ladder, the wood groaning with each step. I crawl over my straw-filled mattress and under an old, worn quilt. Mama hands me my small lantern, and I lie there flipping through my favorite book until my eyes are too heavy to look at the pages.

Memories continue to play out. Faster and faster.

I relish the thoughts coming back to me. Even the mundane pieces I hang onto. The weather, the seasons. I watch as my mother tallies off the days on a piece of parchment.

The sun season, the harvest season, the cold season, and the rainy season. All of them are equally wondrous. Even in the cold season, the snow is only a soft dusting that glistens in the mild sun, the entire world glittering under the frosty blanket. The rainy season always makes time for the sun, too. And the soggiest of days still end up with enough sun for my little feet to play in the mud.

"I'm going on an adventure, Papa!" I yell as I run through the field to the lush green forest with towering trees.

"Be back before the sun goes down. Don't make me search the woods for you again!" Papa yells back from the goats' pen.

I run and leap, talking to the forest animals as I go. Not just animals, my friends.

I reach a calm, clear river with twists and curves, and rocks just big enough for me to jump on. I live for my adventures there. I hop from rock to rock, making my way to the other side of the river's shore. I'm at the last rock, making my last leap, when my vision begins to tunnel, everything getting blurry, then black.

My eyes open and sand grates my raw skin. My head is throbbing. I reach for the source of the pain, my hand coming back sticky and covered in blood. The sky is muted, hazy, and the weight of the heat is already crushing me.

It only takes another second to remember where I am. The wall, the monster that ate people's screams. Falling.

I close my eyes again, willing myself back into my dream. It felt so real. I can still smell the honey and lavender. The smell of the river and sunny days. Tears well up to the point of bursting. I know deep in my being that those were memories of me, my mother, my father, my home. I replay the memories in my mind, trying to follow them further, but it's like I hit an insurmountable wall. My mind is warring—a battle of anguish and loss and longing and panic, all fighting to be the most important.

The obsidian wall ominously looms over me. Part of me wants to let whatever horrors occupy this side of the wall take me. But a different part of me—a stubborn and full of rage—won't allow this to be where I die. I have a home, a family, a forever garden. I can't die before I remember it *all*. I can't die before I get to see my family again.

Mustering up the smallest kernel of energy, I force myself to sit. With each clench of my muscles, I scream and pant and sob. The pain is blinding, causing my vision to flicker before it starts to dim, and everything feels like it's spinning. I lean against the wall, catching my breath.

"No!" I shout. But even though there isn't another soul in sight, I can hear my voice clearly, raw and raspy as though someone has pulled a cork from my ears. My throat is on fire, but I keep screaming, willing myself to stay conscious.

I can't ignore my injuries. Bits of flesh are hanging off my mangled leg, muscles peeking through. My wounds still ooze blood, chunks of pus marring the sanguineous fluid like curdled milk. My stomach heaves at the sight of it. *Do not throw up. Do not throw up.* But my body clenches and convulses, leaving a dry, sticky feeling in my mouth like it's coated in itchy wool.

Gods, what can I focus on that doesn't make me want to wretch?

I realize now that there has been no actual end goal in sight. I thought escaping the first side of the wall would mark some finale. But I was wrong. So wrong. There is no goal, no finish line, no ticking clock, and no map to guide my progress.

My thoughts begin to unravel. *What if the land and terrain just keep changing? What if there is no end? Am I doomed to travel this uninhabitable place forever?* I shake my head violently to dislodge all these panic-laden questions, but this just causes my head to throb even more.

Using the wall for support, I scream as I pull myself up to stand. My "good" leg feels like custard. *When was the last time I stood? Walked?*

There is no movement in the air. No wind. It's almost suffocating how torrid it is. I brace myself and take a step. With the slightest movement, the ground crumbles under my feet. One leg drags behind me as I force the other to keep going, resulting in a strange, limping hop, pain surging with each stiffened stride. There's no sun that I can see, but the air is hot and heavy in this lifeless landscape, the sky a hazy bluish-gray. There are some trees, but no leaves dot their branches, and the bark is black, as if they have all been ravaged by fire. I could use these branches as a splint or a crutch, but as I slowly approach one of them, my breath catches in my throat.

They aren't branches at all. They're bones.

Mounds of land that I had regarded as sand or ash through the haze are actually littered with corpses in different stages of decay. Some are down to their bones, while others are still rotting in the heat. Panic bubbles over. *Are these the people who were on the wall with me? What could have done this?*

I gather the strength to touch them. I don't have anything else to support my leg. As if to confirm my predicament, my toe catches on something and I fall to my hands and knees.

"Fuck." I hiss through clenched teeth. This is impossible. I sigh, then let out a growl, "How am I supposed to get out of this nightmare if I can't even walk ten feet?"

I pull, hand over hand, my leg dragging behind me to the skeletal piles. I dig through the ivory bones looking for any long enough to use as splints and another as a walking cane. My stomach starts to churn again, thinking about the fact that I'm digging through *actual bones*. I close my eyes and press my hand to my mouth to push down the reality of it. *Survive, nothing else.*

I settle on two slender bones—*splints, they're just splints*—about the same length. With pain shooting up my leg and the heat in the air accelerating the irritation of all my wounds, I crawl to a corpse several feet away. This one looks newly deceased, not even the smell of decay wafting up from its body. Dejection and sorrow coat my determination, but I will not give in to hopelessness.

Strange that there is no blood anywhere in sight, even though they are covered in bruises and lacerations.

Using tattered pieces of clothing, I tie the bones to my leg then push back the sweat-drenched hair sticking to my face. My skin is starting to bubble where it has been mercilessly exposed to this scorching air. And my leg, my tattered, mutilated leg, is now clumped with sand mixed with blood, and oozing with yellow and green creamy pus. *I'm going to lose my leg. There is no way this can be saved.*

I can stand on my makeshift brace. It doesn't do much for the pain, but at this point, I'm almost used to it. Strange how the mind adjusts. And the bones—*splints*—really help with the weakness. I'm dragging a little less and learning to move more quickly as I hobble from bone pile to bone pile. I find one long bone to use as a cane, but all I can really scavenge for clothing is a torn shirt and a pair of ripped-up pants. At least I feel a little less exposed. In one pile, I find a long, thicker bone, broken off with jagged edges that I take to use for a weapon.

Braced with a spear at the ready and a support to lean on, I'm finally making progress, and a spark of hope begins to bloom.

Chapter 4 Evelyn

I**T FEELS LIKE** I have been trekking through heat for an eternity. It's only after miles and endless miles that something scratches the earth behind me, and I stop.

I see nothing but the barren land in all directions. Then, something moves. Something huge. As if out of nowhere, a shape emerges, birthed from the desolate land itself. The ground shakes enough to nearly knock me over, its appendages slamming to the ground in a storm of sand and scales as it grips onto the land, skittering forward.

Why can't it be the size of an ant, a mushroom, even a dog, for gods' sake?

No, this...thing has to be about ten feet tall and fifteen feet long.

Four shiny legs and two massive pincers skitter into view. It almost looks like a giant scorpion, with dark brown skin as thick as plate armor. At first, it scampers slowly, making frequent short stops, turning its giant head with two long antennae from side to side, as if looking for something. Trying to *sense* something.

Maybe if I stand very still, it will think I'm a tree? I have lost my damn mind.

I can't even stand still with my jerky movements and complete lack of coordination and I'm not fast enough to catch my makeshift spear as it falls from my hand. It makes only a slight thud, but with the eerie quiet, it echoes as loud as a burst of thunder. The creature's head jerks toward me, its antennae twitching, sensing my exact location. A clicking sound intensifies as the creature sprints towards me, unnaturally fast, snapping its giant claws.

This is the end.

I scream in agonizing pain, my leg spasming as I throw the makeshift cane to the side and grab the fractured bone-spear with two hands. All I can do is hope this is over fast. As the creature closes in, it jumps like it's going to land on me. I thrust the spear upwards as I slid underneath it. I can barely hold onto my spear as it scrapes against the creature's belly. The thing lands just beyond me and whips around, its spiked tail missing my torso by just inches—the harsh, frantic snapping of its pincers a relentless, angry thrum in the air. I briefly marvel at myself, at my sudden strength and agility, but it's cut short by the impending reality staring me in the face.

"What are you waiting for?" I scream at it, but my voice is as scorched as this land.

My hands feel slick as sweat drips down my fingers. My heart is pounding like it will burst out of my chest.

The scorpion creature charges. It isn't jumping at me this time, and I won't be able to slide underneath it again, but my body starts moving with instincts I didn't know I had.

I should be dead.

Shifting my bad leg towards the creature, I lean back, gripping the bone shard in my right hand while my left is outstretched.

Lean back, inhale, aim, and throw on exhale. Do. Not. Blink.

I draw the strength from my core and unleash the spear at the same time as I scream out in rage. It pierces its left eye.

Yes!

I can see black slime oozing out from here. In my brief moment of respite, I wonder how I even knew to do that. It just felt right.

The creature swipes out with one of its pincers and grabs me by my bad leg before I can make a move. A slicing pain envelops me. I can't see straight, bile rises up my throat, and I vomit all over the ground below. Ground that is getting smaller as I'm raised higher and higher. It's so dizzying. The land is starting to spin. The other pincer comes up like it's going to grab me and rip me in two. I instinctively close my eyes and throw up my hands to shield myself. And then I smash onto the earth below.

It dropped me. *It dropped me.*

Where the beast once stood is now a wall of brambles and thorns. It's so thick that I can't see through. I can hear the thrashing of the scorpion on the other side, but it would appear that it has no way to get to me.

Where in the Underworld did this come from? Did I do it?

I stubbornly block the pain out from my mangled, useless legs and use my arms to pull myself to the side of the thorny barrier, collapsing flat onto my back. Sobs catch in my throat in an all-consuming ache. I'm so dehydrated from the heat and exertion that no tears run down my cheeks, but I sob nonetheless.

A second passes before I am engulfed in a tornado of darkness. It's cold, and goosebumps tighten my blistered skin. The air is thin, stealing my ragged breath.

What if my injuries are killing me? What if I never wake again? Never see my mother?

I can see glimpses of a dimly lit room. The ground is cold and damp. There are only metal bars confining me to a room that is too small. For one short moment, I can see clearly, clearly enough to know one thing for sure: I'm in a dungeon cell.

Chapter 5 Evelyn

THE EDGES OF MY dream are recognizable. Pools of thick black ink swirl as I sink into darkness and away from reality.

I'm back in my forest, about six years old, and free of all cares in the world. My feet pound against the earth, and the smooth, warm surface of worn stepping stones caresses my bare toes—a stark contrast to the freezing droplets of water that dance around my feet. The birds chase me as I run. I run and run and run. Run through the years. Through the memories. Until suddenly they begin to slow.

I must be eight, maybe ten. Just a few inches taller than before. I look towards the sky at the dome of curved, towering branches and listen. Sticks are cracking, giving panic to the birds who have stopped their songs. Many fly away.

Something is here. I swiftly hide behind one of the large tree trunks and wait, watching for the intruder in my forest.

Something moves. *There!* It's clumsy. And loud. And clearly not trying to hide.

It's a boy. He's about my age, poking at different plants and running his hand through the river before setting himself on the ground near a small pile of sticks and leaves. I slowly come out from behind my tree and walk toward him, purposely crunching leaves to catch his attention. It doesn't work. He's so captivated by this pile of wood. I make my presence even more apparent by clearing my throat—still nothing. Rocks clink together as he hits them over the stick and leaf pile.

"Hi!" It comes out a little louder than I intended. But I am so excited to see someone new in my forest that isn't a bird. Our farm isn't close to the center of town, and the nearest cottage takes ages to walk to, not to mention the elves that live there have no children.

At the sound of my voice, he startles, dropping the rocks he was holding.

"Hi," I say again. But the boy keeps looking down where the rocks rest in a nest of leaves and twigs. "I'm Evelyn. What are you playing?" I pick up my own rock and small stick, swinging it in the air as I walk closer to him and sit down. "Can I play too?"

His wavy blond hair is tied up, but his pointed ears poke through the strands. He looks out of sorts sitting here, wearing clean and polished leather boots, a crisp white tunic, and brown riding leathers. When his blue eyes look up at me, they're glassy. He's trying not to cry.

"I-I'm trying to make a fire...so I can talk to my fire friend." He stammers.

I try not to giggle. "Oh, is that all?" I sit down next to him, pushing him over a little. "You're doing it all wrong."

Sticks work better than rocks, so I start there. Father taught me to find dry grass and leaves to make the flames catch. There hasn't been rain for days, so this is easy work. I'm surprised the boy doesn't even know these basic steps. Hopefully, he really wants to start a fire, and he wasn't just playing pretend. It takes me less than a minute to get a flame to catch.

The boy looks so much happier, at ease.

"I'm Odin," he finally says. "Thank you. Do you want to stay and meet my fire friend?"

I'm not sure what he's talking about, but if I can have animal friends, why can't he have fire friends? So I stay in the sunlit woods with him. Odin. We slowly start talking. He loves the magick of the forest as much as I do.

"Do you want me to add wood?" I ask as the fire dims. "We haven't played that fire friend game yet! I've never played a game like that. I would love to show my parents at story time tonight."

He looks a little defeated, like he is longing to say something but can't get it out. "No, that's okay." He says, head hanging. Suddenly, I am over-whelmed with the urge to make him smile again. Whatever is bothering him, the forest will help.

We race into the trees, and soon our laughter echoes all around. I show him my favorite hiding spots. We balance on fallen logs across the river. We talk the entire time about the best ways to skip rocks and climb trees, mine of course being the superior methods. I even take him to the shallow cave behind the waterfall, where I like to eat my lunch alone.

It feels like a hundred days wouldn't be enough time with him as dusk lingers, threatening to send us both home. He has been such welcome company, and something inside my little heart pulls as we say our goodbyes. For the first time, I don't want to go home yet.

"Evelyn." Odin says, with a touch of sadness coating his words, "My parents would be angry if they knew I walked so far into the woods." He pauses like he's holding back. Before I get the chance to say I won't tell, he says, "But I'm glad I did." Then he turns and runs back down the river's edge, quickly out of sight.

Right then, clips of dreamy memories start to race past in a ghostly montage. Day after day and week after week, I meet Odin in the forest.

It's an unspoken rule that we get there right after breakfast. I find myself scarfing down my meal hastily and sloppily cleaning up after myself. Then I rush out of the cottage before my mother can even say goodbye. She often yells after me to be home by dark.

Sharing my beloved forest with someone who listens to me is so overwhelmingly exciting and fun. I crave it as much as water. Odin listens to me as if there is no one else in the world. Every time I pause to take a breath, he's staring, smiling, and attentive.

I'm every bit as interested in Odin as he is in me, even though he doesn't talk much at all. His clothes especially pique my curiosity. They're so vibrant and soft. I can tell his family is well off not only by the clothes, but in the way his basket of fruit and cheese is prepared and the trinkets he brings with it. They spin and fold like nothing I've seen before. One even makes music! I don't think my father himself could craft anything like it, not with all the free time in the world. I imagine Odin's farmland is perfect and filled with many workers, all experts in their craft.

My mother and father don't seem to mind the time I spend in the woods. I don't think they believe I have a real friend. My father, the vibrant storyteller that he is, often acts as if he's playing along with a tale I've invented, saying something like "One day you will be a greater storyteller than I!" And mother smiles, assuring me that she does, in fact, believe the story of "the handsome boy who lives in the woods and brings baskets of treasures." I haven't convinced Odin to come back to my house to meet my parents, and I've never been invited to his house to meet his own. I stopped trying to ask. I like that it's just us and the woods.

Time rushes forward again. Now I'm twelve years old. My body is larger, I'm stronger, and I have a clearer mindset. But I cling to my childhood, with no real care in the world—

"No, wait." I hear myself say. I can't tell if I said it in the dream or in the waking world. I'm desperate to grasp onto this moment in time with absolutely nothing to ground me. The cottage fades, becoming inky shadows. My eyes must have been closed, because I slowly open them. The edges of dreams fade entirely, and I'm staring at the dark metal bars of my cell.

Chapter 6 Evelyn

I can't help but think that the slow pace at which my memories are returning is part of the torture. How the Nightmare King must delight in showing us everything we once had, little by little.

I would give anything to be a child in the forest with Odin. To hear my father's stories again and to make soap with my mother.

I find myself sitting with my back against the wall in my cell. I blink upwards, tracing the cracks in the stone, watching tiny water droplets crawl through them. One large plop of water on my forehead snaps me out of my trance.

The Kingdom of Nightmare. Grimm Lodge. *How did I get here? Why am I here? I just need one answer.*

I try to move, but pain pulses through me. The more I take in my mangled body, the more I shake, my breaths becoming so uneven I think I might die from the hyperventilation alone. I hear voices—moaning and crying.

The sounds they make quickly quell any hope I had to reach out to them. Many are screaming, some taking deep, rattling breaths. Surely each is about to die, or has gone completely insane with the pain and frustration of what they have endured.

I hear a whimper, followed by the sound of retching from the cell next to mine. The splatter of liquid on the stone ground reaches me before the stench wafts my way. The cells look dark, but I turn my head any-way—about the only movement I can manage—and spot an elven figure on their hands and knees heaving violently. It's too dark to make out a face, but I can tell that their tunic and pants cling to a feminine build. Between heaves, they murmur something under their breath, but the words are too faint to understand.

I want to reach out to tell them they're not alone. But the truth is, I'm in no position to offer comfort.

If I don't focus on myself, I'll end up dead. No one else here can help me.

I take in my current state. I'm still wearing the tattered clothes and bone brace. Both the shirt and pants barely cover me, and I can feel the chafing from the sand that has stuck to my body, but anything is better than being naked.

Through the evenly placed metal bars are two rows of cells separated by a hallway, and—*oh gods.* Each cell is illuminated by a faint glow from a flickering candle, casting dancing shadows just beyond the bars. Any small area I can see is littered with beaten bodies. Limbs are on completely different sides of their cage. One holds nothing but an upright torso—no head, no limbs, and oozing with rot. A muddy, eviscerated sludge coats the floor. Each cell also has a large stone slab, a bed, if I were to guess. I have one too.

What do I look like from outside this cell?

I try to skitter back, but I'm already pressed flat to the wall. A mixture of panic and despair starts its familiar churn in my gut as I try to block out the scene, the sounds. For the first time since waking up here, I really look at myself. I'm covered in blood, dirt, pus, and...*vomit and urine*. I'm littered in lacerations, deep and shallow alike. On top of the pain, there is a persistent throb in my head and a high-pitched ringing in my ears.

How am I alive?

This is a mistake. I'm not supposed to be here. This is a *mistake*. I feel so out of control. I want to rip the rest of my skin from my body. Pull the hair from my head. I want to scream until someone comes for me. *Someone will come for me, right? Someone is looking for me?*

There must be, but I can't remember anything past that day in the cottage when I was no older than twelve. *Why are my memories scattered like a broken mirror?* I try to piece it together, but the parts where my reflection should be are blank.

"Breathe in. Survive. Breathe out. Survive." I repeat it out loud over and over until my body obeys my commands.

The sound of metal on metal interrupts my thoughts—a grating noise that cuts me deep to the core and makes me cringe. A door further down the hall opens. My mind harshly reminds me that I'm a complete fool as my heart involuntarily lurches with hope.

Two people walk in, the sconces flaring as they pass, as if their movement is summoning the flame. They're arm in arm, and as they get closer, I can tell it's an elven man and woman. The man is a strong, leather-armored guard. Without his helmet, his strikingly beautiful face is on full display. His dark hair is pulled back, and a trim beard lines his sharp jaw. He has a feral smirk, walking without taking his eyes off the woman on his arm, as though a festering cesspool of death didn't surround him.

Surely they can see this too. Can't they?

Wearing a scantily clad, skin-tight green velvet dress that hugs her lean, slender figure, the woman giggles as she meets his gaze. Dark chocolate brown hair grazes her porcelain collarbone as she walks, her round hips swaying more than they should, flirtatiously sauntering through the grime and gore. It's utterly out of place in this mess. They're exclusively focused on each other, swaggering through the blood-stained floors like they're in a dance hall.

He leans in and kisses her. Desperately. They stop walking for a moment, and he practically chokes her with his tongue. Even in my confused disgust, I can't stop watching it. That there is anything else going on besides an unforgiving stone floor and the chorus of death is enough to put my pain at bay. At least for this moment.

The guard runs his hands up and down the elven woman's bare arms, and I watch her open her lips wider for him. She twists her fingers in his hair and pulls him closer, wrapping her leg around his waist. He drags a huge, tanned hand across her thigh and squeezes a little before pushing back.

What is going on here?

"Now, now Hilia," The guard's deep voice growls, like he is still in full-fledged desire for this seductress, even as he stops. "Our guest here looks like she may want to join us. We don't want to be rude."

Are they talking about me? Is someone else watching? Surely anyone alive must be. But join them? Have they lost their minds as well? Why would they even come here and exhibit this type of—

My thoughts are cut short by their unmoving stare. They're looking directly at me, and not at any other prisoner. It's unnerving to say the least.

"Evelyn," I blurt out. "My name is Evelyn, and I'm not your guest; I'm a prisoner. I need help. Please help me. I'm not supposed to be here." My voice wavers to hold back tears.

"Prisoner. Guest. That's just semantics." The woman, Hilia, says. She peels herself farther away from the guard and slinks toward my cell, not caring that her gown is brushing across the filthy floor. She roves her gaze over me with a look of disgust plastered on her face. "What's a pretty thing like you doing in a place like this?" The corners of her mouth curl up, and the guard shamelessly grabs her ass.

She's mocking me. Maybe they're drunk.

Either way, I'm wasting my energy on this foolishness, and pure anger heats my gaze. "I can't do this," I mutter to myself, but she must have heard me, because the patronizing continues.

She stands, pushing her ass into the man behind her, accompanied by a dramatic gasp. He doesn't skip a beat as his hand glides up her body, and he leans down to kiss her neck. "Owen, my sweet boy, did you hear that? This poor thing thinks she has something better to do with her time than talk to us." Lust dances across her eyes, but she doesn't stop looking at me, "I would think someone in your situation would be grateful for this entertainment. It will be the last taste that you'll ever have of something like this," She reaches her hand up around Owen's neck and pulls his face to hers over her shoulder. Her tongue pushes into his mouth, but she opens her eyes and glances at me, as his desire starts to take over. Owen lustfully purrs her name into her neck. My blood boils, both because I'm most definitely *not* interested and because she may actually be right. Not to mention the looming plethora of questions that I'm sure these people can answer.

I have to get them to talk to me. "Can you please just tell me why I'm here? Or how long I've been here? Or how to get out?" I lock eyes with Owen, my nails scraping against the ground as I curl my fingers into fists. "You must have a prisoner log." He barely notices that I'm talking, lapping at Hilia's neck like she's his main course. "Maybe it's just that you can't leave your whore for five minutes to figure it out." I look away again, shocked at my bitter tone and choice of words. Softer, but still laced with hatred, I breathe, "Coward."

Hilia chuckles again. "Whore? Coward? Harsh words coming from someone in your predicament, you ignorant thing. We don't *owe* you anything. Don't forget it. Perhaps before calling anyone a coward, you might take a good, hard look at yourself and remember who is in charge here. Just because I fuck, and I love doing it, doesn't make me a whore. Do you deny that such acts are good for the mind and body? Or—oh, gods, Owen—maybe she's never done this before!" She steps away from Owen and presses herself against the bars, sliding down toward me. She smells sweet but sharp, like mint and vanilla.

"Have you never lost yourself in the feeling of a strong man making you come? Have you ever been kissed the way you watched us kiss? What about being touched? Have you ever had anyone touch you and make you scream their name?" She makes eye contact with me for a moment, but stands before I can thoroughly study her face. "She has no idea what she's missing." It's like a dance, the way they move together without even speaking. His towering size is glaringly apparent against her slender frame. He kisses her neck as she takes his hand and guides it down to the soft white skin of her thighs. The slits in her dress easily push back, exposing her bare skin underneath. Hilia smiles down at me. "You probably wouldn't know this either, but you can't wear undergarments with a dress like this. It completely ruins the look."

She brings his hand further up her thigh until it cups her sex. Owen lets out a breathy moan, still blissfully unaware that they are standing in death's garbage disposal. She starts to let out small whimpers as she lets go of his strong, tanned fingers, leaving him to play with her on his own.

Don't watch this, Evelyn. It's a trap, it's ridiculous. These are sadistic, evil people.

But I can't stop watching. The guard's thumb begins making slow circles over that bundle of nerves at her apex. Hilia leans back into him, reveling in the pleasure. After a few seconds, he slips one, then two fingers inside of her, wetness glistening around them as he pulls them out. She lets out a gasp, then a moan as he places his fingers back inside her and begins pumping faster and faster.

How can anyone get turned on in a place like this? The smell alone is debilitating.

I ask myself this while simultaneously not being able to tear my stare away. I'm sure there is a version of myself that would be appalled and ashamed, but she is far, far away, and my gaze doesn't stray.

"That's it," the guard whispers in Hilia's ear, just loud enough for me to hear, coaxing her on. Trying to push her over the edge. He looks up from his ministrations and locks eyes with me, "show our 'guest' how you come undone with my hands moving inside you."

This is abhorrent. I can't watch.

Instinctively, I turn away and remember that my leg is in dire need of healing. I hiss, prompting Hilia to lift her head and lock eyes with mine. "Watch, Evelyn. Watch him fuck me with his fingers. Yes." She's moaning as her eyes roll back again. "Faster." Owen spins Hilia around, keeping his fingers positioned inside her. She grinds into him as he keeps up the pace, building intensity. Then he kneels, pulls her leg over his shoulder, and pushes aside the center of her dress. He sucks and feasts on her like he's starving while she releases a feral moan that fills the entire prison as she rides out her release.

Hilia pulls Owen up by his hair until he is standing tall enough to kiss. "I love the way I taste on your lips." She says with a grin, turning her attention back to me.

"So you see? This?" She gestures to the guard and herself, "It's my choice, my right to take pleasure in. I'm not ashamed. This is the way of life here. There is no shame for you either in admitting that you liked watching me come. And look! No one thinks *you* are a whore. A little self-righteous and downright filthy, maybe," she says, plugging her nose while grimacing at my oozing leg, "but we can all agree that we share this primal need. And it's so fun! Besides, I love making you watch, knowing you can't enjoy anything like this. Something about it just turns me on." She giggles again as she turns toward Owen. He stands there, smirking like he is in on a joke that no one else knows. He places both his hands in his pockets, his erection pushing against his pants. Hilia makes a move to unfasten his trousers when another set of footsteps sounds on the stairs.

It's another elven man and woman. *Great, is this where everyone in this realm comes to get off?*

It occurs to me that maybe the Kingdom of Nightmare is so horrid, so unlivable, that a place like this may actually be a sanctuary for some.

"Hilia, has no one taught you any manners? How many times do I need to tell you that we have other rooms for this? You're going to fall ill." The other woman says in a casual, clear, and decadent voice.

"Soldier, if I didn't know any better, I would have thought that you were on guard duty today?" The new elven man adds.

Owen stands to attention, doing his best to hide the annoyance at being caught. Hilia shoots me one last grin before changing her own expression to one of an innocent-looking doe. "We were just leaving, Gwen." Owen nods slightly and turns on his heels. Hilia links her arm through his and walks back into the stairwell that they came through.

The second couple comes closer. A flurry of perfect skin, chiseled muscles, soft lips, and luscious hair. They may very well be even more striking than the last pair. They pass my cell, and the new man claps his hands. The sound deep and slow, echoing through the Grimm Lodge.

"Congratulations!" A jovial, thunderous voice booms from him. "If you're still breathing, then you have survived your first Nightmare Trial."

Nightmare Trial, like a game? And this was only the first one. *How many are there?* The elven who was retching in the cell across from me looks up. At least she is also well enough to move her head.

We're both looking at the couple now, the woman hangs on the man's arm, a slight grimace on her face as she looks around, but otherwise completely oblivious to the carnage around her. She's clearly used to this.

The man continues, "Many have come before you, and even fewer have made it this far. Be honored and proud that you are even breathing now. I look forward to watching what is to come of each of you in the future trials."

Is he serious? Pride and honor aren't even on my radar. I need my leg healed. I need to see straight. I need water.

It makes sense that the Kingdom of Nightmare hosts such arrogant and entitled elves, with nothing better to do than torture and revel in it. I assume he's going to walk right back out the way he came after that short, pointless speech. But he doesn't, and I'm able to take him in as he stands right in front of my cell.

His jet black hair hangs to his shoulders in waves. He has deep green eyes and a small amount of stubble growing on his face. The black pants he is wearing hug his body in all the right ways. I can see the bulge in front clearly as my eyes sink all the way to his boots and float back towards his face. He's wearing a black jacket with a white tunic beneath, the top three buttons undone to show his tanned skin below. Holy gods, even in the state I'm in, this elven man makes my pulse drum.

I'm sure his vanity is the only useful thing he has to offer anyone.

I look straight into those beautiful green eyes and spit through the bars at his shoes.

"You are a feisty little thing, aren't you?" He says with a deep growl, not breaking eye contact. "Gwen, look at her." The woman, Gwen, looks up from idly studying her shining red nails. She sways her body to face me. A look of pity in her eyes quickly vanishes, and her expression changes into a thoughtful smile. "She's just our type, don't you think?"

I turn my gaze from this gorgeous, vile man and look at the woman, Gwen, for the first time since they stopped in front of my cell. I assumed she was just mindless arm candy, but the man looks at her with respect, like an equal.

Strange for such an otherwise smug-looking man.

Gwen's tall, but it is hard to tell if it is because I'm sitting on the ground or because of the strappy heels she's wearing. Her silky thighs peek through the slits of her skin-tight red dress. The neckline plunges far past her full, round breasts, putting everything on display, and I notice that her entire back is exposed to her buttocks. As she turns a little, I see the glow of the hall lights catch something on her neck. She wears a simple golden chain with a pendant of a black bird sparkling on it. Her deep brown hair is parted to the side and hangs in soft curls just below her shoulders. Her eyes are the color of honey, outlined in black kohl, and her lips are stained a deep red, the same color as her dress. Being this close to them both, I can smell hints of citrus, smoke, and roses.

Stop drooling, Evelyn.

"I'm not feisty, and I'm no one's type." I spit out. "As I told the other couple that was down here having...relations, my name is Evelyn. Will someone please tell me what I'm doing here? Can you talk to me? Or are you just going to get off in a bloody dungeon, too? I mean, what is it about this place exactly? Is it the smell? The darkness? Or maybe you all just like exposing yourselves in front of helpless prisoners for fun. *Revolting.*"

"My, my, Little Raven." The man may as well have purred at me. "That is quite the mouth you have on you." He pauses, studying my face, and I keep his stare. "As much as I would rather have that mouth on me, I am afraid you are in the midst of the Nightmare Trials, and letting you out of that cell would make the next round of the trials void, and you would either have to start over or be immediately executed."

My insides are swarming again. I feel my face pale even more than it already has from the blood loss. *Doing that first trial again? No. Escaping execution? Definitely not in this condition. They have to be able to offer me something that will help.*

Gwen flashes the man a look like she was...hurt? Concerned maybe? Ashamed of how he was talking to me?

"You may not understand the honor it is to be here, Little Raven. Not now, anyway, with your state of mind. But know that you and you alone are the reason you are here. Maybe that's what's really bothering you. This dungeon, these trials. You put yourself here. So you either need to find a way through it. Or succumb to the nightmares. The choice is yours and yours alone," he says.

I look down at my leg. I barely made it through the last trial. There is no way that I can start another one in this state and make it all the way through without my body completely failing me. Although my insides are riddled with defeat, I bare my teeth at this wretched person before me. "Tell your horrid king he can rot in the Underworld for what he puts his own people through. You're all monsters."

The man just smirks. He *smirks* at me.

"Oh, Little Raven, I do look forward to the next time I see you." He smiles to himself as he starts to walk away. He holds out an arm, but Gwen is still looking at me.

She bends down to my eye level, "Maybe instead of giving up on yourself, you accept that you have come this far. Maybe you got yourself into this because you know that you can get yourself out." Her face looks kind, a mask, no doubt, for the true nature of her character. She holds my stare until the moment she stands to leave, linking arms with the man and strolling out of sight.

It's too hard to keep myself upright and too much work to keep my eyes open. I give myself over to sleep—or death—both a welcome oblivion.

Chapter 7 Gwen

ECHOES OF OUR FOOTSTEPS bounce off the stone wall in an endless, steady beat. It's as though the bounding clicks have no idea that it's such a long, punishing climb from the dungeon. This stairwell is narrow, dark, and damp, all the way to the top.

I usually enjoy the clink of my heels, but right now I would give anything to be wearing flats.

"Cane, I don't train nearly as much as you," I pant. He continues as if he didn't hear me. "Slow down!" My words are a whiny groan. Sweat trickles down my spine, soaking into my dress.

And this is one of my favorites!

He lets out a harrumph, but his pace slows just enough for me to catch up. A smile tugs at my lips. I've known Cane for twelve years. We met in Sallows, the bustling town just beyond the castle. I was eighteen, making my living on odd jobs while Cane was already entrenched in castle life. I'm not sure why he started talking to me. Maybe it was just his kind nature—maybe his undying need to know every single person of the kingdom on a personal level. But I like to think we were connected, even then.

The relationship soon evolved, as it often does with women and Cane. I learned about his open lifestyle, and I wanted to be part of it.

Our relationship now is very…fluid. We share our bed with many lovers. It's a beautiful game, a dance with pleasure in every way. And even though our bodies don't belong solely to each other, I can't help but think there may be a hint of "more" between us. We've just never stopped to assess it. No need to change anything since we are both happy and satisfied. But still…I know trying to lock Cane down would be like trying to cage a hellcat. He's wild, and he loves to explore, and there are enough of his smooth words and confident smiles to go around. I can't keep it for myself. And I don't want to. I like that he is happily himself and that I get even a small piece of his splendor.

Yes, Cane and I are friends with benefits. Really, really good benefits.

The door creaks, and a sudden wash of orange and golden light snaps me from my thoughts. Judging by the way the sunlight floods the foyer, it's midday. Even here, Cane doesn't pause. He strides right through the sprawling front doors and out of the castle, two guards flanking the entrance as we pass.

"Where in the realm are you going?" I all but shout at him.

"I need air. The dungeon smells of piss, shit, and vomit."

"And whose fault is that?" I mutter under my breath.

He finally stops at a small alcove within the castle gardens: the jewel-toned flowers, tightly placed trees, and thick shrubbery shrouding us from any onlookers. A pale stone bench, tucked deep inside the leaves, beckons us to sit. My mind calms with the sound of insects and the chirping of black birds.

The silence between us is comforting and not oppressive, as silence can sometimes be.

"Ravens," Cane says.

"What? The birds? I guess they are ravens," I say, looking up at the three black birds hopping on the tree branches above us. One is still and stares into my eyes with such profound intent that it sends a shiver down my spine.

"There's something different about her, Gwen. She shouldn't have made it out of that trial. Gods, she shouldn't even *be* here. When was the last time you heard of anyone crossing the border?"

Cane had called that woman in the dungeon Little Raven, and now there are three of them sitting with us. Some see ravens as a symbol of death—a bad omen. But I know the truth. I know ravens mean wisdom, *transformation.* Maybe his pet name holds more meaning than he realizes.

"I know" is all I can say. We both already know the answer to the last part. No one has ever crossed the border.

I don't have true power myself, but being near that woman was like being near an open flame. The sensation almost rivals the power I feel when I'm around Cane. He feels like dark shadows and cool caresses, but she feels like stifling heat. We both saw that she bears no mark of Daydream or Nightmare. She's not a magick wielder. *So why does she feel different?*

As if reading my thoughts, Cane rubs at his arm, right over his Nightmare mark, the dark tattoo that appears once a wielder comes into power. I've traced Canes mark countless times, the sharp lines and dots etched into the skin under his shoulder. I used to long for a mark of my own to appear, even when I was an adolescent, well past when even the late bloomers' magick appears. But I've since come to find that even without natural gifts, I can create my own enchanting existence.

Raking his fingers through his hair, Cane lets out an exasperated sigh. "She's going to be nothing but trouble. We should never have let a Daydreamer into the trials. What was I thinking? Have we gotten any word from Daydream on any wayward citizens?"

"No messages have made their way to me. However, I've been busy preparing a room in the council's quarters for whoever wins the trials and then catching up on the healing tinctures and tonics for the clinic. And honestly, Cane, do you think Daydream would ever even try to reach out to you?" I catch Cane's eyes.

"Stop rolling your eyes at me! You know I'm right. How many times have you tried to plan a meeting with their king only to get no response back?"

"And don't get your hopes up too high, Gwen. It's been five years, and no one has won yet. I'm about to make Piscevens come out of retirement to fill the final spot in The Shroud."

I pick one of the deep red roses off the bush next to me. The pad of my finger glides across the delicate velvet over and over. My wandering mind remembers the last time Cane used a rose just like this to trace circles around my nipples, down my abdomen, over my...

"Gwen?

I clear my throat. "This woman, the one who feels different, she's going to win. The Night Shroud will be whole again, and I'm going to make sure she has the best gods damn room in the palace." It's the least I can do for any winner, but especially someone like this.

Ever since I was a child, I've had an uncanny ability to read people. My parents used to say I was seeing their aura, though that never felt quite right to me. It's more than that—a blend of sensing their energy, their power, and something...deeper. I suppose you *could* call that an aura, but to me, it's like each person radiates a unique color, one that bursts into my mind the moment I see them. Cane, for instance, is red—deep, sensual, and intense. There's a strength in his color, something raw and unyielding. I see red in myself, too, but it's different—muted, softer. Maybe it's his magick that makes the difference. I've never met anyone else who can see these colors, so I have nothing to compare them to. Then there was Evelyn.

When I saw her, she glowed white, brilliant, pure, unlike anything I've ever encountered. Her presence didn't just stand out, though; it felt familiar, comforting, like finding an old friend in a crowd of strangers.

It's written that since the inception of the Nightmare Trials, there has always been the Night Shroud, a select order of elite warriors who survive the trials and ascend to serve as the king's personal guard. Their number never exceeds five. When one passes to the Overworld or chooses to lay down their blade, the trials are used to find a new Shroud member in addition to their use restoring balance to the kingdom.

Anyone is permitted to enter the trials. Some come seeking the glory that comes with being in The Shroud, others the boon, a reward of coin vast enough to last a lifetime. But in all the time I've been at the palace, no one has claimed a place among The Shroud. And no one has walked away with the boon.

Cane pulls me to stand, and we begin a slow walk back to the castle.

"I missed the morning council meeting. I'm going to catch up with the Night Shroud for an update. Will you join me?"

As much as I would love to spend my day with Cane, I have business in the alchemy lab. I know more than most when it comes to potions, and the healers' cabinets are not going to replenish themselves.

Chapter 8 Evelyn

MY EYES OPEN INTERMITTENTLY during the following hours, but I never completely break the veil to full consciousness. There are moments where I feel like I'm on the cusp of remembering something—a scent of lavender, the sound of a river flowing, the feel of the sun on my skin—but then I'm pulled back into my dreamless, fitful purgatory. Every time I wake from my oblivion, I crash back into my reality and the pain that is constantly gnawing at me. Elves are known for their resilience, supposedly blessed by the gods themselves with good health, speedy healing, and long lives. Right now, I would give anything to die quickly, like a small rabbit in the woods.

My body involuntarily spasms, burning with fever. My chattering teeth incessantly click and grind together, a metallic taste growing stronger in my mouth from the countless times I've bitten my cheeks and tongue. I'm still between the dream world and reality, unable to fully immerse myself in either one.

One of the times I open my eyes, the kind eyes of a woman are staring back at me. I remember her name. Gwen.

She's standing just out of reach and places a metal tray with a piece of bread and a cup on my cell floor before walking away. She looks defeated. I try to call out to her, but words elude me.

And then I'm waking again to my head slamming into the floor, my convulsions unrelenting. This time, I see Gwen's partner standing outside my cell. He throws me a pair of pants and a shirt, but they are just out of my reach.

I drift back into sleep yet again.

The next time my eyes open, it's to a bucket of water being thrown on me.

"Hilia! What in the Underworld do you think you're doing! I asked you to come help carry the water so that she can clean herself up, not so you could throw it at her."

"She has been in and out of sleep for nearly three days and smells like death's asshole. There was no way I was entering this cell until at least *some* of her stench was rinsed."

I hear an exasperated sigh from the other woman standing beside Hilia. It's Gwen again. "I'll take it from here."

Hilia pats Gwen on the cheek as she walks by, "happy to help." Before turning to leave, she looks over at me and winks.

If I was cold before, I'm ice now. The water saturates my clothes, and goosebumps pebble my arms and legs.

"I was hoping to bring you some water to clean yourself up. But that did not go as planned." She's about to step closer to me, but I see her nose scrunch.

Okay, I get it. I smell. If you don't like it, leave.

"You need to get up, get dressed, eat, and drink. You need to do it now, or you will die in this cell within days. Maybe even hours." She says this as she sniffs at the air, as if the scent alone can track my time left in this realm.

"I'm sorry I can't stay long. I shouldn't be here as it is. I know you understand."

I want to speak. To throw back a witty response, but I don't think that there is any part of my body that works properly anymore.

Gwen quietly leaves, and if it weren't for the water dripping off of me, I would have thought that seeing her down here was a fever dream. After I'm sure she won't be returning, I pull myself to a sitting position. Holding my head to stop the incessant pounding.

Do the rooms ever stop spinning in this awful place?

My scrapes, bruises, and lacerations are in various stages of healing, which is a good thing, I think. And then there's the matter of my mutilated leg. My ankle is pointing outward, and I can't feel my toes to wiggle them. From my knee down is swollen to almost double the size of my other leg. Black streaks shoot up towards my knee, which is the size of a grapefruit. There's a large gash on my thigh where I can see the white of bone through the unhealed edges of the wound. This is much worse than I thought. I can't recover from this. No elven could. I will either die of the festering infection or have to amputate my own leg and die from the blood loss.

I take slow sips of water and a tiny bite of the bread that is still on the tray from the last food delivery. The cool liquid is a much-needed reprieve from the scratching burn that has taken up permanent residence in my throat. The bread nearly crumbles as I eat it, but even stale bread feels like a feast. The food fuels me enough to peel the soiled clothes off my body. I dip the edges of the shirt in the puddle of water from Hilia's awakening tactics and use the moistened shirt to wipe some of the grime.

It's got to be better than nothing, right?

There are no undergarments in the pile of clothes, *of course,* so I first slide on the new shirt. I have to work my way up to the excruciating task of putting pants on.

"You're looking better already," comes a gravelly voice.

I startle, then shake my head. *I'm hearing people now. Great.*

"It's really a wonder what a fresh pair of clothes will do for you, am I right?" This time, the voice trails off into a cough. I immediately look in the direction of the very real voice. As my eyes adjust to the darkness, I can see the person in the cell next to me sitting on her stone cot.

"I'm Sage." She says, as if she has already been watching me this whole time. "These trials are a bitch. I was *not* as ready for this as I thought I was."

"I'm Evelyn." I try to inch closer to Sage, but movement still causes debilitating jolts of pain. She doesn't look nearly as wretched as I do. She may have a wet cough, but at least her limbs are all attached with no threat of an amputation in her future.

She may as well look like a warrior princess sitting there. Her lithe frame is defined by lean muscle, visible through her torn tunic and leggings, every line of her body carved like a statue. Yet despite the strength in her build, something is welcoming about her expression. Her lip is split, and a dark purple bruise blooms on her face beneath freckled skin, the once white of her eye now bloodshot red. Her auburn hair is tied up, matted, and snarled. She lifts her hand to rub her shoulder, and that's when I see it, a long, raw gash across her neck. Jagged. Fresh. Like someone, or something, tried to slit her throat.

I must be staring because she chimes in, "My last trial," like that was the full explanation. I shake my head because what else does one say to someone who almost had their jugular torn open?

"Do you know how much longer the trials will last? Do we ever get to speak with the king? I don't think I'm supposed to be here. I don't know how I got here, but I have the strongest feeling it was by accident." The moment I speak, the flood begins. Every eager, oppressed feeling crashes through the castle gates of my mental fortitude. The sobs start, the burning in my throat worsens, and I think I might die from the weight of it all. I meet Sage's gaze through soggy lashes. I don't know what I was expecting from this stranger, but it certainly wasn't confusion.

"That trial must have done a number on you. Keep your head in the game, girl, it's too early to lose your mind just yet. I can assure you, we *are* supposed to be here."

I mentally sift through everything I know about the Grimm Lodge, but just like the rest of my life, I'm at a loss.

I go back to fitting the new clothes to my body. *Maybe I should just keep quiet.* And that's when I notice a glass bottle in the pocket of the pants.

I angle my body away from Sage's so she doesn't see what I have.

It's a small vial filled with purple shimmering liquid that seems to pulse with warmth when I touch it. There is a small piece of parchment attached to the bottle with a piece of string: Drink me.

Might as well read "bad idea."

It's probably just part of their nightmare games. Take it, and enter the wondrous world of being at the bottom of the food chain. I place the bottle back in my pocket and quickly try to forget about it.

Sage keeps talking.

"It sure doesn't taste good, but it's better than nothing." She says as sandy crumbs fall from her last bite of bread. She stands from her cot and begins to do stretches in her cell.

I wish I could even move a little.

My bone splint is still in place, but I wonder if it's doing more harm than good to the rest of this festering mess. I unwrap it, and without thinking, I grab my left foot and jerk it back into place. My scream joins the agonizing chorus of voices in the dungeon as stars flit across my vision. Heat burns under my skin, and nausea bubbles in my gut. I'm confident that if I were standing, I would pass out completely.

I scream at no one. But the world stays bleak, cold, and stinking except for that little vial of color and warmth emanating from my pocket.

"Oh my gods, you actually did it!" Sage says and walks over to the bars between us. Her hands still have a strong grip, despite the battered nature of her skin and nails.

"I didn't think you would, to be honest. That looked like a tough break."

It felt like one, too, Sage.

Without even trying to hide it this time, I uncork the vial and drink the purple shimmering liquid in one triumphant gulp. If this is what kills me, then so be it.

A wave of heat and contentment washes over me before I can even get the top back onto the vial. My eyelids start to feel heavy. I still hear Sage talking, but her voice is far away. I quickly put the vial in the cup before I slump over, and real, comforting sleep embraces me.

Chapter 9 Evelyn

THIS TIME, I'M HERE. An observer watching as my dream—*memory*—play out.

I watch my twelve-year-old self playing in the yard surrounding my home while my mother tends to the gardens. That delectable lavender and honey smell infuses the warm sunny air. Near the woods, the river sparkles with the sun, so bright I can feel its dry warmth caressing my skin. And just before time flashes forward, I see him by the trees. Odin.

Time is so different in dreams, like a living fog that pushes and pulls in every direction, both instantly and infinitely.

I watch as my younger self runs through the woods to meet Odin for a picnic. We play as prince and princess together, fighting dragons and sitting on thrones of gold. We add wood and leaves to the fort that has become our home away from home. The moments pause long enough that I can hear our laughter, which overlaps the river, which overlaps the creaking branches. One such creaking branch holds my little body as I climb and climb without a care in the world. But then the branch breaks, and I fall like a stone to the forest floor. Odin is instantly by my side and lifts my head into his lap. There are tears on my cheeks—I can't remember if it's from pain or shame—all I can tell is that I'm trying to wipe them away. I notice my leggings are torn, and there is blood trickling down. Odin notices too.

"Shh, shh, you're okay. It's only a small scratch," he says.

My younger self sits up, looking at her leg. Whatever she's feeling is tossed to the wind, and she starts shouting at the sight of herself.

"My favorite leggings are ruined! My mother just made these for me; all my other leggings are too small. She's going to be so angry. And look at that cut! It's going to scar. I'm such an idiot."

Odin picks twigs out of my hair. He reaches into his pocket for a small knife and cuts away the fabric clinging to my cut.

"It's really not too bad. And look," he says with a wide grin on his face, "It almost looks like a heart!"

I wipe the tears from my scowling face and take a closer look, but before I can see anything, Odin takes the protective cover off his knife again. He starts to roll up his pant leg and presses the knife to his skin.

My younger self screeches, "What are you doing?"

"I'm making a heart on my leg too, that way we'll always match."

The edges of sense and time start fading. I can't hear our voices anymore, and as hard as I try to hold on to this memory, it changes. The world quickens, and in another flash, I'm an adolescent, maybe fourteen. Odin and I are still together and running through the forest, as we always have.

It feels like days pass as the dream spins through the essence of my memories like whispers. Sometimes I see myself with a sketchbook and remember drawing as Odin makes trinkets with his carving knife. Sometimes we're silent, but I remember the utter contentment I felt in those moments.

How could I have ever forgotten this? My best friend.

The dream morphs again into a montage of Odin and my parents. I remember when he finally agreed to come home with me to meet them, and then all the days after. Milking the cows, tending to the garden together, all of us sitting in my cottage, laughing over dinner, the way Odin steals glances at me and my parents' knowing smiles.

Home.

I could watch this for eternity. I want to stay for as long as the dream allows me. In this particular slice of time, Odin and I are sitting close to my parents, listening to my father tell stories by the hearth. This story is my favorite—the tale of the realm's hero, Istvan.

"Istvan had not one, but both sources of great power from each realm. From one hand, he controlled the smoke and shadows, and from the other, luminescent beams of light. The power of nightmares and daydreams flowed through this one, formidable being. And he used this power to back his persistent promise of peace. No kingdom dweller would dare challenge his force, not because they were afraid, but because he was so loved. For centuries, the realm put its complete trust in him. He created and maintained a land so peaceful that we were able to sustain open trade, and everyone could travel freely from one kingdom to another. The entire realm of Sallix was thriving."

Father had been standing, using his hands like puppets to animate the story as he always did. But here, he lingers for a moment and sits down, like he lost something important. He continues from the chair, "One fateful day, however, Istvan's peaceful reign did indeed end, as all things do." He snaps out of his stare and returns to loom over us. I smile to myself because I still love the theatrics. "A group of unknown beings from unknown places crept into our sacred lands like a plague. No one knows how they got in under Istvan's rigorous watch. But came they did, and they intended to plant lies within the open minds of the realm. Slowly but surely, they convinced anyone willing to listen that the realm was on the brink of attack from evil outsiders and that Istvan himself was planted here to take over and aid in the downfall of the realm."

Odin interrupts. He must have been holding it in for a while because his voice bursts through the room. "And the townsfolk believed the strangers? They were so easy to manipulate? Did they even ask who these beings were? How did they just betray someone they all looked up to like that?" My father was taken by surprise at the outburst, but he, too, studied Odin's face, and with his usual grace and understanding, his features softened. "Sometimes, the pure of heart are the easiest to take advantage of. The people were nurtured; they learned to trust one another, and they discovered that truth and kindness were the best ways to prosper. They truly had no reason *not* to believe them. And there will always be those wild hearts desperate to thrive on mayhem. It's easy to whisper in the ear of someone willing and looking for chaos. All it takes is one citizen to change sides, and then more always follow. It didn't take long at all for one whisper to become many." Odin's expression worsens as he looks toward the ground, eyes wide and brows furrowed.

It looks as if he himself feels betrayed. As if it were the first time, he truly understood that elves are not always purely good.

"Rumormongers," Odin mutters under his breath. A laugh bursts from my younger mouth, "You're a monger, Odin. A rivermonger. No! A cowmonger." And she shoves his shoulder playfully. But he doesn't laugh.

My father continues a moment later. "Istvan, of course, denied such threats and sent his own army to find and interrogate these strange newcomers. Before he could find even one, many of the townsfolk from both kingdoms had formed their own alliance—an army big enough to overpower Istvan—as if numbers were any match for his powers. In the cover of night, they stormed right up to Istvan's home, where he lived quietly in the middle of both kingdoms. Even though he pleaded with them to understand the falsities, to, at the very least, question them, no one listened. The mutinous crowd needed the satisfaction of their quest, no matter the logic behind it. He never resorted to violence. It was remarkable, the way he swore to the gods themselves that every single living soul was good at its core. The mob parted, and a group of creatures dressed in robes came forth. The same *rumormongers* who started this riot." He looks toward Odin again. "They dragged Istvan from his house. He let them, even as he screamed, begging his people to listen, hoping for just one good soul to be brave enough to step forward. He swore that the accusations were false and that his goal had only ever been to keep the balance." He took on the role of poor Istvan here, acting as if he were being painfully dragged. He clutched Odin's arm, "Please, Odin! Don't listen to them! Dear Evelyn, I love you and I love this kingdom!"

I can't help but smile as I watch myself and Odin, barely breathing, hanging on his every word. My father's voice is low, his face close to ours when he continues. "In one last desperate effort, he cast a spell. It's said that the glow from the ball of light in his hands blinded anyone who looked directly at it. He cast the light out in a blast that changed everything. No one knows what he said, but that blast separated into one wave of shadow and one of light, splitting the realm in two. No part of the land was left untouched."

My father's hands are outstretched and straining, and he throws his head back to shout, "I vow to protect you even in death!"

I look at my beautiful mother. She is staring at my father, a small smile gracing her face, but her eyes look like they are miles away.

"The people froze. They could feel his magic all around them. There was a heavy pull, with the force of a thousand winds, that pulled the people of Daydream towards their side of the realm. And the same for the inhabitants of the Kingdom of Nightmare. 'No! No. No. No.' Istvan shouted as he was relentlessly dragged further away. With each pull of his body, the realm divided, and the ghastly wall shot out from the soil. Marring our realm to this day. Forcing us to live separately."

"At least we are far from the monsters and shadows that curse the dark, dank Nightmare wasteland," Odin murmurs.

"Ah, but Odin, what do you think that the Nightmare people say about us?" My father retorts.

Without my control, the dream—*memory* skips forward again. I try to grasp at the places that pass, to see the faces of my family and Odin, but nothing works. It only stops when I'm back in the forest. I'm about sixteen now, with more curves, and my golden hair has grown to my waist.

Oh, Odin was so handsome with his tall stature and blonde hair, falling in waves to his shoulders.

There is an unmistakable yearning in his gaze, barely able to keep his eyes from the swell of my breasts. And the younger version of me loves it. I move in so close it's like I'm in the moment all over again.

I watch as my adolescent, doe-eyed gaze roves over him. Everything we do is dripping with longing. Every laugh flirtatious, every stare lingering. The sun is streaming in from the tree tops. I can hear the birds singing and smell pine needles and soil in the forest air. I watch as we lock eyes, and I turn to stare at him as well.

Gods, I remember these eyes—the beautiful blue, sparkling and alive like the wild ocean waves.

He tucks a loose strand of hair behind her ear. His gentle touch visibly sends shivers across her tingling body. He leans in and breathes her in before he kisses her.

My young eyes widen, but they soon close as I watch myself relish the feeling of their lips together. She wraps her arms around his neck and pulls him in closer, deepening their kiss. His hands move up to her face and caress her cheek. She pulls back just enough that their kiss breaks, and he opens his eyes. They sit like that for a moment, just looking at each other. Lost in the ecstasy of just being, finally, together.

I was forever changed at this moment. Ignited.

My younger self moves to kiss him again, but a blood-curdling scream slices through our paradise.

The woods fall silent, and all I can hear is our mingled breathing. I can't tell if it's coming from me or my younger self. She jumps up and starts running.

"Evelyn, wait! I'm sure everything is okay!" Odin yells as he chases behind her.

I follow them. I run through the woods until I'm on the forest edge and can see my cottage in the field. Suddenly, I'm at the front door. My younger self has already opened it, and what lies in front of us is nothing short of shocking.

I no longer pay any attention to my younger, wailing self and look instead at the crushing details of this room. There is blood everywhere. It's coating the floor and walls. There is so much of it, I can smell it, *taste* it. I start shouting

"Mother! Father!"

I hear myself scream over and over again. They're nowhere. I feel frozen in place, but the memory continues, and I'm suddenly with my younger self in the barn. She's still screaming their names—still nothing.

It's so strange, wanting to comfort myself. All I can do is watch as she sinks to her knees, screaming, overwhelmed with panic.

Odin is suddenly by her side, helping her up. "We have to get out of here. Now."

I follow as they hurriedly walk down the road.

This just doesn't make sense.

I think my younger self is still screaming, but I can't tell. I watch in sorrow as her tear-stained face contorts and her body physically shakes.

I remember this, a feeling worse than death.

Then we're at the Daydream castle. Odin is still holding her up, helping her along. His face is determined, but gentle.

The guards let us walk right in, and Odin leads us to the throne room. The King and Queen of the Kingdom of Daydream are casually perched there, talking amongst themselves. It's only once we barrel in that they gasp in surprise.

Stunned and fumbling over words and emotions, I watch as my younger self glances at Odin as if to say, "What in the Underworld are you doing?" but instead she blurts out, "I am sorry, My queen, My king, I am not sure why my friend has brought me here. This surely is not a concern for you."

Odin steps forward.

"Mother, Father. This is Evelyn."

Chapter 10 Evelyn

I try my best to focus back on everything else in my dream. On Odin. But the blood-stained cottage has taken permanent residence in the forefront of my mind.

I sit up, bracing for the familiar agonizing pain. But it doesn't come. The blisters and minor cuts on my body have faded to nearly nothing.

That purple vial must have been a healing potion! I may also suffer a slow, painful death while trace amounts of poison eat away at my insides. Only time will tell.

Gods, I feel so much better. Excitement laces through my ribs at the thought of being able to sit without suffering.

And, really, I'm still not in the greatest shape. The large laceration on my left leg is still open, but I can no longer glimpse the bone protruding through the tissue; the black streaks that were racing from it earlier have now vanished. I notice that small heart-shaped scar and rub my fingers over it, loving that its twin exists on another leg, on Odin. I keep thinking of that day, trying to burn the details into my memory. That boy, Odin, must still mean something to me, something important. I think I love him. Before I can explore my memories more, I notice the state of my ankle.

It's completely reattached like my tendons and muscles had never been severed. I can wiggle my toes and move my foot up and down. Nothing could accurately express the storm of utter gratitude and relief brewing in my gut. I don't know whether to laugh or cry. I owe my secret healer my life.

Who left the vial? Was it Gwen?

"Look at you. You'll be running in no time!" Sage is nearly grinning at me as she claps her hands up and jumps her legs together.

Is she doing jumping jacks?

"How long was I out this time?"

Sage continues, her slight, sharp intakes of air, clap of hands, and slap of her feet on the ground being the only noise for several seconds. She uses her hand to swipe away the perspiration that dots her forehead. "Hmm, they only came down with food once since you passed out, and food has been coming about once a day, so I'd say you were out for a day or so."

"Are the trials over?" I ask my question more as a plea. As a desperate prayer. A manifestation.

A laugh echoes throughout the dungeon, bouncing off the walls and settling into my gut like a heavy stone.

Sage is doubled over. Like her already exhausted body can't support the laughter. She looks up, her gray eyes glistening as she catches her breath.

"I needed that." She breathes out. But when I don't laugh or giggle or even smile, she says, "Evelyn, it is Evelyn, right? The trials are only just starting."

It's odd, my body mending in front of my eyes as I endure countless uneventful days with nothing to do but watch. At one point, I even heard an audible *tha-wump* type sound, like suction, before seeing an entire wound close up. There have been no more pompous speeches, no secret healing. Food—if you can even call it that—appears sometimes after I have been sleeping. There haven't been any new dream-memories. It's like they left me with the most horrible memory on purpose. A part of me now has to carry this new insatiable void of grief.

Thankfully, Sage is quite the conversationalist, usually talking about nothing of consequence and oddly skittish when I ask her questions about why she's here. But she seems so resilient, much more than I'm. As if being here is a walk in the gardens.

"One," *grunt*, "two," *grunt*, "three..." Sage trails off her counting, but her grunting between each sit-up continues.

"How do you do it? How can you wake up, not even know what time of day it is, and just train?" She uses our meager accommodations to her advantage, chin-ups with the cell bars, jumping on and off the stone cot, push-ups, and lunges. If you can do it in a small confined area, *she* can do it.

"I have to be ready for anything. I *am* going to win. I'm going to take the boon, move to a nice house with my family, set up a small farm, and never look back." She continues to do sit-ups as I just gawk at her sheer will.

My ears perk up. *Boon? She has never mentioned anything about a boon.* I level my voice before speaking. "Do you think the prize is enough to last a lifetime?"

"It damn well better be! I didn't train for this for the coin to run out before I'm old and ready to leave this world. I'm done working for others. This is my chance to live for myself."

"Wait, you're telling me people have gotten *out* of the trials. There really is an end?"

Sage looks at me and laughs, and she only stops when she realizes I'm not laughing with her. "I really need to read your face better. Of course, people win the trials. Why else would we be here if we didn't think we could win?" Sage finally stops her chuckling and begins her sit-ups again.

"I can barely even remember who I am. I don't even know how I got here. I certainly don't have muscles like—" I swish my hand in a gesture at Sage and her many toned muscles.

"I just want to go home. I...I keep having these dreams. But they're memories, *my* memories." I may as well tell her everything I know. My story pours out of me, and Sage listens quietly. It's only when I've practically worn a hole in my tunic from anxiously toying with it that she speaks.

"It must be hard, these dreams you're having, not being able to put all the pieces of yourself together, but right now, the only thing that you need to focus on is not dying. You won't find any of your answers until you get yourself out of here." I can hear the gentleness at the edges of her vibrant voice. I want to hug her, but I can't, and a sob wells up in my throat.

"Why don't you get up and train with me?" I don't move at first, still fighting back the tears threatening to drown me. And then her gentleness is gone. She's back to her vibrant tone, loud and beautifully piercing, maybe even a little stern.

"Get up, Evelyn! No rule says only one person can win. We're going to be the first to make it out of the trials together, and that means we're done with tears. Starting now."

I know she can't touch me. I could sit here and fester and ignore her completely, and there would be nothing she could do. But something about her voice reaches deep within me and empowers me to stand.

"Where do I start?" I say, as the first glimmer of hope blooms in our shared knowing, smile.

Gritting my teeth, I force myself upright, pushing past the weakness and the ache in every limb. A scream claws at my throat, but I swallow it down, willing my body to be stronger than it is.

"Go on. Scream, swear, let it all out. You'll feel better," Sage says. She arches an eyebrow at me. "Do you even know how to swear?"

"Of course I do." Even thinking the coarse words makes them taste sour on my tongue.

Sage grasps the bars of her cell, looks me in the eyes and screams a string of "fucks" that echo off the dungeon walls.

"We're in the Nightmare Trials, living in the Grimm Lodge. There is no better time to say 'fuck it all' than right now. So say it. Scream it."

"Fuck" it slinks out on a weak breath, but a thin thread of relief loosens inside me.

"No, not like that. Scream it. Let the guards hear you. Let them know you're here and not going anywhere." She flashes me a wide, reckless grin. "We'll do it together."

"One, two, three—"

"Fuck!" We scream together until our lungs are raw. Over and over, chiseling away the layers of pain and agony and frustration. It's raw, it's reckless, and we do it until we're both on the verge of losing our voices. Laughter bubbles into the dismal space. And I really, truly, do feel better. "Fuck that felt good."

"There you go," she says, satisfied. "Now you're ready to start training."

After so many days, *and days and days,* of absolutely nothing, the sudden activity is daunting. Sage tries to ease me into it, but it feels more like a battle. I start small, like pushing my body up and down on the stone slab while I sit on the floor, or tensing my abdominal muscles to crunch myself up to a sitting position.

And all the while, Sage is my valiant crusader, pushing me and cheering for me.

I was reluctant to do anything strenuous with my legs, but Sage doesn't see them as an obstacle. She is relentless.

"You can stand."

"Get up."

"Walk. Go slow if you need to, but do it."

And I do. The first step was a little tender, but the more I stretch and flex, the more confidence I have. Not only can I stand and support myself, but I can pace the entire cell in seconds. Sage smiles more and commands less as the days pass. I even start jumping on and off my cot without a word from her. It's like I have a compulsion to make this woman proud of me, and I think I have.

The tedious routine is exhausting, but it doesn't do much to keep my mind from wandering. I wonder why Gwen and that other horrid woman, Hilia, haven't been back down here. I wonder why I haven't had another dream-memory. I wonder if Odin and I would have stayed friends, or perhaps even lovers. Any time my mind wanders to my family, it also wanders to that day at our cabin—the blood.

Thank the Overworld for Sage. I couldn't do this without her.

Chapter 11 Evelyn

A SWIRL OF DARKNESS surrounds me, slowly dissipating as blinding white light bursts into my field of vision. I blink several times to adjust. It's an infinite open field, no dark prison cell in sight. But despite the inviting scene, somehow I just know.

Another trial.

The soft blades of grass are tickling my feet, and an endless blue sky stretches above me. I tilt my head back, letting the warm rays of sunshine caress my face, reveling in the calm air. But just like all nightmares, the scene in front of me changes in a blink. Suddenly, there is a wall of hedges with an opening, just the right size for a person to enter. The rapid intrusion of brambles is unnerving, yet it seems so still; nothing is trying to hurt me.

"I'm going to have to go in there, aren't I?" I say to myself. My eyes involuntarily roll in exasperation. *At least I'm not naked.*

Inhaling a deep, full breath of fresh air and letting it out in a long sigh, I slowly head toward the hedge's entrance. The shrubbery seems to grow taller the closer I get to it. Double my height, maybe even more. The branches are twinned together, and the greenery is so thick that I can't see through to the other side.

Oh, wonderful, they are also covered in thorns.

"Let's just get this over with," I say out loud, my voice testing the space. I should be scared, but mostly I feel resigned.

I fill my lungs with what could be my last breath and breach the opening. One moment passes. Another. But nothing happens. It's still just more towering hedges and eerie silence.

There's a path to the right, and one to the left. Neither shows signs of another opening, and there is no end in sight. I turn just fast enough to see the entryway knit together, a crunching mass of branches locking me in.

A maze, then. A trial of wits, I can do that!

My instincts pull me to the right, and I go with it, hoping that quick decisions will get me to the heart of this nightmare faster. But I continue on endlessly. Hours pass on *and on and on and on.*

So much time passes that I start to feel...*safe.* Maybe the nightmare was intended to be the fear of not getting out. And while one day it may very well drive me mad, I can't get enough of this painless, sunny stroll. If there were no thorns on the hedges, I could see myself lazily running my hand through the leaves and spinning in circles as the sun kisses my skin. The thought alone has me smiling.

When was the last time I truly smiled? I wish Sage could see this.

I spin in a circle with my arms up, just laughing. This may very well be the beginning of my complete and utter madness, but gods, it feels *so good* to be outside!

Snap. Crunch. Snap. The snap of twigs beneath heavy footsteps breaks the silence behind me. I push myself against the hedge, the bite of needle-sharp thorns sinking into my back. The snapping and crunching keep getting closer, and I'm frozen with fear and indecision.

"What would Sage do?" I whisper to myself, and I can almost hear her voice telling me to move.

It's then that I feel a cool caress down my face, like a hand guiding my head to turn. And there, up ahead, a new path has opened.

I make haste, moving as quietly as I can. Each heartbeat booms in my ears like a relentless drum as sweat slicks my palms. The putrid smell of spoiled meat and the metallic tinge of blood wafts towards me. Suddenly, there is a ferocious growl, wet and hungry. My muscles tense, sweat beads down my back, and a race of tingling sparks runs down my arms. My fingers are numb as terror envelops me. *Where did it come from?* I start to run. A root catches my toes, and I crash onto my hands and knees. The smell burns my eyes and makes it hard to breathe.

A shadowy creature emerges, with paws the size of my hands, tipped with razor-sharp talons. Patches of jet black fur and festering wounds stretch over a lupine body, nothing but sinewy strands of flesh holding its limbs and bones together. Small craters have formed in the grass beneath it, sizzling with putrid ooze. I follow the trail of dripping liquid right to its snarling maw that's lined with teeth the length of my finger. I let out a strangled cry when I see that this death dog's eyes glow red, and I remember what they are called—

Barghest.

Creatures that prowl the night, hunting down the souls of those who have cheated death and dragging them down to The Lord of the Underworld himself, Erebus. It is he who will decide the magnitude of your suffering and damn you to endure it for eternity.

Once, Lord Erebus was one of the divine architects of the very land we walk upon, but insatiable greed led to his downfall. He demanded more power and was willing to go to any means to get it—including the creation of terrible beasts like the one before me. For this, he was cast out and condemned to the eternal darkness of the Underworld.

I get up and run as fast as I can, the barghest's giant paws inching closer with each sprinting leap. I practically crash into the walls as sudden lefts and rights open to me throughout the maze. And I do. Not. Stop.

I dig my hand into the sharp hedge wall and gain purchase on a branch. Thorns like daggers, violently shredding my palm as I grip. I climb as fast as I can, trying to ignore the fact that it feels like I'm scaling an angry wasp nest. I remember Sage back in our cells, *"Every second counts."*

I get to the top just as the beast pounces upwards. The barghest can only look up and growl at me as I triumphantly gasp in relief from the top of the thick hedge. He wails. Howls. Drools. But doesn't climb.

My clothes never stood a chance—there are tears scattered all over my tunic and leggings. Red spots appear on the fabric and swell as the lacerations bleed. I reach up and pull a twig out of my hair and wince at yet another prickly thorn.

The shrubbery continues to bite at my legs as I crawl across the top of the maze, the barghest stalking me all the while. One weak branch and he will devour me whole. The endless paths before me move and change, some disappearing, others merging. I'm completely disoriented, and my internal compass went quiet hours ago.

As if the maze knows that I'm evading death, the wall begins to thin out. My arms and legs start to fall through the branches, which grow increasingly thornier. I'm going to have to change my methods. *Now.* Luckily, my option is an easy one. The creature's on my left, and there's an empty path to the right.

I make the decision quickly, like Sage taught me, and jump off the brambles to the empty path. I brace, waiting for the barghest to attack out of thin air again, but I don't hear anything, or smell it for that matter.

The pleasant weather hasn't changed, but gone is the luxury of a leisurely stroll. I barrel forward, trying to put as much distance between me and it as I can. Turn after turn. Row after row. Only when fatigue threatens the promise of vomit do I pause and brace my hands on my thighs. My breath is hot and heavy, sweat dripping from my face to the grass.

Before I get the chance to regulate my senses, I hear the same sound of paws on the ground behind me. I can smell it and feel the heat of its breath as the beast pounces. I move fast, but it still claws at my pant leg, tearing the fabric off.

"I just fucking regrew this leg!" I think of Sage as the words fall from my mouth. And damn she was right. It makes me feel better.

I spin around and kick the beast in the snout, causing a vicious growling whimper to come from its chest. I kick at it again and again, the squelching, thudding sounds promising surrender but never delivering it. My foot scrapes across its teeth, drawing more of my own blood.

And my gods, it burns.

Burns like its teeth are from the fires of Erebus himself. Its talons drag across my legs, blood splattering under me. With one last kick, I strike it right in the eye, causing it to yelp and wince back. I take my chances and start to run again.

Dammit, my limp is back.

Suddenly, a new opening in the hedge appears, and I dash through it, landing flat on my belly, my face in the dirt. The opening starts to knit itself together, but not fast enough. The hound must notice because he howls with rage and lowers himself to pounce.

Come on, come on, come on. I urge the sentient hedges. The creature's eyes are locked on me as each branch slowly grows into a solid wall. The hole is getting smaller, but the barghest is getting angrier. It leaps toward me with its mouth wide open, only to crash into the thorns. All I hear is the echo of a pained whimper.

It worked. *Gods, it worked!* Sage was right. Never stop moving, be ready for anything, survive. I could kiss her. I'm so grateful. I can't wait to tell her every detail. For the first time since I learned I was trapped in the Grimm Lodge, I feel like I can do this. We both can.

Chapter 12 Evelyn

A TALL, GRAY, OMINOUS house now mars the otherwise perfect landscape. It's as if the realm shook, and the house appeared from the quake.

This should count as two nightmares.

There are four windows on each of the house's two stories. A wrap-around porch displays two rocking chairs that sway even in the perfectly still air. It looks to be hundreds of years old, with its chipping gray paint barely clinging to its rotten wooden sides. Untamed vines break through the shutters as they weave in and out of the splintered wooden slats. Almost all the glass windowpanes are broken and sharp. Despite its rotting state, I'm drawn to its charm.

I bet they weren't counting on that. My father was excellent at telling ghost stories.

The familiar voice in my head tells me what I already know: I have to go in.

The wood groans under my weight as I slowly step onto the front stairs. The rocking chairs halt once I reach the porch and creak like someone sitting on them has repositioned. The air grows cool and heavy, raising the hair on my arms. Something unseen tracks my every move.

"H-hello?" I say into the wind, but nothing changes. "I don't mean any harm." I want to continue, but my voice trails off, and the feeling of something watching me swells.

Unlike the rest of the battered house, the front door is a work of art. It's a deep mahogany with woodworking that could rival our old barn door. The wood is warm when I touch it, and I feel a hum of what can only be magick. The bronze handle looks recently oiled, paired with a skull-shaped bronze door knocker in the center.

I reach for the doorknob and a quick flash of light sparks from my fingers.

Did the door just do something to me?

I don't have a second to think, my dread so thick it's suffocating. I can feel the electric, buzzing charge of energy that tries to consume me. The rocking chairs start frantically moving, turning slightly with every erratic thrash. I swear I see something dark lunge for me as I open the door and slam it shut behind me in a thunderous, narrow escape.

It takes a minute to steady my breathing. A minute to realize the ominous presence is absent on the inside.

It's just me.

Me and...my cottage?

Not just my cottage, but that day, the one where everything ended. The day my parents...

I see the kitchen, the sitting room, the hall leading to my parents' room, and the ladder up to my loft. Everything coated in stinking, sticky blood. It's dripping from the ceiling and pooling on the floor.

This is worse than I remember.

There are pieces of flesh strewn about. Arms, legs, fingers. I see a trail of intestines leading down the hall. There is a sound that comes from nowhere and everywhere, and it's getting louder. A beating drum. It isn't until I look down at my feet that I find the source of the sound—a still-beating heart.

It's then that I scream, my body curling in on itself as I cower. *This isn't what happened!* I have to get out.

But the beautiful door I came through is gone. It's just a wall covered in splatters of blood. I spin in circles, running from wall to wall, from window to window. The blood makes the floor slick, and I move slowly to keep from falling into the gore. Every time I reach a window, it's suddenly gone, only returning once I get to the opposite wall. The back door is jammed shut, the handle covered in oily crimson. My hands are covered, slipping, and no matter the effort I put into it, I can't break it open. The thumping of the heart is maddening.

I run to the hall towards my parents' door, a severed piece of an intestine squelches beneath my foot, and I fall. There is even more blood up close. A warm, viscous pool that is constantly rising and coating me.

Gods, the smell.

It's a mix of copper and rancid meat. It hangs in the air and sinks into my skin.

I pull my hands up, but threads of heavy, wet flesh appear in stretched webs across them. As quickly as one breaks, another grows. Pieces are rapidly falling from above me, clinging to my hair and splashing blood onto my face. I can't wipe it off fast enough before more strings come together.

I can taste the fleshy pieces that cling to my mouth.

I frantically pull at my hair only to come back with a finger in my grasp. I'll never forget the sound it makes as I throw it against the wall, or the way I scream as it plops to the ground. I need to get up.

Get. Up. Evelyn.

I reach upward with all my strength, breaking through the bloody web, but it's not as fast as I am. Each snap of the sinew makes it a little easier to lean against the wall. My vision begins to clear without the grotesque puddle sticking to my face. I can see the door to my parents' room from here. If I can just get past this puddle of flesh, I can get inside.

Still dripping with the sanguineous fluids, I trudge toward the door. The clammy, wet putty of skin continues to grow, clinging to my feet. With every step, I slam my foot into the stew of flesh, shaking some of the pieces loose. They still reach for me in a tight, sticky grasp, but I have done so many jumping jacks that ripping my feet away isn't as hard as it should be.

As soon as I get to the door, it disappears. The sticky puddle subsides, but the door is completely gone. *I have to get in that room.* I need to save them. I back up, and the door appears again. I close my eyes and lunge forward, but slam into a solid wall.

The sound of the heart begins to speed up.

"Shut up!" I frantically shout.

The pounding doesn't relent, and I'm running out of options. The gore is so thick over my body. I can't rid myself of the dripping slickness; it clings like oil. Even as I thrash my arms, it just weighs down my limbs.

I slam into the door over and over again, willing it to burst open. Relenting, I rest my forehead against the space. The door remains this time but refuses to unlock. Toying with me. I can smell the oak, feel the grain of the wood, of home. I can't stop crying.

"Please, please open," I whisper as I turn and slide my body down the door to sit.

I curl into a ball, spasms taking over as I sob.

Lub dub. Lub dub. Lub dub.

The panic is a boulder on my chest.

Lub dub. Lub dub.

"Where are you, Mother?"

Lub dub.

Then, quiet. I'm not sure how, but I knew the deafening silence was final.

Gone. They're gone.

Tears continue to stream down my face. I failed them again. Silence beckons for me to just give in.

What could possibly be worth all this?

A thunk rings out in front to me as another door appears. As if being dropped into place.

Like the front door, the wood is a deep mahogany with a well-oiled bronze doorknob. I stand and reach for it without thinking. No light flickers as I twist it open, which happens easily, and reveals nothing but darkness.

As soon as my foot passes the threshold, I know it's a mistake. I'm met with no resistance and instantly begin to fall. A scream is wrenched from my throat as my stomach drops. My back hits the water first, slamming into it like stone. I sink immediately into the watery depths. I start swimming, kicking, and pulling, and kicking more, hoping the direction I'm heading is up. With every reach of my arms, the pressure builds in my chest, my lungs screaming from the lack of air. My lips begin to part when I finally break the surface. My desperate gasps are ragged and painful, just barely keeping me alive.

I tread in place, trying to keep my body afloat as fatigue weighs me down. At first glance, I think I'm in some type of cavern, but as my eyes adjust to the dim lighting, I can start to make out the walls of smooth stone surrounding me. A cylinder that extends up, and up and up. I frantically twist in the water until I realize there is no break in the wall, no path or stairway. I'm stuck at the bottom of a well.

The jet-black water is frigid. I constantly sink like I'm far heavier than I should be, like stepping through quicksand. Just before my head is completely submerged, I see a familiar, handsome face at the top of the well.

"Odin!" I scream. The water floods into my mouth, but the sound is still a mixture of relief and urgency.

Odin looks down at me and smiles. But it isn't his smile. It twists up, unnaturally wide, and he starts to laugh. And it isn't his voice. It's much deeper and angrier—an *evil* sound.

No.

My muscles are screaming with the unrelenting weight of my limbs. I'm so weak.

Was that really Odin? Or was it just a trick of the trial?

Water creeps over my face as I lose my battle with the pull, and I start to sink. I instantly relish in the heavy silence of being submerged. Maybe I can just drift into nothingness and be done. *At least this part is peaceful.*

A burning ache interrupts my solitude, and my eyes involuntarily open wide. Now there is only darkness, and I have no idea which way is up. Panic laces through me. No matter which direction I try to swim, nothing changes. The pressure in my chest rages until I can't take it any longer, and I have no choice but to open my mouth and let water flood into me.

This isn't peace. It's agony.

Smooth iridescent scales brush up against my foot and then skitter between my legs. *Just eat me, beast!* I pray to the gods. *Stop toying with me and end this!*

This thing glows with bright greens, pinks, and yellows. Some sort of eel, maybe? I can see the end of its tail, swirling like silken ribbons of light, and just barely make out the creature's torso: a skeletal elven-like being with thick silver strands of hair. Atop her head is a crown of bone, jutting out like it's attached to her skull.

In one last agonizing pulse, my lungs exhale, and I await my fate.

This mermaid of darkness slithers up my body as I start convulsing, and presses itself to me. I can't swim away, I can't breathe, and I'm uncontrollably heaving. Pausing as if to study me, the creature flashes her fangs before leaning in. Her hair floats around us in a silvery fog as she presses her bony mouth against my lips in a kiss. The graze of her sharp teeth nicks my skin, her head turning so that our mouths are fully locked together. And suddenly, air bursts into my mouth. Glorious, full, living breath nourishes my lungs. My mind clears, and with it so does my vision. I'm not as far down as I thought. *Was the surface always that close?*

The creature rips away from my mouth, disappearing into the darkness below.

I breach the surface, and a rope ladder appears. I climb each rung, making my way to the top. Just as I tumble over the edge of the well, my insides turn, and all of the water within my lungs spews out.

There is an open room that wasn't there before. The door I walked through is nowhere to be seen, disappearing along with Odin. It's just this new room, the size of a small bedchamber. No furniture. The walls are covered in stained floral wallpaper, and the hardwood floor is soiled with what looks like blood and, given the smell in the room, urine.

I think I'll call this scent "torture's grime." It's so common in this wretched place that I barely even mind it anymore.

Something stirs in the far corners of the room. Two unnaturally thin elven-like creatures are clinging to the ceiling, their heads tilted all the way backwards, looking at me with upside-down faces. So reminiscent of the flesh demon from my first trial, they begin to scuttle closer to me in twitching movements, their joints popping in and out at strange angles. They look like spiders, the way they move over the ceiling. As they get closer, I recognize their faces. They are King Edward and Queen Vanessa of the Kingdom of Daydream, Odin's parents. Their lips aren't moving, but they open their mouths wide, and scolding voices start screaming at me.

"You killed your parents, you wretched thing."

"You are disgusting inside and out."

"Everything they went through is because of you, you selfish pig."

I know this is all part of the design meant to break me, but I still feel it as though it were real. They're right. If I hadn't been pursuing Odin, I would have been there. Even if I couldn't have saved them, we would still be together, even in death.

My throat starts to burn as the *things* get closer. Blood drips from their mouths and lifeless eyes as they flit across the stone ceiling. There is nowhere for me to retreat. I close my eyes, letting the tears spill over as the room fills with their taunts and the skittering sound of their appendages.

Scratch. Click. Scratch.

"This is your doing; if it weren't for you, they'd still be here. You know it's true."

"You aren't even worthy of this test, or any redemption."

"What would life even be like, living with such guilt?"

Click. Scratch. Click

Closer and closer the sounds come.

"You were not meant to be in the woods that day; you could have saved them if you had been home."

"You are a worthless girl, and now you have no family."

Scratch. Scratch. Click. Click.

"Stay far away from our son. He deserves the world, and you are but the lowest filth of the land."

"I love him!"

Panting, I force myself to look at each of the despicable creatures on the ceiling. Somewhere in their furious accusations, my mind started to remember. I saw Odin. I saw him in my cottage. I saw him in the woods. I saw us holding hands as we walked through the wildflowers. We were in love. I know it with every part of my soul, even though I can't remember it all yet. Even though all I can recall is up until that horribly wretched day when my parents were taken from me.

I start laughing. "You have no idea the gift you have given me, because above all else, despite your efforts, I remember our love. That one thing is stronger than anything here in this nightmare. And absolutely nothing you can say to me will change it."

They're right above me now. Their blood drips, raining down around me. As it reaches the floor, it hardens slightly, turning into a rope of fleshy, sinewy, bloodstained tautness. It begins to take on a life of its own, wrapping around me like a spider's web. It's just like the puddle from the cottage, but stronger. So much stronger. They're going to trap me here.

Arms thrashing, I roar and start breaking the threads, but they regenerate almost as quickly as they snap. Pure adrenaline takes over, fueling thrash after manic thrash. I scream, and a burst of blinding light shoots out around me, filling the room. All at once, the strands disappear, the room is silent, and the creatures fall from the ceiling. They land in a wet thump on the floor in front of me. Just lying there, eyes fixed on the ceiling, unmoving.

Where did that light come from?

I look around for any change. Maybe it was someone else in the trials. Perhaps I am dead and I just don't know it yet.

I look at my fingertips. Dirty, but otherwise fine. I stretch them out in front of me, weary of what might explode from them. But nothing. I try again, faster, with more muscle. Left, right, one hand, the other. Nothing.

It must be something about the Nightmare Trials. Maybe I passed this part of the test, and that is just how it ends.

As if answering my thoughts, a foggy black cloud seeps in through the cracks in the walls, an instant confirmation that this is over, for now. And just like it never happened at all, when my eyes open, I'm on the floor of my cell.

Chapter 13 Gwen

I DOUBT EVELYN EVEN realizes there's an entire council watching her through an old magicked mirror. Safely tucked into lush black velvet armchairs—sipping mead, debating politics, fucking—while hellhounds are hunting her through the cursed maze of her nightmares. The walls burn red as firelight flickers across writhing, naked bodies. I enjoy pleasure as much as the next, but not here, in this room. I hate when the Nightmare Trials come around. The anticipation leading up to them. The stress and exhaustion it places on Cane.

The Trials began generations ago, longer than anyone still alive remembers. They were an honorable challenge to test strength and spirit. Only the best were selected for the Night Shroud, an elite group of warriors and strategists that serve on the king and queen's council and provide protection to the royal family. But then the realm fell into a dark time known as the Sundering. Our once unified Realm of Sallix was fractured, our kingdoms cast apart, and everything changed. The Kingdom of Nightmare was holding its trials at the time of the power shift. When chaos swept the land, the trial was twisted by the unstable energy. Contestants went mad, slaughtering each other in a blood-soaked arena. Not even the most powerful could control the insanity. From this chaotic energy, the Nightmare Trials were born.

At first, the king and queen put an end to the quinquennial games, banning a centuries-old tradition to protect the kingdom's people. But they soon discovered that the unstable magick coursing through the land had other plans. The arena itself became a never ending battlefield. When one person fell, another was dragged in to take their place. The chaos chose its victims at random, even children. People would go to sleep in their own beds and wake in the center of the arena, crazed and bloodthirsty.

Desperate to halt the madness and uncover the source of the realm's instability, the king and queen sought out an ancient crone. She led them to a relic, an orb that glowed in response to chaotic energy. Through it, they learned to contain the chaos until it reached a crescendo, at which point they could intentionally trigger the trials, shaping the madness into something structured, if still brutal. It was as though the trials themselves were a bloodthirsty beast, one that had to be fed, or else true insanity would overtake the kingdom.

Over time, the king and queen found ways to temper if only a little. Contestants no longer had to fight one another to win the games, but instead faced themselves, battling their own nightmares. With a single drop of a contestant's blood, pledged willingly, they were transported to the Grimm Lodge, where they remained until the trials concluded, either in death or in victory. Yet even with these changes, the brutality of the accommodations could not be eased. Once the trials began, there was little the crown could do to interfere. Victors were still offered a place in the Night Shroud, of course, along with a sizable boon meant to entice citizens to volunteer.

But the kingdom's energy has changed in recent years. I know it—Cane feels it too. The chaos is growing wilder, more torturous. So severe that fewer are brave enough to enter, even as Cane increases the boon to the point where it promises wealth and freedom for eternity.

To make matters that much worse, there has been a significant rise in Night Terror Golems. After the Sundering, the creatures infested our kingdom. They emerge from the leylines in our land and increase in numbers ahead of each trial, another signal of the chaos to come. They have been appearing more frequently, and the orb never fully dulls as it used to.

It's sickening to watch the old elves laugh and trade jokes while Evelyn is pushed to the edge. Exhausting her mind and body to just inches from death or hysteria, or both. Their amusement, their detachment is *wrong*. Their *colors* are wrong, all blends of muted greens and grays, greed and self-righteous sophistication—nothing like the bright, vibrant colors I see in Cane, or even Evelyn.

Cane stands beside me, eyes locked on the mirror, silent and focused. I know it pains him to endure this even more than me. I wrap my fingers around his. With every scream, every shadow that flickers across the glass, I squeeze a little harder, clinging to his warmth and safety.

And still, the laughter behind us rages on.

As the event continues, my chest tightens, and the anticipation in the back of my throat burns almost to the point of suffocation. There is no way Evelyn can survive this. Blood cocoons her in place. The arachnid beasts skitter closer. Burying my face into Cane's shoulder, I take a steadying breath, letting his toasted sugar and vanilla scent ground me. I just barely miss the bright flash of light. Was it the mirror? Or something else? Before I can really see anything, Cane stands, snaps his fingers, and the mirror swirls to darkness. The trial is over. And Evelyn won, again.

"Gods, I can't believe she didn't die in there!" I whisper-yell at Cane. We make our exit first, leaving the mob of lost bets and sweaty bodies in the stale air of the viewing room. I know it's not Cane's fault, but I just want someone to *do* something. I've tried everything I can to help Evelyn in the trial, when technically I'm not supposed to help her at all. The healing tincture was definitely against the rules. I've become attached to this contestant. Willing her to win. Every time I see her, I get this feeling that she's meant for more than this, and I'm meant to help her. Cane thinks it's absurd, but I think he's just afraid to hope.

We make it to his room, and I can see his muscles relax, if only just a fraction. "You know that I can't interfere once they're in the trials. My hands are tied, even on this one." Cane remarks as he pours amber liquor into a crystal glass.

He says this as if it means nothing to him, but I can see that he's more disturbed by this last trial than usual. Neither of us wants to see anyone fail.

There is a loaded silence as I stare Cane down. But then guilt washes over me. Sage. I didn't even think to check the mirror for her. "Did Sage—" I begin to say, but Cane gives his head a shake, a solemn look on his face.

Evelyn and Sage had made it further in this trial than most. I didn't know Sage well, but that woman held her own in there. Until she didn't. Even she couldn't survive the physical horrors of her last trial. If Sage couldn't do it, "How did Evelyn make it out?"

Cane's eyes widen a little as if searching for an answer in the room. "I'm not sure. There was a glitch in the mirror, some light interference, I couldn't see what happened. I just know she passed."

I link my arm in Cane's and start walking towards the door. "We should go check on her, see if she needs anything."

"Our Little Raven has proven herself resourceful. You can't interfere, Gwen. Trust that whatever happens is meant to."

I roll my eyes. "Can't you just *be nice*?"

"I'm not being malicious. Besides, nice is for my people, nice is for you. Evelyn is not one of us. She is a puzzle that I have not pieced together. You need to remember that. You forget what I can do. You forget how I manipulate these trials. When Evelyn crossed our border and I looked into her mind, her memories, you know what I saw? Nothing. Every path I took to find out who she really was would end on a cliff's edge. This was nothing like the way one loses themselves when they're old or sick. This was unnatural. Like someone cut me from those paths."

I quirk my head at him, urging him to continue. *Why didn't he tell me this sooner?*

"So every night, I've been walking into her nightmares and piecing her back together, bit by bit, brick by brick. I've taken those mental walls apart, and do you know what I found?"

I shake my head, knowing I won't like what I hear next.

"She knows King Odin, Gwen. She was *with* him. I've only been able to piece together through her adolescence. She grew up a farmer's daughter, playing with the fucking prince in the forest behind her house."

"So she escaped from Daydream then?"

"Escaped? She practically begged the guards to put her in the Grimm Lodge. No, there is more to our Little Raven than even she remembers, and I plan to find out first."

Maybe she was placed here for a reason, but I know that there is something special about her, and I plan to find out what.

"You may be right, but she deserves to finish the trials. To win. It doesn't matter who she is. We need to show her who *we* are."

Chapter 14 Evelyn

ANY FALSE SENSE OF comfort instantly disappears as the bleak and utter silence surrounds me in the dungeons. No screams or moans. No wailing.

I scramble to my feet as the throbbing in my head settles into a steady ache. Lurching toward the side bars of my cell, I grip them hard. "Sage. We did it!" My voice is raw, raspy. The words echo off the cold, stone walls, and the thick, metallic scent of blood floods my senses. My fingers curl around the iron bars, knuckles blanching. My eyes adjust to the darkness at a maddening pace.

I see mutilated body parts strewn across the floor, discarded like old pieces of clothing. And the blood. So. Much. Blood. There is a pile of bones, muscles, and flesh. I see auburn hair that's attached to what used to be her head. Her fearless features twisted into a grotesque, lifeless stare. *It can't be. It just can't be. It's not fair.* Something sinks heavy in my chest, like despair, but darker. And then I scream. It's from the darkest part of me, the kind that only exists in the worst of nightmares. But this isn't a nightmare. This is real.

We're getting out of this together.

I huddle in the corner of my cell, squeezing my eyes shut, rocking. I try to picture my forest, my parents, and Odin. I try to hold on to just one happy memory, but each smile I pull forward transforms into Sage's deformed face. I begin counting. *One, two, three...* Anything to clear my mind. At some point, my consciousness wanes, and I fall into a dreamless sleep.

Sage's body has been removed from the cell, cleaned like she was never there at all. Maybe she was just a hallucination, part of a nightmare. But I know it's a lie, my mind trying to ease my own despair.

Sage was in much better shape than I am. She *trained* to be here. And who am I? *Gods, I barely even know that.* I'm a farmer's daughter, not a warrior. If she couldn't do it, how can I? It's not fair. She had no right to give me all this false hope. Anger rises all the way up to my head, burning and livid. Who did she think she was, offering so much companionship and then leaving me here alone? What's going to happen now? I'll never get to thank her, she'll never know what she meant to me, and I'll never get to see her smile outside of these walls. And for what? These horrible nightmare elves destroyed a beautiful soul and a powerful warrior. And probably countless more. The first thing I'm going to do when I'm out of here is destroy this dungeon. Burn it to the ground until every last nightmare is ash.

There is no reason to hold back tears, and it feels good to let them fall. My mouth twists in torturous sobs. First, I cry for the life I miss, then I cry for the life I can't remember. I cry for Sage and my parents.

How long will this last? I would complete one hundred bone-shredding trials before having to endure those awful twisted faces again. The king and queen—*my* king and queen—spewing such hate. I know Odin is still important to me; I can feel it. I don't know how long we've been apart, but I need to get back to him.

Click.

I halt, the sudden noise an unwelcome invasion in my now silent purgatory. "Hello?"

My cell door swings open. Still, no one is there. I wait for a tray, for some disgusting display of sexual taunting, a monster...but nothing emerges.

I stand up and scurry towards the open door, pausing at the entrance, waiting for a sign that this is a trap. I have only ever seen anyone come from the door to the right, and now it's wide open, taunting me forward. *I should at least try to escape.*

Without a second guess, I sprint for the opening and am met with a set of steep stairs. My already exhausted body struggles with each step I take. Wood creaks under my feet as a cold, stale draft wafts down from above. As hard as I try, I can't make out where the stairwell ends.

Suddenly, light pierces through the darkness as a door creaks open, casting a long shadow that stretches ahead of the figure stepping into view. I wince as sharp pain lances through my eyes, the bright, painful intrusion causing them to blur, and I'm unable to make out the person standing before me.

Then I hear it. Clapping. *I am such an idiot.*

"You made it so much further than I thought you would, Little Raven," the pretentious man says. "That last trial was horrid, I thought for sure I would be peeling you off the bottom of the stairs." I can see his face now, eyeing me with an amused smirk.

"You mean like you peeled away Sage?" I still can't really see his face, but I see his shoulders sag before straightening.

"You have more willpower than I thought," he continues as he saunters down towards me. "Let's go back down to your room." He says this as if

I'm a child who got out of bed in the middle of the night. He takes me by my elbow and leads me back to the cesspit below.

I spin out of the man's grip, almost losing my balance and tumbling the entirety of the way.

No. I will not go back.

He catches me, sensing my panic and will to flee.

"My room?" I spit out. My rage boils over, and I think of Sage as I say my next words, "You mean my fucking cage? Why bait me with freedom? What the fuck is the point of this? I finished my trial. Is that not how one gains freedom? Are Sage's stories of passing the trials just to get people to join so you can brutally torture them?" I'm shouting through sobs welling in my throat.

I just want one gods damned answer.

He doesn't say anything at first, keeping his smirk plastered to his stupid face. "If you must know, this was to see how far you would make it if given the chance. To see if you *wanted* to be out, to be free. To see if you were broken from the anguish, the torment, the complete torture of your last trial." He says that part like a performance, waving his free hand around. "I can see now that you are not so easily broken, Little Raven. Even I have underestimated you."

"My. Name. Is. Evelyn." I grind out through clenched teeth.

The man chuckles. "That it is, Evelyn. Come, let's get back. I have a gift for you." A basket appears on the elbow of his free arm.

"Why can't I see anyone else here?"

"Don't worry yourself with the others." It's strange, but I swear I can feel a shudder run through him like it pains him to speak of the other people here.

"How can you be so cruel?" I growl under my breath.

He doesn't argue with my insults, just gives me a tight-lipped smile. "I know so much more than you could ever understand, *Evelyn*."

My cell door's still open—the man motions for me to sit on my rock-cot.

"I prefer to stand," I say

"As you wish."

He places the basket on my cot and opens it. Inside, there's a fresh pair of black leggings and a deep purple long-sleeved tunic. Undergarments too. The sight of these fresh clothes almost brings a *thank you* to my lips, but I quickly bite my tongue. I won't show him any appreciation. He continues to pull things out. A brown canteen, three small wrapped parcels, and a large, clear jar with liquid and a cloth inside.

"This is for you, for your bravery and determination." He pauses, sending me an expectant look.

If he is waiting for a thank you, he can wait for an eternity.

He speaks as if I have missed something, as if I can't see the basket.

"As you can see, there's a new set of clothes, fresh water, bread, cheese, dried meat," I remain scowling and silent as he continues. "The jar is magicked. It contains water and a cloth for cleaning yourself." More to himself, he says, "You are emanating quite the stench, if I do say so myself." He looks at me with something like pity. "The water will stay clear, and you can drop the cloth in as many times as you need; it will emerge clean. When you are done with it, just leave it by the door, and it will be retrieved. The magick only lasts a few hours. You will know that it has run out because, well, the water will turn as filthy as you are now."

Disbelief starts to chip at the wall of stubbornness I've built.

"Why are you doing this? Why support me, but not free me?"

The arrogant twat smirks at me. A dark, alluring smile that I'm sure turns most women into puddles.

"Oh, Little Raven, the magick of the Nightmare Trials does not allow me to pull anyone out once it has started, but I can contribute in small ways."

He looks around the dungeon, murmuring to himself, "Sadly, I can not control the accommodations." But then he shakes his head and stalks closer to me. A predator locked into its prey.

I think he is going to pounce, but instead, he just sighs, pausing for longer than necessary. "You put *yourself* in my trials. Believe it or don't. I can't set you free."

I feel my skin pale. "What do you mean I'm in *your* trials? Who are you?" Through the man's laughter, he says, "Oh, have I not introduced myself properly? I'm Cane. Although some call me 'His Majesty' or 'Sire.' It's a pleasure to make your acquaintance."

I scoff at his declaration. "Oh, so now you're a jester? Those titles are for kings..."

I'm not sure what my face is doing, but my insides are whirling.

A wry smile crosses his face. "That's right, *Evelyn*. I am the King of the Kingdom of Nightmare." At the declaration, he flicks his wrists, and wisps of shadows flow off his fingers like fog rolling in on a cool harvest evening. And just as quickly, they retreat with a snap of his fingers. "As I was saying, this is my gift, my power. I know you, Evelyn. I know everyone here. I know your secret fears and your darkest pleasures. I can bring them to you and take them away just as quickly."

I remain standing in the middle of the cell, petrified, collecting my thoughts. He circles me. Cane—the king—flicks his wrist and shadows uncoil from his hands, forming hundreds of small spiders that begin crawling towards me, circling.

"I can create any fear, any nightmare," he says as his shadow spiders skitter over my feet and up my legs.

I let out a screech that echoes throughout the Grimm Lodge and jump onto my stone cot. Spinning in circles, I kick and flail my arms. All the while, a sound of laughter rings through in the background.

"Get them off of me!"

The spiders continue their climb up me, covering my legs, abdomen, and making their way up my neck. I slap at my neck and my face, but the shadow spiders are relentless. I close my mouth and eyes, shaking in anger and fear. When suddenly, just as quickly as the spiders covered me, they're gone.

I open my eyes and watch as a lingering tendril of shadows retreats up the stairs. Following Cane, *the king*, as he departs.

Was that entire encounter a nightmare?

The only sign that Cane was actually here is the basket still sitting on my stone cot. The water he mentioned, that's real too, and it's warm to the touch. I start with my hands, wiping away the mixture of blood and dirt that's stained into the grain of my fingerprints like crusted paint. Scabs come free from between the hairs on my arms and legs. I scrub at myself harder and faster as the grime lessens. The liquid pooling on the cell floor is a burnt muddy red, and he was right, it's rancid. I start to see clear skin between my newly forming scars. I take a moment to trace the heart-shaped scar on my thigh. I close my eyes, picturing what little I know of the girl I used to be.

Satisfied that I'm as clean as I can make myself without a full bath, I slip into my new undergarments and clothing. They fit perfectly, and the feeling is ecstasy.

I finally lay down on the stone slab, events of the day still bombarding my mind. Although I often linger on the trials, my thoughts keep straying back to Cane. He puts on a face of arrogance, but he also came to help me.

An act that I know he didn't need to do. An act that is well below that of a king.

Despite his taunting nature, I want him to come back. I have so many questions. I want to plead with him to set me free. To tell him that this was all a misunderstanding.

I roll to my side, thinking that sleep will elude me after the torment of the day, but my body is completely exhausted, and I'm pulled into my dreams.

Chapter 15 Evelyn

I'm thrown into my dream like an angry storm. My tormented emotions reach a crescendo as my panic continues to rise.

I'm back in the throne room.

My body is sixteen years old, and Odin is holding my hand by my side.

"Mother. Father. This is Evelyn."

My head whips around to Odin. I know he can see me staring at the side of his head, but he doesn't turn to look at me. He keeps his eyes on the dais where the king and queen are seated.

"Son," the queen says, ignoring his introduction. "Why do you look like you have been frolicking in a pig pen?"

I feel invisible and garishly out of place all at once.

"Mother," Odin continues, "this is Evelyn. She lives at a farm on the outskirts of our kingdom. She was in the woods today when she heard screaming and discovered her parents were gone from her home." He looks at me tenderly for a moment before looking back to his mother. Softer, he adds, "There was blood. Everywhere."

The king and queen still appear unfazed, like they are painfully waiting for him to get to the point.

Odin takes a steadying breath. "I have been meeting Evelyn in the woods near her farm since we were both young." The queen's features twist now as she looks down her nose at him, her mouth beginning to open. "*Don't,*" he spits out. "I will answer any questions you have later. The only thing you need to know now is that she is important, maybe the most important thing in the world to me. She is not just some farmer's daughter; she is my dearest friend. As the crowned prince of the Kingdom of Daydream, I offer her sanctuary here with us." His words come out with such graceful elegance. So different from the boy that I've run carelessly through the woods with.

I want to be so angry with him. But more than that, it hurts to watch. He puts on a mask with his parents. They have no idea who he really is. He can't show his own family the Odin I know.

Neither Odin nor his parents backs down. I clear my throat, bringing Odin's attention back to me. "Odin, we don't even know for sure they are dead. We didn't see them. Only the aftermath of whatever occurred in my house. We can still find them."

I look up at the king and queen, their glaring eyes locked on me now, with so much mistrust behind them.

"Your Majesties, you can send guards out to look for them, can't you? If you please." I try so hard to sound proper, but I have absolutely nothing to offer them, and urgency fuels my desperate tone.

The queen is quick to answer, but I see it written all over her face. Pity. "Oh, dear child. I am afraid that if what you say is true, then there is no hope for your beloved parents. You see, there is a known deviant evading our capture who has been raiding the local farms. It was only a matter of time before they reached yours. And the attacks have yielded no survivors.

Just disgusting, gory remains." I'm holding back tears with near insanity. "You must be so grateful that you weren't in the house when it happened. You surely would have been terrified, and probably—"

"Mother!" Odin interrupts, probably to keep her from saying "nothing but a pile of meat." The more I'm around the queen, the more I understand Odin. I would have kept her at a distance, too.

She inhales, still staring at me, before finally deciding to change the subject. "Although we will not be able to save your parents, rest assured that we will do everything in our power to find and sentence their murderer. We have already been on his tail, sparing no expense."

Why hadn't we heard of the other attacks? The king and queen knew? Why didn't they warn anyone? We could have been prepared for this. My parents could still be alive.

Something the queen said sinks heavily in the pit of my stomach. *Murderer.*

I was just with them this morning. I gave my mother a peck on her cheek before telling her that I was going to the woods to meet Odin. I watched my father carry buckets of water to the shed for the chickens. Has time stopped? Moved faster?

My parents were murdered today...My parents...were murdered today...

I hear the thoughts, I feel them, and I remember them all in the same moment.

I sink to my knees. Tears stream down my cheeks, and Odin's arms envelop me. I let him scoop me up and carry me away.

I can't even think about my exchange with the king and queen—*Odin's parents*— as we enter a cozy, quiet bedroom. Still in his arms, against his chest, and through tears, I unravel so many questions. "You are a prince, Odin? Your parents are the king and queen? And you never said anything to me? I thought we trusted each other. You always said your parents were busy, but you never once mentioned that it was because they were *royalty*."

"Evelyn." His strong, tender voice soothes every bone in my body. I'm still frantic with the day's events, but he anchors me. I wonder if he knows just how important he is to me, even as I don't filter the outrage in my questioning.

"Did you know that an attacker was raiding the farms? How could you keep that from me?" I am so angry. Angrier as the realization sets in. "We should have been at the cottage! You knew it was dangerous!" I'm shouting now, and I pound his chest with my fists as I push off of him. "You knew! You could have protected us! We could have protected my parents. Why didn't you tell me..." I sag back into this chest and sob. He doesn't say anything for a moment, just holds the back of my neck close and rests his head on mine as I shake with grief.

"I cherish our bond more than anything else in this gods forsaken world, Evelyn." He says in a soothing, gentle tone. "What we have built together in our short lives is something that I could never find from anyone else, I don't *want* to find in anyone else. Not even my family. It is sacred. It is ours alone. If you knew I was royalty, who knows how that might have changed. I was young, and I didn't want you to see me as anything but Odin the boy. Not Odin the prince. And as we grew and more time passed, I didn't know how to tell you."

There is a long pause. Filled with the sounds of my sobbing and sniffles. "You asked if I knew about the farms being raided." Cupping my face, he locks his gaze with mine, his sky-blue eyes glistening with unshed tears. "I did know. I am so sorry, Evelyn. I didn't want to believe that it would ever come to your home. It was always a whisper of news happening far away. We hear about criminals constantly. I didn't want to worry you or reveal my identity in that way. I never meant to reveal it this way either. And I am sorry. I wish I could change it. I will spend every day from this day forward making it up to you."

My cries continue for the hurt I feel pushing down on my heart, but I ache too, to forgive my best friend. I yearn to feel at peace with *something*. So when he pauses, I blurt out, "What makes you think being a prince would change anything about the way I feel for you? I have loved you, my wild forest boy, since we first met in the woods. Before I even knew what love was. I would die for you, Odin. It's *me*. You trust *me,* don't you? You just said we have something that is ours alone. You said it! Did you not mean it? How could you feel that way all the while hiding your true self from me?" He is quiet, guilt painted across his pain-stricken face. I don't want to admit that I understand, but I do, and I hate to make him feel any more hurt than he already does. But I hurt. So much that nothing matters but quelling the pain, even at Odin's expense.

Silence sits heavy between us for a moment. "You can't ever lie to me again, do you understand? Not ever. No secrets. I can't bear it, and I could never forgive you." It just pours out of me, even though I'm not sure I mean it. But I hold my stare with his perfect crystal eyes as I shake with sorrow. He hesitates for just one second, but doesn't break the stare.

His eyes soften, and he pulls my hand over his heart. "I swear to you, I won't hide anything from you ever again. My heart is yours. Has always been yours." He hardly finishes speaking before I press my lips firmly against his, still wet from tears. I'm so desperate for the feeling of home that this man gives me. He pulls my head upwards, and we stay like this, locked together for the first time since the woods. I can feel him breathing. The warmth of his body, his tongue gently exploring my mouth. I pull back slightly and press my forehead against his, our eyes closed. I wish we could stay here forever, for this and every lifetime, connected wholly.

He lays me down in the soft, silken sheets and then lies beside me. My hand rests over his heart as if it has a mind of its own. I'm so grateful for this bit of peace. His breath steadies as he drifts off to sleep, his body relaxing around me.

I let my grief push through, here, where I'm safe.

Tears steadily cascade down my cheeks as I push closer into Odin. Hoping the warmth and stillness of his body will help soothe the ache in my heart and soul.

Chapter 16 Evelyn

THIS DREAMING MEMORY SEEMS longer than the others. I'm thrown from one glimpse to the next as the moments unravel in the hours following my parents' death. I'm never thrown into consciousness back in my dark dungeon cell. I continue to live through my memories like they are happening anew.

Time slows, and I see that, thankfully, the queen and king hold true to their word. Not two days after my parents' murder, Odin and I are following his parents to the dungeons. His hand holds firmly to mine, squeezing every few steps in silent reassurance.

An elven man lies on the floor of a cell, cackling to himself.

The king steps forward. "He, dearest Evelyn, is the one who slayed your parents. He admitted as much when we caught him breaking into another local farm."

Something about this person feels wrong. He seems broken and completely out of his mind. I feel uneasy just being this close to him, but Odin squeezes my hand again. I see his jaw clench, holding back his fury. His eyes are glazed with the sheen of unshed tears, but he keeps his composure, as I'm sure he's needed to his whole life.

The man has moved to a crouch in his cell—the murderer who took my parents from me. I want to scream. I want him to know that he is despicable, the vilest of creatures. When I look at him, though, all I see is a husk of a person, not even capable of malice. His clothes are in tatters, covered in mud and blood. His blond hair resembles a nest as it mats around his face, and his skin looks like gray leather as it stretches over his hunger-stricken frame. When he opens his mouth to speak, the smell of decay wafts out as I glimpse his rotten and cracked teeth. *How could he have done this?*

"Death to all, death to all. He is coming and there will be death to all." He laughs to himself.

I can't bear to look at him any longer. My parents deserved a longer life, and I deserved to watch them grow old. My future children deserved loving grandparents. To lose so much to a frail, crazed, maniac…I still can't believe it.

I look up at Odin, pleading for him to take me away. And he does, but instead of going back to the castle or for a walk through the gardens, he offers to bring me back to my cottage to get my belongings.

"Maybe now's the best time to say goodbye?" He is so eager to support me, to guide me, but my heart thrashes against my ribs and a burning wells in my throat at the thought of going home. I do my best to smile, and it's enough for Odin to squeeze my hand and lead me to my home.

⟫⟫⟫ ⟪⟪⟪

The sole of my shoe barely touches the frame of the door. I can hear Papa's soothing voice as he reads stories to us. Hear the fiery crackle beneath his words. Mama's chair creaks in high-pitched notes that move just slightly faster when she's really into his tales. Everything she knits smells like sheep's wool and dried herbs. I can still see those herbs hanging over the window in the kitchen—the spot where Mama and I would make dinner every night.

"I can't do it." I look up at Odin with pleading eyes. "Please don't make me go in there. I can't do it. I can't go home without them."

He pulls me into his chest. My panic turning into wailing sobs, my tears soaking into his white shirt.

"Shh, shh. You don't need to do anything you're not ready for. I'll have someone come and gather your belongings," as my knees buckle and my grief becomes all-consuming. He catches me.

My memories cascade forward to a point in my life where I still feel the grief, but it has begun to ebb. Always present but not consuming. I'm enthralled by the life that Odin lives, the life that *we* now live. I have my own bedchamber with a sitting area and a bathing room. Someone always helps me draw my bath and lays my clothes out for me. And the *clothes*. They are the most delicate and beautiful fabrics I have ever laid eyes on. It's a strange feeling, letting people dress me, serve me, but it's a welcome one. It's a distraction I'm happy to bury myself in. Every day, I push my grief aside with busy work: shopping, walking the gardens, reading books in the library about star-crossed lovers and flying beasts.

Odin and I are inseparable. Our attraction isn't only physical; it runs so much deeper than that. As if without words, we both know we would give anything to be alone in the woods again. We pledge ourselves to each other in every way we know how. He'll find me in a library window seat just to pepper kisses along my neck. He once declared I will one day be his queen so boisterously that his joyous voice caught the attention of the librarian. She quite literally chased us out. If it weren't for the Daydream marriage laws, we would have wed the second we turned eighteen. Royals must wait until they're thirty to marry. It gives time to ensure the best match for the kingdom is secured, and that children don't hold the fate of the people in their hands.

I try to help him any way I can. He is a prince, after all, and he bears the weight of so much responsibility. If I can take even the smallest of tasks off his shoulders, I do. Our burdens are ones we carry together. I often attend meetings with the local townsfolk and soon become a liaison for the palace. Odin says that I'm better at talking to people than he is. That I have a softness because of my countryside upbringing. Even that makes me ache for him. He is still so afraid to be himself in front of anyone. Like if they are faced with a "prince," they may no longer see him as a person at all. So I attend banquets and dinner parties and report back on anything important. Doing this together fulfills something within me that I didn't know I craved. It gives me a purpose beyond shopping and meandering the garden. And I'm helping the man I love run our kingdom.

The dream glitches again. I'm in a room with sheer black curtains, and the soft hum of stifled sobs fills the air. Odin is beside me, our hands naturally clasped. Tears streak Odin's cheeks, and I feel them coating my face as well. Up ahead, where the king and queen's thrones once stood, are two marble altars covered in silks, the king and queen displayed, lying in wake. The room is thick with somber murmurs.

"Such a sorrow at twenty-three to have your parents taken."

"How can a king so young rule our entire kingdom?"

Just as I twist to look behind me, another glitch, and now I'm staring at Odin on the throne. He's sitting there with a crown atop his head and his hand outstretched to me. Odin, my wild forest boy, is now my king. He whispers in my ear, "Are you happy, my love? You are everything I have hoped for. You are my best friend, my lover, and you have always been my queen. Now we can officially live out our dreams together."

Even though we are both still healing, I *am* happy. I can see our future, and I know we'll make the kingdom strong. "I'm elated, Odin. We get to be King and Queen of Daydream together, just like we pretended we were in the woods. I don't tell you enough how I am constantly awed and honored that I get to share my life with you."

With Odin's coronation comes more duties and more training. Odin has always attended daily sparring lessons, but as the king, he's expected to not only be able to hold his own in a battle, but to lead his army to victory. I train too. Every day starts with a run through the gardens, and then I head to the training field for sparring. And I enjoy sparring so much, I think some of the guards are actually starting to fight back. I hone my aim with a bow and arrow, and master the halladie dagger. Where most of the ladies in court bear soft lines and delicate features, my body tells a different story. I'm more toned with defined curves and the faint roughness of calluses forming on my hands. I know I won't ever be sent into battle, but I crave this feeling of strength. Of never feeling as helpless as I did that day my parents were murdered.

My memories keep flashing by. I spend more and more time working with Freyr, the castle gardener, to incorporate my favorite flowers through this floral sanctuary. He is a short, elderly elven man, and he often greets me with a smile and a freshly picked tulip. Sometimes he even places a hibiscus in my hair, tucked behind my ear, or a lily in my braid. We adore each other's company, and the company of the flowers. My mother would have loved him.

The garden is magnificent. In the center is a large weeping willow with branches so low that you can hide within them. There's something about it that always pulls me in. It makes me feel alive.

The surrounding grounds are covered in all of the colors of the rainbow. Some plants are specifically for butterflies, and they flutter about gracefully, illuminated by the sun. Others are for the bees. I hear them pleasantly buzzing from flower to flower. I use their fresh honey to make mother's soap, and it smells almost as sweet as when we made it together in our cottage.

I glance up at the massive tree and something startles me. At first glance, it appears like half the tree is glistening with dark, oily sparkles instead of the pearly, opal grays that paint the green leaves like crystals. But one blink and it's gone. As I get closer to it, I see someone coming towards me from another path.

Odin? I thought he was at a guard's meeting today.

I can already see his smile, mirroring mine. As we get closer to each other, he grabs my hand, looks around, and pulls me through the willow branches. Underneath the tree canopy is an entirely different world. It smells of flowers, soil, and sunshine. The light filters in from between the willow branches, but we're virtually invisible here to anyone walking by. There's a soft fur blanket lying on the ground, complete with a bottle of wine and two crystal glasses. On a silver platter lies fresh cheese and berries.

My heart squeezes. I spin around, reveling in the beauty and abundance that is my life. My gaze lands on Odin as the skirt of my dress swirls and settles around me. He's always been breathtaking, but as we have gotten older, he has become harder and harder for me to take my eyes off of. I have to stand on my toes just to look into his crystal blue eyes now. His pants are tight-fitting and accentuate his buttocks, and he always leaves his tunic undone, showing off a small patch of his well defined muscles.

As he gets closer, I yearn to run my hands through his wavy blond hair. He usually keeps it in a plait, but today it's loose, framing his face down to his shoulders. His blue eyes twinkle when he looks at me, and his mouth parts as he licks his bottom lip.

"My, my, my. I had no idea anyone would be out here on this fine day," he says with a mocking grin.

I let out a pretend gasp. "My king, it is I who am surprised. I didn't think I would see you until dinner," I say as I run my hands down his arms.

He wraps me in a tight embrace—the safest place in the realm. I rest my head on his chest, and he strokes my hair with one hand while he continues to hold me with his other. After a moment, he touches my chin and lifts my face to his. "Since we have met here, totally coincidentally, would you care to join me for lunch?" He presses a soft kiss to my temple, my cheek, and then my lips. I let out a breathy moan, and my lips part slightly. His kiss is soft and sweet, deep and sensual. He trails his mouth down my neck as I run my hands through his hair.

"I will have to check my schedule, it is *very* bu—"

Before I can finish, he sweeps me off my feet, and my euphoric laughter fills the air. He lays me down on soft furs, bracing himself over me. His arms cage my head as soft kisses pepper my lips. "Gods, you look divine today. You know I can't resist you when you wear red."

His lips trail down my neck and I let out a soft groan.

"Call me king again," he says with a feral grin. But I wait, I like watching him want me. I think he senses my attention when he whispers into my ear, "I love you, Evelyn, forever."

"I love you too, *my king*."

He growls as he unties my camisole, my nipples peaking as the cool air hits them, and continues his ministrations across my collarbone and down my chest. When he reaches my breasts, my eyes roll back. The warmth begins to spread from my belly down to my core. I watch as he takes my peaked nipples to his mouth and suckles with such tenderness. He drags his lips in lazy kisses down my belly and towards my folds—already slicked with moisture.

The speed of my breathing picks up. On each exhale, I let out airy moans as he gets closer to my center. I sit up and let Odin pull my gown off completely. I lay beneath him in only my black lacey undergarments as he traces the lines of my body with his eyes. He's seen me undressed more times than I can count, but that look always does me in. I feel his hot breath and lips on my undergarments and down my thighs before trailing lower, kissing my heart shaped scar on my leg. I sit up and pull at his tunic, untucking it from his pants. He takes a small step back, reaching over his head to pull his shirt off. The sight of his bare chest makes my mouth water. I need more of him. With slow, nimble fingers, I watch as he unties his trousers and slides them off. He is not wearing any undergarments, and his hard cock springs out. I stroke his length, a bead of moisture instantly forming at its tip. I want to take him into my mouth, to taste his pleasure, but he pulls back.

I smile as I bite my lower lip.

Lying me on my back, I feel weightless in his arms. He's so careful to position the blanket and pillows around me as he aligns himself over my opening.

"Are you ready, my love?"

I wish he knew I always want him, all of him, in every way. Odin's love is softness, sensuality, and safety. I love that he respects me and wants our closeness to be about our love and not about primal needs.

I wonder sometimes, though, if he is so nurturing because he is afraid to hurt me. I wish I could let him know that he doesn't have to be so guarded. Not anymore. We can learn more about each other. I trust him. I want to continue to explore what gives this man pleasure and what doesn't. I want to learn what else I like, too.

The minute the tip of his erection brushes against me, I start whimpering. That first feeling of our bodies joining is a bliss I would recreate every minute of every day if I could. Odin rests his head against mine, "Beautiful, perfect, and mine. You are mine, Evelyn, and I will worship you every day of this life and all the ones that follow." He whispers.

Odin moves slowly at first. The gentle stroke of his hardness rivals the consuming brush of his lips against mine. I can feel him swelling inside of me, brushing right up against that most sensitive spot, building me up higher and higher. I begin to writhe under him. My body bucks up to meet his slow strokes, looking for more pressure, but he presses me back down, teasing and taunting me. He knows what I want, what I *need*. The movement is torture, but one I would succumb to any time. I want release, but I want to feel his body on me, *in* me, more than I want this to end. Grabbing my hips, he pulls me closer, seating himself to his base and holding me there for just a moment before pulling out and sliding back into me deeper and harder than before.

I groan, the pressure building and building. It's too much and not enough. It's bliss and pain and ecstasy all in one.

I can tell that he's almost at his peak. Our moans are a chorus through the branches.

"Gods, Evelyn, I fucking love you. This body—*you* were made for *me*."

He starts to move faster, his arms wrapped around me and his head buried in my neck. Holding me above the ground with one arm so that the roots don't dig into my back. His thumb lightly caresses across my nipple as he turns his head and captures my lips in his. I crave to fall over the edge. I reach down to touch the sensitive bud at the apex of my thighs. Using the moisture from our mixed arousal to circle and glide over the bud, bringing my release closer and closer. I cry out his name as my climax rings through the willow tree, the sound bouncing off the opal leaves like the sound of wind chimes. It's enough to drive Odin over the edge.

He collapses next to me, sweat on his brow, panting. Before I've regained my breath, he looks at me, "Am I not enough for you, my love?" I wasn't expecting that. "Why did you need to touch yourself while I was inside you? Can I not pleasure you well enough?"

"Oh, Odin, of course not. It was perfect. As are you, in every way. I love you. I think I just wanted to play a little with you, but you are always enough. More than enough."

Odin grins. "Good, my soon-to-be queen." And as if to let me know it was okay, he slides my hand back between my legs.

"Then show me how a queen worships herself."

❧⟫⟫⟩⟩ ⟨⟨⟨⟨❧

We lay there, our bodies still slick with sweat. I rest my head on his chest as we come down from the euphoria of just being together. I would stay like this all day if we could. Lying under the willow branches, watching the sunlight flicker through, the shadows and light playing on his gleaming skin.

Odin breaks our blissful silence. "Ugh, the day is getting ahead of us. I have so many meetings with commanders and officials who only care for their own needs. The time we have together reminds me of who I really am. I'm not sure anyone else sees me for anything but the king. They see me as someone with the responsibility of power, someone who has all the answers. Most of them don't even trust me. What I would give to just rest after such a romantic afternoon."

I look up at Odin. "I can go for you. I'm not yet a queen, so they still see me as a loyal friend. We have done it before, and I'm not even remotely tired. Let me do this task so you can rest, and I will see you at dinner tonight."

Odin stares at me, I can practically see his thoughts churning. "I can't ask you to—."

"I wanted to go shopping in town anyway."

"The gods have truly blessed me with you, my love. Thank you for being exactly what I need, always." Odin stands to dress, and as I look up at the canopy around me, there's that dark sparkle in the branches again. I blink my eyes twice, and when I look up again, it's back to its rich greens and yellows, coated in glittering rainbow gradients.

Odin glances down at me with his eyebrows raised. "Something in your eyes, my dear?"

"Oh no, I just thought I saw something. Probably just still seeing stars after that amazing lunch date," I say, and everything around me begins to fade.

Chapter 17 Evelyn

"Odin" escapes my lips as I wake and open my eyes.

I slam my fist on the cot. Solid rock.

My sweet Odin. The King of the Kingdom of Daydream. My king. My lover. I'm instantly drawn to the heart-shaped scar and touch it as if searching for any connection to Odin.

Gods, Odin must be tortured with worry for me. What if he finds out I am here and risks his life and our kingdom to get me back?

I have no idea what the people of Nightmare are capable of, what they have already seen. I can't dream about Odin again while I'm here. I instinctively clamp my mouth shut as though it will somehow hide my thoughts. I concentrate on my more recent memories.

This damp, cold cell, my injuries, my recovery, my unanswered—wait. I'm not alone. A shuffle of feet blares through the silence of the dungeon and the storm in my mind. The second I whip around, I find Cane leaning against the bars to my cell, staring down at me from the other side. I can't read the look on his face. It's like he's deep in thought, intrigued.

"You are so peaceful when you sleep, Little Raven. Tell me, what was making you moan? Were you thinking of me?"

Gods, how long has he been standing there? Did he hear me yell out Odin's name?

"Get over yourself. What kind of creep watches his prisoners sleep?"

And with that, he simply walks away.

⟫⟫⟫⟶   ⟵⟪⟪⟪

Days pass uneventfully, with no company but my tortured memories. Sage, then Odin, then my parents, and then Sage again.

They don't ration my food or water anymore, and I track each day by the predictable meal schedule. I even get clean clothing. No one comes to visit me. No new prisoners emerge.

I send up silent prayers to Sage every day. I hope that wherever she is, she can hear me, because I'm going to get out of here, not only to get back to Odin, but for us too. Training in this cell is easier now. I have everything Sage taught me, and everything I learned in Daydream. *No wonder I had those reflexes in the trials.*

I'm always sure to talk out loud to myself. Some days, the tune to a lullaby drifts into my head and I hum the melody. At other times, I recite passages from my favorite tales that my father would read to Odin and me. The sound of my voice keeps me company, and at least when I can hear it, I know that I still have one.

Chapter 18 Gwen

THERE IS SOMETHING SO calming about the smell of herbs mixing with tonics and infusing the air with earthy sweetness. I love my bedchambers here in the castle—and Cane's—but my favorite room is my alchemy room attached to the healer's quarters. I wasn't born with Nightmare magick, but my tonics don't need me to be blessed to provide aid.

I have something better.

Cane gifted me with a book the first year we met. A spell book unlike any I had ever seen. Unlike anything *anyone* had ever seen. The book's exact history was unclear, but it can be assumed that a powerful crone owned the grimoire. It's known that when the gods and goddesses created the elven people, they also created witches and crones: beings not imbued with magick themselves but able to pull magick from the land with charms and concoctions. According to legend, it has been countless years since this type of magick was truly practiced.

Cane says this book has been passed down in his family for longer than what's recorded in their history, just moving from shelf to dusty shelf.

"Look at it, experiment, explore. If anyone can have fun and learn something at the same time, it's you. And if you find anything in there that makes me even more charming, you'd better let me know." He said with a wink.

And I have had fun learning from it ever since.

Today I'm desperate for the smells of chamomile, echinacea, lavender, turmeric, feverfew, and yarrow root. The earthy fragrances soothe my frayed nerves. It's just barely enough to distract me from stomping up to Cane's room and smacking him in the face.

Cane, who took me in simply because I had nowhere else to go. I wasn't royalty, I wasn't even nobility. I was just a runaway with no money, no food, and a family I wished to forget. I had nothing to offer him, and he did it anyway. So, the fact that he is following such strict rules with Evelyn *irks* me.

I suck in a large breath of warm, herbal air and regroup behind closed eyelids. *I will focus on work.*

My simple navy dress is covered with the same off-white apron I've used for years. The pockets full of ginger root tea that I give to the pregnant women in the village. It's easy to lose myself in the routine, humming a light tune as I tie each tiny bow that seals the pouches. I push my brown hair off my face, the tendrils that have fallen from my bun tickling my brow, and look at my finished products. They're all lined up in neat rows, and my space is clean before I blow out the candles for the night. Just as I reach the last candle, a draft of cool air brushes against my skin. My spine straightens, and goosebumps pebble up my arms. It's followed by a low creak from shadows in the corner of the room.

What I wouldn't give for a touch of magick right now so I could re-light all the candles I just blew out.

Reaching for the edge of my work table, I wrap my fingers around the closest object I can find—a stone mortar and pestle. Then I run for the door. Icy tendrils circle my legs, down to my feet—anchoring me to the ground.

"Are you fucking kidding me!" I scream as all panic ebbs from my bones, only to be replaced with pure annoyance.

I sense his smile before I can see him. "I got you real good that time, love," Cane says as he creeps out of the dark shadows of the room.

"That was *not* funny!" I say as I throw the mortar as hard as I can at his head. It whizzes by him, and he lets out a deep laugh. A laugh that hits me right in my core, but I'll be damned if I let him know that. I cross my arms in defiance. "You can call back your little nightmare shadows now."

"You've been ignoring me. If I let you go, you'll run back to your room. I think I like you just where you are."

"You're insufferable." My huff echoes off the cabinets, causing Cane to chuckle even more.

"Why have you been hiding in here?" Cane has never taken well to being ignored. The lone candle casts flickering light over his frame. His brows are furrowed, and the deep green depth of his eyes don't cast his usual arrogant playfulness that I'm so used to. He's let his facial hair grow out a bit, giving him a more rugged look. I want to tell him that I haven't been hiding, just busy. But truthfully, I was avoiding him because I know I can't stay mad when I'm close to him.

I've missed talking to Cane, *being* with him. I ache to run my hands through his dark hair, to pull him close and feel his lush lips on mine. I know that I must be losing my mind because it has only been a week at most since we were together—the morning of the last trial—and I could have had him any time; it was my own doing to stay "busy".

He looks so tired, and his usual crisp attire is wrinkled like he just woke up for a nap.

So instead of answering his question, I ask, "Are you okay?" I want to reach out and touch him, but his dark tendrils still anchor me.

"Why have you been hiding here?" He asks again.

"I couldn't stand by and watch you torment Evelyn—"

"I gave her the basket. I delivered it myself, Gwen. She's clean and fed. It's the best I can do."

"You could have done something better, you're the king. She's suffering. Did you really have to let her see Sage? You have *always* been one to give others the benefit of the doubt, but with her, it's like you want her to fail."

"Evelyn is from Daydream!" He shouts at me. I flinch at his words. Cane has never raised his voice to me like that. I watch him run his hand down his face, so drawn and lost. "I'm sorry. I didn't mean to yell." The shadows around my legs unspool, and I wobble with their release, catching myself on my worktable. "I have a whole kingdom to protect. It's not my fault that she's here. I can't break tradition and risk my people. The castle. *You.*"

I close the gap between us and slowly cup his cheek.

"What happened? What's wrong?" I plead, setting aside my own frustrations.

"I am so tired, Gwen. So fucking tired. I love this kingdom. I love our people. But these trials. I can't do them anymore. All the pretending. Pretending to the counsel and the kingdom that we have the golems under control, pretending to myself that Daydream is not trying to overthrow my kingdom."

I pull Cane in a tight embrace, letting him rest his head on my shoulder, as I run my fingers through his soft hair. I wish I could make a potion that would just tell us what to do.

"And you know what I have been doing every night? Walking in her dreams, her nightmares. Putting her back together." Pulling back, he looks me in the eyes. "Evelyn is Odin's betrothed. All her memories are ones of love and closeness and loyalty to him. I just can't for the life of me figure out what her mission is. She doesn't even know herself! Why would Odin do that unless he had some terrifying plan? Is she a trap? I can't break the rules for a person that may very well bring down the entire kingdom as we know it."

"I know this doesn't look good. I know that everything points to danger. But I feel something, Cane. Right here," I say as I poke myself in my chest. "I feel that Evelyn is different. And even though you don't know her, you do know me. I've always been good at reading people, sensing people, seeing their inner colors. She has this brightness that I can't explain, but I *know* she has good intentions. When have I been wrong?"

Cane plants a gentle kiss on my forehead.

"Give me a chance. If she makes it through the last trial, let me show her our kingdom. Let's just see what she does. Maybe she'll learn that we aren't a threat. If she decides to trust us, and she has any influence over Odin, it could be a step toward real peace. I'll be careful." He doesn't answer right away, and instead takes a long, full breath.

"Gods, woman, you know I can never say no to you." I can't contain my smile. Now Evelyn just has to make it through the last trial. And I need to win her over. But first, I need to change the subject before Cane changes his mind.

"How have Hilia and Catherine been? Have they missed me in your rooms the last several nights, or did they take advantage of your extra attention?" Catherine is more of the meek type, soft and submissive. Hilia, on the other hand, is rough around the edges and exciting in bed. I wonder how differently they act when I'm not there.

"Do I look like a man who has been lavished by beautiful women lately?"

"You do look exhausted."

"Are you jealous? Only okay with sharing if you're there too?"

I feel the blush as it creeps up my neck, the heat of it across my cheeks.

"Don't flatter yourself," I say as I push off him and start to turn.

Cane catches me by the wrist right before I get away, spinning me back to him.

"I was thinking, what if it were just us tonight ?" He places a hand on each of my thighs, slowly pulling them apart.

"You make it sound like it has never been just us before." The feel of his hands on me sends a surge of molten heat to my core. Gods, I missed his touch.

"It's never been just us on this table before." He slowly inches his hand up my thigh. I let out a small gasp, but don't stop him.

I have never been happier that I cleaned up my worktable before leaving for the day.

"Gwen, you are so warm, are you wet for me, love?"

Cane continues slow caresses over my dress, my breath becoming shorter and my body trembling.

In one move, he grasps me under my buttocks and hoists me up. I wrap my legs around him and drown in his toasted sugars and vanilla scent. His deep green eyes bore into me and light my chest on fire with lust. Gone is the brooding man who first came into my alchemy chambers. The man wrapped up in me now is all confidence and finesse. His jet black hair falls in front of his face, and I push it back. His lips, gods, I want those lips on me. Without thinking twice, I pull myself closer and press my lips into his.

He opens for me, and I swipe my tongue in. I swear I can taste the sweetness that he emanates. I let out a low moan. Turning us both, I hear a loud crash as the few ledgers and my inkwell clatter to the floor.

The feeling coursing through me is ravenous. Cane always has that effect on me. I have had many lovers. I still have many lovers, but the pure fire that burns within when Cane touches me is like nothing I have ever experienced. It's a high that I chase over and over.

All sense is lost, and there is nothing but my body's insatiable need. He grabs the hem of my dress and pulls it over my head, throwing it to the ground. I'm utterly naked, lying on the table, splayed out like a meal that he is going to devour.

Cane lets out a growl. "Gwen, gods, you look delicious."

In the next breath, his mouth is on me. Sucking and flicking at my nipples. They instantly pebble from his touch and become so sensitive that each flick of his tongue sends jolts of pleasure through my body. My head falls back as the feeling of pleasure builds in my core. With my eyes closed, I'm surprised when two of his warm fingers suddenly dip into me.

"So fucking wet for me, love. Were you thinking of me fucking you while you were working? Or are you always just this ready for me?" In and out, over and over. He consumes my nipples and strokes my pussy. This is complete bliss. I feel his mouth leave my nipple and trail down, all the way to my apex. His fingers never stop dipping in and out of me as he captures my clit in his mouth. He has me arching my back off the table before he hooks his fingers inside of me and touches that one spot. It sends lightning skittering across my vision. I scream in release, panting, a sheen of sweat covering my skin.

He removes his fingers and crawls back up my body. "Open up, love."

Gods, I love this side of him.

My lips part as he takes his two glistening fingers and puts them in my mouth. "Lick it off of me." I look him in the eyes as I hollow my cheeks and do as he says. "Such a good girl." I can feel his cock pressing against his pants, straining with need. His pants fall to the floor, and then suddenly his hands are back under my ass and pulling me forward.

He leans over me and whispers in my ear, "Hold on tight."

I grab the edges of the table with both hands, which pushes my breasts up. And then he thrusts his cock into me.

"Oh, fuck" I scream, feeling him fill me, buried to the hilt. He moves my legs so they rest on his shoulders and holds my hips as he continues to thrust, deep and hard, over and over. The feeling of him in me, stretching me, filling me, is borderline painful, but the pain only causes me to moan louder and want more.

I let go of the table, needing to get closer. He thrusts, and I almost fall, but I move my legs and wrap them around his waist. I pull up and wrap my arms around his neck, and he carries me to the wall. With my legs still wrapped tightly, he re-adjusts and starts fucking me against it. With this angle, his thrusts hit that sensitive spot inside of me that tears me apart.

"Gods, Gwen, you take my cock so well."

"Please, Cane, gods don't fucking stop."

"That's right, I am your god right now, come for me."

Just the sound of his deep, sultry voice is my undoing, and I'm breaking on him, my release echoing off the walls, pulsing around him. One more thrust, two, and he groans, pulsating inside of me. I can feel his come, warm and slick, spill into me.

We're both panting and sweat-slickened. He carries me back to the table where he gently lays me down. His eyes still have the look of heat and passion as they roam over my naked body.

"Gwen," His voice sounds breathy. "We made a mess," Cane says, looking down between us, the come dripping from us both.

"Holy gods, I don't know the last time I came that hard." I moan, standing and looking for my clothes.

"I take offense to that," Cane says as he throws my dress at me.

I walk over to Cane and kiss him. Slow and deep. Taking my time to really relish the feeling of his lips on mine. He softens again, wrapping me in his arms as we breathe the same air.

"You know it's going to be alright, don't you, Cane?"

"If you say so, love, if you say so."

Chapter 19 Evelyn

I BARELY NOTICE THE swirling blackness ebb as large hands clamp beneath my arms, and I'm ripped off the ground like a rag doll.

Why must everything happen like some startling wake-up call?

As naturally as anyone who is yanked from sleep, I punch the first person I see square in the face, landing a pretty good blow to someone's jaw. I can hear the crack of his teeth hitting together.

"Bitch!" the man calls out.

As hard as I try to back away, the space is now uncomfortably stuffed with two seedy-looking guards, and there is nowhere to go. Their broad shoulders block the exit, and the smell of stale ale and bad breath stifles the air. One of them is still rubbing at his jaw, and a trickle of blood drips from his nostril.

I hope Sage saw that.

The guard I punched is ready to strike back, but the other person gives a quick shake of his head. More to him than me, he says, "The king has ordered us to retrieve you. You can walk with us, or we will drag you, but either way, you are coming."

"You could have just asked nicely," I mumble to myself. They turn to face me, and it's as though their stature grows with their fury. "I'll go. Lead the way, bog-breath." The one with a bloody nose looks even more furious.

At the top of the stairs, we're met by four more unwashed trollspawn, each guard uglier than the last. We climb two more staircases and pass countless dungeon cells before we are on the first floor of the Nightmare castle.

"Is climbing really the only way? Can't you conjure up something to fly us up here?" No one answers. "You guys are pretty fat for guards who walk up and down so many stairs so often." The one that I punched thrusts a spear just under my chin. "Shut your whore mouth." I smile because he is so stupidly easy to rouse. And because I know they won't actually kill me unless the king says so. I give him a wink but keep my mouth shut. *I just winked at that man with a spear to my throat. And I thought it was funny.* How different from the soft and sensual girl I was in my dreams.

A large wooden door waits around a corner, and the bright light that shines on the other side assaults my senses.

Outside?

It's been days, weeks, maybe months since I've experienced real brightness. It's blinding. Through my burning vision, I notice the castle towering over us first. Its peaks and turrets glisten in the light. The stone path we walk on leads through an onyx gate to the rich colors of the land beyond. My eyes feast upon a vast tapestry of deep, jeweled greens, rolling hills, and secret valleys that unfold endlessly. It's like a living, breathing dream. *Nightmare.* I can't forget where I am, but I secretly vow to myself to never, ever, take the outdoors for granted again.

The sky is entirely different from what I'm used to. At home, it's the richest of blues, speckled with puffy clouds. But here the sky is a cascade of color, like harvest season but brighter. Yellows, oranges, and reds bleed into one another and emit a warm glow around every single thing. The sun isn't the same bright yellow but rather a pale orange orb. It's a blanket of amber, both comforting and ominous.

Just past the gate, there is a black covered carriage drawn by two black steeds.

I would do anything to stop for just one more minute outside, but there is no way to resist being thrown into the awaiting carriage. It's nicer than I would have expected for a prisoner: curtained windows, cushioned seats, and even has the savory scent of cedar. I'm tugged up and pressed down onto the bench.

I'm a little disappointed that the person I punched sits at the front with the horses and not inside with me. "What, did I scare him?" I jest to another guard.

I can tell at least one of them wants to smile. Another is exuding a stoic, loathsome expression. "I can't wait to watch you die." I try to keep a lighthearted and carefree smile on my face, but something about the way he says it makes me uneasy.

The rest of the painfully long trip is silent.

I hate to admit it, even to myself, but after being alone for so long, I'm bursting with gratitude for the company, even if they *do* want to watch me die. But the fear of the unknown strips me of my confidence, and I can't think of anything worth saying.

Instead, I try to look out the window. The curtains are shut, but I still get glimpses of colors and shapes, my eyes finally adjust to the small slivers of light seeping in through the slit. I was taught that the Kingdom of Nightmares was dark and drab. That the buildings were abandoned and run down by the constant feuding and chaotic rage. Full of black, rotting creatures roaming the lands that would eat you alive if they saw you. But this place is nothing like that; it looks pleasant.

Must be an illusion. A damn good one, too.

I'm shocked by every quaint, colorful house and shop. The cobblestone walkways and the most gorgeous lanterns illuminating them. The colors are so vibrant. It's like the air itself glows a rich ruby red, and the rest blurs into garnet, emerald, and sapphire. Precious gems seem to be the only appropriate comparison. I'm unsure of the time of day, but I suspect it's late afternoon or early evening. Like a perpetual dusk, the sky is fading from the pale yellows, pinks to deep violets with streaks of orange and red throughout.

I wonder what it looks like at night? Can they see the stars like we do in Daydream?

The carriage stops abruptly, and the door swings open—my new angry friend gestures for me to get out. When I don't move right away, he pulls me up, spins me towards the door, and kicks me with such force I don't even touch the stairs leading out before I slam into the ground. The sting of gravel and the jolt to my bones are worth every ounce of annoyance on that man's face.

The landscapes and beautiful towns have long since passed, and I now stand before a giant arena. The crowd is already rowdy inside, chanting words that I can't make out from where I stand.

The curved tan stone walls of the stadium reach up to the sky with notches in the walls where small windows are carved, thick bars covering them. There's a portcullis that's open, revealing a glimpse of the rows beyond rows of seats brimming with people standing and shouting.

I try to look around for an escape route, but trees surround this path on all sides. The canopy is so thick that there is no light illuminating what may lie beyond the forest's edge. I actually feel safer inside my wall of stinking guards.

"Who is fighting in there?" No answer, just continuous ushering forward. The grip on my arms is unforgiving, as is the blank expression on their faces.

They're like machines.

"Why would the king bring me to an event like this?" The words fade away before the thought finishes, as I realize they are not bringing me to a spectator's chair. "Oh, fantastic, more stairs," I grumble. The feeling of fear is scraping at my insides, and it only gets worse the farther down we walk.

At the bottom, the walls are gray, and the air is cool and moist. The only noise I hear is the distant chanting and the occasional *drip, drip, drip* of water from the ceiling. They shove me into a cell, locking the door as they leave.

"You're not even going to say goodbye?" My tone is mocking, but it still makes the panic rise when not one of them turns before they disappear from my view. My swallow echoes in the new silence.

My new cell is clocked in shadows, but there's enough light from the hallway lanterns that I can make out small details. On the back wall, there is a wooden door with what appears to be pulleys to draw it up. Even though I don't have hope of moving it, I brace my hands on the damp wood and push. My feet slide from under me, dewy moss making the stone slick. I take steps to gain traction, with absolutely no luck. I turn and brace my back against the door and again, push, slide, push some more.

The crowd above me suddenly goes quiet. As I press my ear to the door, the wood groans and starts pulling upwards. Suddenly, I would take anything, *anything,* over this door opening. Light begins to seep in across the floor, until its rays reach my head and beyond, filling the entire cell.

No. No. No.

I put my hand up to shield my face as I hear the chanting crowd.

"Ev–e–lyn, Ev–e–lyn, Ev–e–lyn"

There is nowhere to go but out. A heavy weight rapidly grows in my chest as a swift realization hits me that this could be the last thing I ever experience.

I should have so much more time.

I try to conjure the vision of Odin. We don't have to be together for him to give me strength. But my godsdamned, trembling hands and the unrelenting chant of the spectators make it nearly impossible to hold onto the image of his perfect face.

I walk onto the floor of the arena. It's covered in black sand that looks like it's sparkling iridescently with all the colors of the rainbow. An unnatural wind blows, the tiny black diamonds stinging my face. Rows of seats circle the center arena. They start about fifteen feet up a stone wall and rise even higher. It's too bright to see where they end, but doesn't look like one seat is empty. It's unsettling how quickly the crowd falls silent, looking at me. I'm alone, dirty, and unarmed, standing in the middle of the arena that is sure to be my final resting place. The energy here is bursting with eagerness. But there is something dark underlying the exhilaration. It's like everyone here knows with certainty I'm utterly unprepared for whatever is coming next, and they love it.

There is an ornate balcony perched among the rows of seats directly across from where I entered—a prime spot for spectating. Cane appears there with Gwen and that vile woman, Hilia, at his side. I don't try to hide my disdain for the trio as I glare up at them with all the fury I can muster.

Cane sweeps out his arms, "People of the Kingdom of Nightmare! Today, you will be feted by my dear friend, Evelyn. She has conquered her fears and overcome some of her worst nightmares. Her determination, coupled with her strength, has landed her here before you. Such admirable traits are surely enough to conquer one more nightmare, isn't that right?" The crowd roars, and he lets them go for a long moment before putting his hand up, halting the noise once again. "Today she will prove she is worthy of this kingdom by fighting in this arena, not unlike our ancestors did so many years ago when the trials began."

My eyes have finally adjusted to the light, now making it possible to see the crowd all around me erupting with screaming and clapping. Some are completely drunk, spilling ale, some are howling.

How can they let children watch?

The people closest to the edge of the arena look like they are gripping the edges of their seats, leaning forward, waiting for...something.

I focus my gaze toward the king. I think he is looking at me, too, until his head swings to the side. The people in the stands follow his stare. Something appears in the middle of the arena. Three wooden stakes rise from the ground. They are as tall as a one-story cottage. In the middle of each stake is a person, bound tightly with a large, fat rope. My heart pounds again. And again. Until I swear, it completely stops.

Mother.

Father.

Odin.

How did he get them? Alive? The memory of my parents, the blood that was real, wasn't it? If Odin is captured, is Daydream already overtaken?

A long metal javelin appears in front of me.

I grab it and spin in a circle. There are other doors in the wall of the arena, but none are open. *At least not yet.* I can't waste time.

I snatch up the javelin and run faster than I have ever run in my entire life towards my family. Faster than I ever thought my legs could run. "Mother! Father!" I'm screaming. Screaming because I want to save them. Screaming because I don't know how I will bear it if I can't. They're each bound to a stake, and their mouths are gagged with cloth. Their eyes are open, but they aren't moving. They're not looking at me, or at anything, and they're not struggling to break free. They must be drugged or under some sort of holding spell.

I'm about twenty feet away from them when I hear an inevitable door opening. Across from the stakes, on the other side of the arena, I see the giant, festering snout of a blue dragon.

Chapter 20 Evelyn

THE SCALY BEAST LUMBERS forward into the arena, each massive talon slamming into the black sand with a bone-shaking crack. The ground quakes beneath its weight, and with every step, a cloud of glittering sand erupts, dark, choking, and alive with menace.

I swear to myself that I will write a storybook about this sight should I live. The dusky sky grows darker with the enormous shadow cast by the beast. All I know of dragons are the tales from my father's stories of Istvan. I never once thought that they existed here, or on any plane at all. But here it is, prowling out of the cell, steam trailing out of its nostrils. Sun ripples off the midnight blue scales, so iridescent they seem to be moving, trembling with each thundering step of the dragon's legs. Its underbelly is a deep purple with flecks of black, and it has razor-sharp talons, each longer than my leg and ready to strike. One swipe would eviscerate me. Its black eyes are like a depthless abyss, bulging through a thick, leathery hide.

Please let this be a nightmare.

Its head sways from side to side, sniffing as it moves. With each huff of breath, steam bellows out, heating the arena and causing the spectators to roar. In less than one second, he homes in on me, his prey. He bellows with such earsplitting vibrations that the entire arena seems to quake. I should be scared, but I'm captivated. Even as he bares his giant serrated teeth, some stained with what looks like fresh blood. In one bound, the dragon is in the air, but he doesn't fly away. There must be some sort of magick dome containing us here.

I realize too late that the dragon's intentions are not toward me but toward the stakes with my parents and Odin.

Fuck.

Once more, I take off towards the beast, my feet pounding into the shimmery black sand. When I feel that I'm close enough, I halt my movement, planting my feet in the sands and using the momentum of my run to power the throw. My javelin, aimed perfectly, sticks into the dragon's tender underbelly.

The dragon shrieks in agony, unleashing a torrent of searing fire from its jaws. I'm unarmed now, but as it crashes to the ground, it starts to look toward me, not my family.

The roar of the crowd is a deafening storm of voices, but even their cries are a mere wind beneath the piercing wail of the beast. My ears are ringing. And above all the noise, my pulse pounds. Somehow, I'm still standing.

The dragon's hind legs slam into the ground first, and it rears up, claws slashing at the javelin lodged in its flesh, smoke coiling from its nostrils. The fury of battle surges through me. My hands tremble, and every breath comes in ragged gasps.

It doesn't notice me getting closer. The wind from his constant thrashing is so powerful, and I know with one wrong move, I could be catapulted into the air or slammed against the arena wall.

I get my chance as he opens his wings wide to gain more balance. The javelin is low enough for me to reach if I can get there fast enough. I race forward, lunging past the dragon's thrashing limbs. Black sand from the arena floor rises in thick clouds. The grains are like tiny razors on my legs, my arms, shredding my lips and grinding into my eyes. I just keep sprinting. The javelin is right in front of me now. I wrap both hands around the shaft and wrench it from the dragon's thick scales. It tears free with a sickening squelch, warm blood splattering from the wound, coating my face and arms.

Crimson sanguineous fluid pools in the black sand around me, the metallic stench permeating my senses. Now that I'm right in front of the beast, I begin to question everything I have done. This creature is easily four times my height.

How do I save myself and my family? What if I have to choose who I save? How do I live with that decision?

I will not let my parents die again. This is my chance to save them, to let them know I wanted to save them before, and that I am so, wholeheartedly, sorry. And Odin. My dear sweet Odin. I can't let him perish here. He can't die until I've shown him exactly what he means to me. I'm the only thing that stands between this beast and my everything.

Frantically grasping for the perfect strategy in my head, I land on one that might work.

If I'm lucky.

I spin on my heels and sprint in the opposite direction from the dragon. When I'm far enough away, I grasp my javelin and slam it deep in the ground in front of me, keeping my grasp on it firm. My hand glides over the blood-slickened grip easily, and I use my momentum to swing around, facing the dragon once again. I wrench it from the ground, pull back, and launch it as the beast, aiming for its eye.

Time slows. My plan hinges on landing this throw. My breath is loud, pounding my lungs. The javelin arcs through the air, another perfect execution. It's going to land, forcefully, exactly where I aimed. But then time catches up to me, and faster than you would imagine a dragon of this size could move, he rears up and knocks the javelin to the ground like a twig.

A loud gasp rings out in the arena, and the crowd around me goes quiet.

He's in the air again and heads straight for the stakes that hold my family.

"NO!" I scream so loud and long that my voice is the only sound I hear—a war cry for a fallen army. But the fallen army is just me. And the cry changes nothing.

"I'm over here, you giant fucking monster!" I shout and run towards my family. Each step pounding beneath me in time with the rapid pace of my heart. The pounding spreads over my body, my arms, shoulders, and chest, aching and burning.

The dragon circles the stakes and blows a ferocious gust of fire at them. The curling flames and smoke appear like a struck match and quickly turns into a raging bonfire that is torturing them, torturing me.

"You can't have them," I whimper to myself as I fall to my knees, defeated.

Through the wavering, smoky air, I can see all three bodies, charred and bare. No skin or hair remains. Some bits of ashen muscle cling to blackened skeletons. Some of the bones had already turned to dust. Even with no facial muscles remaining, agony resonates from their gaping jawbones. I can't get any closer to the blazing heat, but I question whether I should just burn with them. Run into the fire, give the crowd what it wants, and be with my beloved family in the afterlife. It's only fair that I suffer the same fate. Maybe I don't even deserve the peace that the afterlife offers. Maybe this really is what I'm fated to endure. I stay there, kneeling, staring, sobbing. Silently begging the gods to take me. The burning and pounding in my arms and chest increase, but the pain is nothing compared to the pain in my soul.

The earth booms. Dust bursts upward, an iridescent cloud of darkness across the arena. The dragon has descended and landed not even five feet away. I can feel the heat from its maw getting ready to scorch me as it did my family. Instantly, a pang of furious anger fills my chest. The purest form of hatred I have ever felt. If I die, this wretched beast will keep killing. Keep destroying families. Cane will know that he has the power to break me and everyone else who comes after.

I can see the ball of fire pooling in his stinking, open jowl. Pain doesn't even matter anymore. I throw my head back and release another explosive, carnal scream. Something in my voice is different this time, alive with its own energy. Tears flow from my eyes, burning and cleansing. I don't know how I have any breath left.

I keep screaming.

It turns into a sound that isn't natural. It echoes, sending waves of sound so loud that some people cower, covering their ears. But I feel satisfied, full. My soul is calling out into this horrid place, and it feels free. Light flashes so brightly that I wonder if my life has, in fact, ended, and the gods have granted me entrance to the afterlife. I scream my lungs dry, until that glorious sound is no louder than a whisper, and the regular daylight returns. What unfolds before me is impossible.

The sound of my scream materialized, turning into dark shadows, like something tangible came directly from my throat, still trailing out like my very essence is being drawn from me. And my hands. They felt like they were bursting because they *were*, with light. They are still glowing even now. The dragon is staring down at me, close enough to incinerate me with one puff. But its expression is vacant, and it's silent. There is pain in its relentless stare. I look beyond his gigantic head and see his hind legs disappearing. No, disintegrating. Bluish, dusty ash works its way up to its neck, hollowing out its form. Bit by bit, its face crumbles, until nothing but one single tooth falls to the ground in front of me. The light and the shadows completely leave my body. I feel heavier and so utterly exhausted. After a moment of silence, the crowd erupts. I reach down and pick up the giant tooth, my entire body shaking.

The king steps onto his balcony and snaps his fingers. As he does so, he looks me in the eyes and says, "Well done, my Little Raven". He doesn't shout, and yet his deep voice reaches me as though we were standing face to face.

The familiar black fog circles me, and I open my eyes to the ceiling of my cell in the Grimm Lodge.

Chapter 21 Evelyn

I CLING TO THE desperate hope that what just happened was an actual nightmare, and not something real. But I can't ignore the nagging feeling that part of it, maybe all of it, *did* happen.

I was driven there in a carriage...wasn't I?

I lower my gaze to my hands—hands that just moments ago pulsed with an otherworldly glow. But now, there's nothing unusual about them. Just dried blood and clinging black sand, stubborn reminders of my failure to save my family. To save Odin.

It had to have been a nightmare.

The sound of footsteps breaks my reeling thoughts. Expecting it to be the king, I'm surprised to find Gwen padding down the hallway to my cell.

I hate to admit that her voice sings when she speaks. "Come, our Little Raven. It's finally time to take you to some better accommodations." How can she be so joyful after knowing what just happened to me? "These cells are utterly disgusting. Definitely not fitting for a champion of the Nightmare Trials."

Is this going to bring me to another trial? Will there be another battle?

"I can see the wheels turning in that head of yours." She pauses, ensuring that I truly see her and not just hear her words. "This is *not* a trap. Follow me. I have something to show you."

She's completely unguarded as far as I can tell. Maybe I can escape easily. Or maybe this is another trap.

"Come on! You can't think there's anything worse waiting for you than what you have already been through."

"I'm not leaving this spot unless you force me to. Every time I do, your people delight in my torment. If you want me to leave, drag me out the same as you have each and every time before."

Something like remorse paints her joyful expression just for a moment before she fights it off. "Evelyn, I'm here alone and unarmed. I practically had to beg Cane to let me come down here personally with nothing but these gods-awful heels to get you. I knew you would win from the first time you entered the trials. I didn't know you'd slay a whole dragon, but still, I'm here. An unarmed woman in heels and you, a mighty dragon slayer. I haven't trained a day in my life, and I'm well aware that if you wanted to, you could probably kill me in one blink." Gwen looks tentative. Beautiful, and unmoving, but seemingly, afraid. Of me. Our eyes are locked. Mine full of anger and mistrust. Hers hopeful and uneasy. She takes a small, heeled step forward.

"I'm not going to force you. No one is. I just thought, since you won and all, that the rest of your experience here could start with me. Some of the guards are so old and ugly, and they forget that a strong young woman like yourself needs some tenderness."

I still don't trust it. But so far, I haven't been able to avoid the trials. Can this really be a trap if I'm already in the worst possible position? And if this is just a new nightmare, I might as well get it over with. So I stand up. Gwen smiles like a child who has just been given sweets, and clicks away towards the door. We make our way up the stairs and out of the dungeon. Gwen takes her time with her strides, looking back and giving me a small smile every few steps. The pace allows me time to soak in the striking architecture and unique build of the castle. The stonework is black, completely precise and polished, each stone with a mesmerizing, glittery sheen—pillars of the same onyx line the hallway, glistening from the fiery sconces. The giant foyer at the end of the hall manages to impress me, and my mouth opens lightly while my eyes trail up to the ceiling.

I thought the palace of the Kingdom of Nightmare would be nothing but rot and cold. But this...this is the opposite of that. Nothing haunts me; there are no menacing creatures. Maybe it's only the royal lifestyle, and the real chaos lies with the townsfolk.

There is a giant crystal chandelier covered in candles, rubies, and black diamonds hanging from the ceiling in the middle of the room. The colors blend into a glorious warm glow that fills the entire entryway. There are floor-to-ceiling windows that line one wall, and through the intricate black panes, white-tipped purple mountains span. It all flows so beautifully, with such welcoming, sparkling warmth. The walls are a deep burgundy damask, and the floor is a polished gray stone with flecks of crystal sparkling throughout. Along the walls are settees covered in black velvet, and between them, gold vases burst with deep-red roses. Blood red. Doors line the halls, all firmly shut. As we pass each one, the faint echoes of moans and the slapping of skin brushes against my ears, sending a flush to my cheeks. Abruptly, reality snaps back, and I remember I'm in the Kingdom of Nightmare. I just need to focus on following Gwen.

She leads me to the large staircase in the center of the room.

It's impossible not to notice the way the light captures Gwen's curves as I follow. She is breathtaking. A pang of jealousy stings my throat because I look nothing like her. Even with my dungeon cell training sessions, my frame has gotten sharper since I've been here, trapped in the Grimm Lodge. My legs and arms are muscular under stretched skin. There is nothing soft about the way I move. Even if I were at the height of my health, my breasts could never fill out a low-cut gown, and my hips have never swayed. How could they if I grew up training them to climb trees? I'm the opposite of this bewitching creature in front of me. In all my memories, I have never seen someone who exudes such smooth, sensual grace. She saunters down the hall with an air of confidence, but not arrogance. She is an exquisite hourglass, and I'm a splintered wooden shield.

I've definitely been staring too long, so I pretend to marvel at the intricate railing that lines the hall instead. We pass door after door, but all are closed, and Gwen doesn't offer an explanation of what is behind any of them.

As we round the corner, two women pass us. They're wearing dresses that hug their bodies, leaving no room for the imagination. One of them is Hilia, and my blood runs cold. Her hair is worn in rivulets down her back, and her dress is sheer black lace. If it were not for her black undergarments, you would be able to see the curls of hair between her thighs. It doesn't matter that she is wearing a top piece, because her nipples are peaked and pointing. The swatch of lace she is wearing sweeps the ground and swishes as it brushes the floor. My eye catches the sparkling diamond necklace draped around her neck as it shimmers, casting prismatic colors across the ceiling and walls. *If she weren't such a bitch, she would be beautiful, like everyone here apparently.*

The other woman is equally stunning, with hair unlike anything I have ever seen. It's lavender and held up in a series of plaits that wrap around her head like a halo. She's wearing a cream chiffon gown that cascades to the ground, a slit up her leg that extends to her thigh, showing off her warm brown skin, so high you can see the crease where her thigh meets her hip as she walks. Her dress is sleeveless and has a high corset back, accentuating yet another swaying, hourglass figure. She is made up with kohl lining her eyes, rouge on her cheeks, and her lips stained bright red. I'm surprised to find that neither is wearing shoes.

How long have I been staring at them?

Hilia snickers to the other person. "I heard she screamed like a baby, and it was pure luck that she made it out alive."

The one with lavender hair looks me up and down. She gives me a slight smile before turning back to Hilia. "I hear they're calling her the Dragon Slayer."

"Don't mind Catherine and Hilia," Gwen says, noticing my glare. "They're harmless once you get to know them. I personally find gossip senseless and tiring. Soon enough, you can decide for yourself!"

"Doubtful," I mumble.

We finally stop at one of the dark wooden doors. Gwen pulls out a key with a skull-shaped tip, unlocks the door, and opens it. Then she spins and hands the key to me.

"I'm not to be locked in here?"

She shrugs and gives my shoulder a light squeeze, "You won the trials, you're free."

I'm more than skeptical, and she can certainly tell.

"I don't jest, and this isn't a game." She waits for me to take the key, but I'm still cautious.

"Well, it isn't a game *anymore*. I promise." And she shakes the key towards me again.

How do I know there isn't some beast lurking behind this door? That the key won't blow off my hand as soon as I grasp it. The casual way she speaks sends my instincts wild.

She takes my hand. "I can see you are confused. You really need to work on your poker face. Just listen to me. No one here wants to, or has ever *wanted* to, hurt you. We didn't put you here against your will; it was you who came to us." She's smiling, staring at my face with those piercing golden eyes, willing the truth of her words into my very soul. I feel my expression soften, my mental walls unlocking. But her words bring me back to my biggest question. *How* did I get here? *Why* am I here?

And damnit, she's right, I can't hide my emotions very well.

She gestures towards the open door, ushering me into the room. I just stand there.

Apparently, residual fear has affected my motor skills, and my feet won't move an inch. I have no idea what is real, what awaits me in this room. I can't tell if it's a guise, and I just feel so trapped.

Gwen takes my hand in hers, mine sweating profusely, hers as soft as silk, and quickly wipes a tear I didn't know had fallen down my cheek. "Stop dwelling," she says.

Dwelling? Didn't my entire family just burn to ash in front of me not one hour ago?

I gawk at her.

How can she not know what I must be feeling?

"Come! This is your new room!" She says as she pushes open the door. From inside, she says, "I've been spending weeks setting it up for you, praying for your victory! Welcome!" She squeals. Finally, I take a step toward the door frame. The room emanates brightness and comfort. My fear involuntarily ebbs, and is replaced with warmth. It's like this is the first time my heart has relaxed in centuries.

So, I step further. And nothing horrid surprises me. There is nothing but this warm, colorful space before me.

The walls are painted with light colors that capture and reflect the daylight. There is a canopy bed that is large enough for at least five people to sleep in. Along one dandelion-colored wall is a row of huge windows and a pair of doors. The doors are fitted with glass panes, each fracturing the light into tiny, dancing patterns on the floor. Through them is a balcony that overlooks the mountains. The large desk is already stocked with a journal, paper, quill, and inkwell. Gwen instantly heads for the armoire. She opens the doors to reveal a massive amount of new, clean clothes. There are elegant dresses fit for balls, day gowns, leggings, and tunics. There are riding leathers and leather armor. Slippers and boots line the bottom.

In the corner of my room is a small sitting area. There are two armchairs with a table and a lamp between them.

"Close your jaw, Little Raven, you're going to drool on the carpet," Gwen says with a smirk.

"It's Evelyn," I whisper, but Gwen's ongoing excitement whisks away my voice as she opens another door. She is quite literally bouncing on her toes, looking from me to the room that she just opened.

I peek around her to find a bathing chamber containing a claw-foot tub large enough for two and a shelf lined with vials of oils, soaps, and lush towels. The entire room smells like a wildflower field.

"The water is magicked. If you tap on the lever three times, warm water will flow into your tub. Similarly, there is a sink with fresh water for freshening up and a chamber pot that empties itself." Her excitement is oddly comforting. Like she is confident that the lingering feelings from all the trauma I just went through will absolutely fade. She shows no signs of guilt, she isn't afraid of me any longer, she doesn't pity me. She acts like we've known each other for decades. It would make anyone forget that this place, the kingdom this woman lives in, is the Kingdom of Nightmare.

She motions for me to sit in one of the armchairs in the main room. And it's like sitting on a cloud. I let out a moan as I let my weight sink into the fabric. Gwen lets out a little laugh and sits down as well.

After a few silent moments, she says, "You have a choice to make now. You can stay here, in the palace, as part of the Night Shroud, or you are free to go. And don't forget the treasure! If you choose to leave, you will be given enough treasure to last a lifetime! If you stay, you will have everything your heart desires. Food, clothing, more clothing, more food! You have seven days to make your choice. At the end of the week, there will be a ball where you will announce your decision to King Cane." She lights up brighter when she mentions the ball.

There is a deep sense of longing, of needing to get home, of getting back to Odin. But the idea of fleeing doesn't sit right. It's like my mind is screaming at me that I know what I'm supposed to do, but I can't pull that thought forward.

She taps the table with her long, delicate fingers. I feel like she wants to say more, but all she says is "I bid you farewell for the evening, Little Raven. I look forward to spending time with you. I have a trip to the village planned for tomorrow so we can go shopping! Have a bath, and I'll have Catherine bring food up for you."

I realize as she leaves that I have barely said one word since entering this room, caught between having too much to say and having nothing to say at all. She starts to close the door, but just before she goes, she peeks back at me. "There was never a doubt in my mind that you would win those trials. Not one." We make eye contact for a moment before she softly smiles and closes the door.

I let out a deep sigh as the thought of a warm bath and clean clothes makes me happier than I have felt in weeks. If death's mermaid comes for me in there and the water turns to lava, so be it.

I need to bathe.

By the time I exit the bathing chamber, the sun has already set. I look out the window and see the sky's purple hue as the last rays of the sun sink below the mountain range. The view would stop a charging bull in its tracks. The deep purple sky is splattered with more stars than I ever imagined I would see, twinkling and pulsing as if they were alive. If it weren't for the savory smell coming from my room, I would have gazed at the sky all night long.

A silver tray of food sits on the table in my sitting area, filled with meats, cheeses, fruits, and roasted vegetables. There is also a glass of water and a chalice of wine.

It still feels strange to trust something like this. But my hunger drives my body forward, despite any lingering reservations. The food is delectable. If this is a trial, it's undoubtedly the most satisfying one. There is a very real possibility that I'm weakening with every indulgence. A monster might be waiting to devour me at any moment. Or maybe the doors will lock and close in on me. Maybe it's nothing so sinister. Maybe the food is just poisoned and serves as an easy way to rid their kingdom of me. I start to sweat as my thoughts reel.

Calm down.

I remember that there was a journal left on the writing desk. Even though I don't want to relive the trials, maybe putting it on paper will soothe my inner voices. If I can organize my thoughts, I may even find a clue as to why I'm here.

And what if I forget everything again?

I force myself to go over to the desk and lift the quill. *I am Evelyn Aria Stone, and I have just completed The Nightmare Trials.* My words pour out, almost like they have a mind of their own. I want to write down every detail, but I'm not fast enough. As time passes, it becomes more about what I'm feeling rather than what happened. Thankfully, the drowning feeling of fear and dread eases as the words spill out of me. I must have written for hours, just letting every bit of what happened to me bleed into the cream colored pages. My mind is at last calm enough to feel tired.

I close my journal and tuck it under my arm. I need to keep all those thoughts and feelings close to me, to remind myself this is real. That *I* am real. I blow out the candles and lie in the luxurious bed. My eyes grow heavier as I sink into the silken pillow.

Chapter 22 Gwen

❯❯❯❯❯ ❮❮❮❮❮

"G reat job," I murmur under my breath. "You're supposed to be winning her over, not scaring her even further."

I can't begin to imagine what the trials were like for Evelyn. Most who enter have time to prepare—time to train for this particular type of unfortunate torment. They go in knowing that the risk of failure is high. But Evelyn? She threw herself in without a second thought. She looked toned, yes, but not like most participants, not like Sage. And yet, she emerged victorious.

"Gwendalin, are you talking to yourself again?"

I snap out of my thoughts to find Hilia standing before me. She's made a quick change, now dressed in loose, sheer black trousers and a cropped, fitted top—her faint Nightmare mark clearly visible. The look hasn't caught on yet, but Hilia wears it with ease. She excludes sensuality in whatever she wears, from her bedroom eyes to her flawless curves. It's no wonder Cane enjoys having her in his chambers.

I step forward, hugging her and giving a quick kiss on her cheek, and she returns the gesture with a practiced smile. Hilia has been slinking around the castle for about five years now. She's the daughter of a wealthy family that owns land outside our main town, Sallows. Cane agreed to let her stay at the castle in exchange for her family's resources. Specifically, their carriages and strongholds, to help move crops up the coast to the rockier towns that can't grow enough on their own.

She was to be a liaison between her people and the castle, but really, the only thing she liaises with is herself in the beds of anyone who catches her eye. It's not her sex life that bothers me. It's her aimlessness. The way she glides around the halls like she owns the place, with nothing but selfish intent.

At first, it was nice having another woman around. Her bright yellow colors bring warmth to my day. But it took no time at all for her to grow colder. Jealous. Now she has greens that leech into her yellows. She joins us in our...*escapades* together, but if she hears that Cane was with just me—or with me and Catherine—her eyes gleam with something sharp. The fleeting dalliances don't bother her as much. It's the intimacy that stings.

I know she must be hurt. Someone must have poisoned her soul. So I try to reach her with kindness. I can't figure out how to make her feel safe, give her purpose beyond sex. But I'll keep trying.

"Where are you heading off to?" I ask, though I already know. She's walking straight toward Cane's chambers.

A wicked smile plays across her lips. "Why, to service," she pauses, eyes glinting, "I mean, serve, my king." With a flick of her wrist, she sends tiny shadow tendrils dancing across my cheek. Her magick is on the weaker side, capable of small feats like lighting candles or conjuring a faint breeze, but the shadow tricks are her favorite. Perfect for little theatrics in the bedroom.

I flash her a teasing smile and wink. "Save some for me."

As I pass her, I catch the parting of her lips, as though she wants to deliver a biting reaction, but Hilia has never been one for clever comebacks.

Tonight, I throw myself into planning the perfect outing for Evelyn. I want her to see the best of Sallows, to understand that the Kingdom of Nightmare isn't the cold, terrifying place that she believes it is. I've already mapped out a tour in my mind: my favorite bakeries, hidden dress shops, cozy corners of the market. I'll give her time to wander, too. I want her to fall in love with this place—not because I told her to, but because she discovered it herself.

By daybreak, I realize I must have only gotten a few hours of sleep. My excitement kept me up much later than I anticipated. I never did seek out Cane and Hilia. Maybe it's good for her to have some alone time. My mind is too occupied with Evelyn and our adventure today anyway.

I practically skip down to my apothecary chambers, a linen bag slung over my shoulder, filled with teas and tinctures. I'm planning to drop them off at the healing clinic in town during our outing.

Oh! Would Evelyn want to see the clinic?

It's usually bustling with small children and elderly elves. The children need constant mending from their daily mischief, while the elderly come and seek salves for aching joints. Some days, I spend every waking moment there. The fulfillment I get from helping others—it's what grounds me. It's what keeps me whole.

I can hear Cane's voice now, *"Always helping others, never yourself."* He says it every time he finds me still working after hours, a babe on my hip, coaxing a healing tonic between their lips while their mother rests on a nearby cot.

I tighten the strap of my bag and head towards Evelyn's room. On the way, I spot Isla and Aidan, two of the Night Shroud, and wave as they pass.

"Don't let Cane get into any trouble today," I call over my shoulder.

They both chuckle. "Since when do we control anything the king does?" Isla shouts back.

Chapter 23 Evelyn

MY JOURNAL IS STILL clutched in my grasp as I peel open my eyes. For the first time in ages, I wake up naturally, enveloped by white, silky sheets and a powder-blue duvet. I stretch, arms reaching overhead as my spine arches. Cool morning air brushes my skin, and for once, there's no pinch, no pull, only ease. A slow breath fills my lungs, and I'm actually able to settle my thoughts. I feel like a willow leaf, drifting to still water.

Maybe this isn't a nightmare.

I can't tell how long I slept, but with the way the sun burst through the giant windows, it's likely late morning.

And gods, I will never get used to that sky.

The colors of evening, but the brightness of day.

There's a rich, warm glow caressing every detail of the room. The pale pastel colors on almost every surface shine brightly in return. Elegant and inviting. The yellow walls now have a faint shimmer to them, like they're coated in a sheen of pearl.

I pad over to the two armchairs that sit a rug's breadth away from the fireplace and sink into the soft, dusty pink velvet fabric as my toes melt into the plush cream rug. *Think of all the books I could read in this chair!* A perfect place to pour over all my thoughts and memories I put into my journal. As much as I don't want to leave this cloud of a chair, I know it will be even better with something to read, tea, and maybe a blanket.

Just as I grab the journal off the nightstand, I hear the door to my room open. Naturally, I spin around and throw it as hard as I can at the intruder.

The book misses her, and she doesn't even flinch when it hits the wall and falls to the floor. "You really should lock your door. Gods know what kind of creature will seek you out for pleasure in the middle of the night."

I blanch at the thought that anyone could have come in here when I was asleep.

Had anyone?

Gwen saunters over after casually picking up my journal, winking as she hands it back to me. "You missed."

She's dressed much more conservatively today than in her previous outfits. Even in leggings and a tunic, she possesses such otherworldly beauty. It's magnetic. Her deep brown hair is in a plait down her back, and except for a small line of kohl accentuating her eyes, she's not made up. She dons all deep purples and pastel lavenders, save for the linen bag that is slung over her shoulder.

Gwen looks me up and down and pouts.

"How are you not ready yet?"

Ready for what?

I must look as dumbstruck as I feel, because this insufferable woman comes over and tousles my hair. "It's time to go shopping! You can't go in your nightgown. Well, technically, you could if you really wanted to... Do you want to?"

I still can't answer.

"Well, at the very least, we should fix your hair!"

I burst out in uncontrollable laughter. Gwen looks at me and cocks her head to the side, eyebrows furled together like I'm insane.

This is just so ridiculous and must be exactly how Sage felt talking to me in the Grimm Lodge.

I was lost for words last night. Shocked. But now I can't hold back.

"Let me get this straight, Gwen, is it? *Your* people threw me into a dungeon, one that resides in *your* kingdom, ruled by the king *you* worship. All for reasons I conveniently can't recall. Reasons you refuse to tell me. I was chained to a wall for a flesh-eating demon monster to suck out my soul. I mean, the thing ate screams before shredding its victims to pieces! I almost died of pain and infection. Do you even know what that feels like, Gwen? To literally die from pain? Not to mention being tormented, *again*, by my parents' death. Maybe you forgot the dragon, the one that killed everything that I love, just *yesterday*!" I'm laughing so hard that tears run down my cheeks, and I can't catch my breath. "And you want to go shopping?"

I barely recognize my voice, and I don't have a name for this maniacal emotion racking my bones.

I'm only making myself look crazier.

I stop reacting when I realize Gwen hasn't done anything but watch me. And then internally scold myself for thinking I'm the crazy one here.

Pull it together, Evelyn.

"Look, I get it," she says while she riffles through the drawers, pulling out pieces of clothing.

And yet she still thinks I want to shop?

"What you went through, it was cruel, yes, torturous even, and," she raises her eyebrows and swallows hard like she's going to gag, "*gross*. But once you enter, there's nothing we can do. You are strong, brave, resilient. You won, Evelyn!" she says as she turns and shrugs at me. "I knew you would. *You* must have known you would, or you wouldn't have been in the trials to begin with. Try to dwell on that part and forget the rest. You are capable of amazing things, and you have proven that you can literally slay dragons. Or *poof* them...whatever that was. And *that* is gods damned brilliant."

She says it so matter-of-factly. Like, "Hey, I know chopping that wood was hard, but look! Now we have pieces for a fire!" And not at all like I was just inches from death, and mentally ravaged. I'm supposed to just forget that and be content enough today to go shopping. "And, there have been so many years without a winner. So yeah, we are celebrating."

Celebrating. The word feels so foreign. To be able to celebrate, I would have to feel joyous and happy. But all I feel are warring emotions. I can't find a way to express myself and overcome this. All the words I try to use are out of my grasp. Like they are at the top of my willow tree, and I'm bound to its roots.

"Sage was brave and resilient. Will she be shopping with us, Gwen?" Pain washes over Gwen's face. "I feel the same way about every soul that enters the trials, and Sage was no exception. If I could save you all, I would. She didn't deserve her fate. But as I mentioned, there is something different about you. You don't compare to other contestants. I knew that, even though I couldn't save you, you would save yourself. No one wanted to see Sage die, but once she started her trials, we couldn't interfere."

I can't bear to look at her. I want to hold onto Sage's memory. She can't just wash her away because 'there was nothing she could do.' "You were down in the Grimm Lodge for months. I thought you might like a day out. A day away from all you went through. Tomorrow you'll be presented at dinner with the king and his court. And even though you have an entire armoire of clothing," she says, tossing the pile of clothes on the bed next to me, "I thought you would like to go out and find something that you would like to wear for tomorrow. Something *you* pick out. Maybe like nothing you've worn before." She makes a feathery *swoosh* with her hands, adding brilliance to her words. "If you would rather sit here and sulk and replay the trials that are in the *past,* then so be it." She says it with a playful nature, as though it was most definitely not too soon or too sore a subject for me to handle. "But *I* am going shopping and will probably also settle for a good mug of mead at the Wretched Hollow if you care to join me."

Gwen grabs her linen satchel and leaves me standing alone in the middle of the room.

Suddenly, the very real idea of drowning in my own sorrow is staring me in the face. So I get dressed before the panic sets in, throwing on a pair of black leggings, a silken grey tunic, and black boots. *I might as well get to know this new prison of mine, right?* Maybe this will help me figure out why I'm here.

I run out of my room, catching Gwen as she heads down the stairs into the castle foyer and out into the courtyard.

I'm almost brought to my knees by the sweet smell of the morning air, the fragrance of the lush rose bushes lining the walkway permeating my senses.

Gwen doesn't slow down, but looks back at me and smiles. I don't smile back and instead focus on the garden.

Some of the roses are so dark they could be black, and others are a shimmering aubergine. I expect to find a carriage or horses, but to my surprise, Gwen walks right through the wrought iron gates. Bursts through, really, with that same electric energy and love of life that seems to surround her at all times. It's intoxicating and slightly annoying. We walk along a pebbled path that soon turns into worn dirt. Its edges mark the beginning of rolling fields covered in emerald colored grass—just like what I glimpsed in the carriage on my way to the arena. In the distance, I see the outskirts of a village with giant looming trees surrounding the speckles of buildings.

"That over there," she says, pointing at the buildings in the distance, "is Sallows. It's the main village in Nightmare. Many of the trade goods come through town for inspection and then are sent out to the rest of the kingdom either by carriage or small shipping vessels. The port is about a quarter of a day's ride from here. Kyustos isn't too far down the road that way," she points to a path that veers into the forest, "but it is definitely *not* a place you will want to visit. There is something about Kyustos that creeps even me out!"

"Why? What happens in Kyustos?" My mind runs through all the terrors it can conjure. Murder. Kidnapping. Torture. Illicit sex acts.

"Oh, I didn't mean to frighten you. You're safe here at the castle and in Sallows. And probably even Kyustos. Cane has been trying to help for years, but the town seems to be a magnet for all the wrong people. No one really knows why; maybe it's the cheap brothel or the old tavern owner. Trouble always finds itself there."

Safe. I try to hide my scorn at hearing her say that.

Eventually, the conversation shifts from kingdom lore to stories of the Nightmare Trials. I'm less eager to hear about that. With every word she speaks, I have to hold back the recent memories of my own experiences.

The only thing I really glean from this conversation is that for the last five years, no one has won. The Night Shroud has been down to four guards, impatiently waiting for a champion to fill the last spot. Over that time, only one other prisoner has even made it to the last trial, but they were eaten by a Chimera.

A Chimera.

I need to sit before I pass out. Gwen must be able to sense my unease because I hear her clear her throat as she changes subjects. "But I'm sure you know all about the prior trials. The stories make their way all over the kingdom," she says, giving me a look that makes me uneasy.

"But it was nice to hear a more firsthand account, you know how stories change from person to person."

I'm grateful for the ability to once again let my mind wander as she fusses over what color looks best on me, and whether I'd look better in a low-cut dress or a backless one. Soon, she's talking about bedmates and sexcapades with the king, and I can't help but listen to *that*.

Gwen is apparently one of the king's favored.

Shocking.

My cheeks blush when she talks about sharing his bed with others, too…at the same time.

How does she talk about this so freely, and with a stranger, nonetheless?

It's making me feel involuntarily voyeuristic. Gwen tells me that in addition to frequenting the king's bed, she is also part of his court. She is the castle's best alchemist and one of the king's closest confidants. I have so many questions about that, but I hold my tongue. I'm not interested in making friends.

I finally blurt out, "Why can I not recall all of my life before the trials? I remember pieces, like where I lived. I know my name, and recently, my family. But so many details continue to elude me."

She stops rambling for a moment. Her expression is perplexed and inquisitive. But all she says is, "Interesting." I continue before she starts pointlessly jabbering again.

"Is that not a normal side effect of the trials?" Her airy disposition and carefree gait completely halt now while she stares directly into my eyes. It's invasive, but I can't look away from her beautiful face.

"No, it isn't," she says as though her mind is elsewhere. And then all at once her glow returns, and she's twirling towards the village with her buoyant gait. Of course, I'm not satisfied with any of this, but at least Gwen talks to me. If I can just get her to trust me so I can get some real answers, I might just learn something.

Chapter 24 Evelyn

As we approach Sallows, the worn path turns into a cobblestone road. Tall, busy buildings built into enormous trees and sparkling with light line the streets. A colorful, bustling energy roars from the elves in my periphery. But above all else, my eyes linger on the lanterns. They're crafted from obsidian with beautiful whirls sculpted into the cage. Like the edges of a dream have caught a beating heart, they are pulsing with fire right in front of me.

The lanterns are the perfect complement to the thriving vegetation, saturating the colors so that they practically vibrate with luminance. The entire town is sparkling. Wildflowers coat the distant fields not with the yellows and whites that I'm used to, but deep purples and dark blues. It's beautiful in a way that I never knew was possible. There is a hint of cloves and sugar in the warm air that gives me a sense of calm. All I've known was that this side of the wall was full of black shadows and monsters, with the smell of rot that clung to the air. The scene laid out before us paints an entirely different picture. It gives me the feeling that something just isn't right.

Why would the gods fill generations of Daydreamer citizens with the idea that this place was depraved?

A few of the trees around and in the village loom so tall you can only see the tops if you crane your head back all the way. They make a natural roof over the bustling village streets, and some have trunks so big that entire shops are carved into them.

My head cannot turn fast enough to memorize it all.

I've done at least two full circles before looking back for Gwen. She casually sways her elegant figure and waves to everyone she passes. She holds such a presence that I can actually see waves of people gravitating toward her. And she knows each one personally, talking about specific details of their lives, and picking flowers to hand to giggling children.

The people here are a living rainbow of colors. From skin tones to hair colors, not one person looks the same. It's like the effervescent hues of the landscape have seeped into their being. For the first time, when my gaze falls to Gwen in the crowd, I don't immediately scowl or look away. Her face lightens for a second, and it's not until she winks that I tear myself out of this stupor.

These are not your friends. Gwen is not your friend.

In all my awe, I didn't notice that we had reached the center square. Here stands a tall, large willow tree, its beautiful, sweeping branches swaying down toward the people. It reminds me of the tree I love in the Daydream castle gardens—thoughts and memories of my sweet, safe Odin flood my mind. Odin and I wrapped under the shelter of the branches. The sound of our moans echoing off each of the leaves. I try to tamp down the blush rising to my cheeks and the tears welling in my throat.

The only difference in the tree before me is the color. This tree's bark is glittering, near black, and the leaves an iridescent purple and gray. I remember that part of my dream where my willow tree shimmered with leaves just like this, just for an instant. *How odd. Have I seen this tree before?*

Gwen links her arm through mine and swings me towards one of the side streets. There are shops that sell everything from small treats to horse saddles. The trees lining the cobblestone walkway shimmer in the breeze, the air is sweet and bustling, and for this moment, I completely welcome the beautiful distraction.

⤜⤜⤜ ⤛⤛⤛

We spend our day shopping and walking around the town. I watch people walk down the streets seemingly carefree. It's like they have no agenda other than to love their neighbor. Some are so loving that they stop and kiss in the middle of the street—and not just a peck on the cheek. Some couples take it a bit farther, partially masked in the shadows, pressed against buildings, limbs blending together. I try my best to avert my gaze, but that's where my stare gets caught—between strong hands and tree branches and vibrant lights and full breasts. It's all happening here, on the main road.

"Close your mouth," Gwen whispers in my ear as she pulls me into one of the shops nearby.

There is a small tinker of a bell, and I'm met with a wall of decadent smells as the door swings closed behind me. The smell of fresh bread and sugary berries floats in the air. There are several small circular tables scattered where we walked in—customers sipping tea and eating gooey breads and pies—and along the back wall, a counter with a display covered in pastries.

"This is the *best* bakery in town. Cane often has Tabitha and Richard, the owners, make muffins and biscuits for the castle. My favorite is the chocolate croissant."

Gwen takes my hand and pulls me up to the counter. "Hi, Tabby!"

"Gwen! It's been too many days since I've seen you."

The older-looking elven woman leans over the counter and pulls Gwen into a tight hug. Her gray curls spilling around them. She pats her hands on the apron covering her light blue dress as she pulls back.

"I was just here two days ago!" Gwen says with a chuckle.

"I hate to tell you this, but I just sold the last chocolate croissant. If I had known you were coming, I would have saved it for you. But I do have fresh biscuits, berries, and cream."

"You know me so well, Tabby. I would love that. I want you to meet my new friend, Evelyn."

"Do you think I live under a rock? We all know Evelyn. How do you do? It's nice to see a new face around here. What can I get for you? It's on the house!"

Everything looks so delicious, I don't know where to land my gaze. There are cookies and pies. Tarts and scones. Pastries covered in fruits and others drizzled in chocolate. If I could, I would try one of everything.

"I think I'll try what Gwen's having."

"And a cup of warm chocolate coffee to go with it." The kind woman says. "I'll bring it out to you girls when it's ready."

We take a seat in one of the only open tables. Gwen is already catching everyone's attention, sending winks and giggles and waves to all the shop's guests. I try to relax into the back of the chair, but the back's too short, so I lean forward, fiddling with the edge of my tunic.

There are cups with spoons stirring on their own, and children making shadowy figures as the adults chat away. When I was younger, I used to wish that I had magick like some of the other kids in town. But mother and father always said that magick does not make you any more or less important. I wasn't sure I believed it, but it never mattered at home. Gwen doesn't have her own magick, and she doesn't seem any less important. Still, sometimes I just wish I knew what it felt like.

"You are going to love the coffee. Tabby melts down the chocolate and mixes it in. If the gods were still walking our realm, I think they would bow to Tabby for this creation."

As if conjuring up our treats, Tabitha walks over with a small silver tray carrying our biscuits and coffees, causing my mouth to water.

"Let me know if you girls need anything else." Gwen reaches into her lined bag to hand her a few coins, but Tabby refuses, saying that Cane pays her too much for her deliveries as it is.

Steam wafts off my mug, carrying the rich smell of coffee and chocolate to my nose. I take a sip and nearly melt in delight.

"This may be the best drink I have ever had." I take another sip before trying the biscuit. The moan that comes from my mouth is borderline inappropriate. "I told you so" is all Gwen says before she, too, is moaning over her biscuit, fruit, and cream.

"We *have* to come back here. I need to try everything now." The words leave my mouth before I know what I'm saying.

Am I so easily swayed by sweets?

I look up at Gwen, and she's just smiling at me, like I alone just made her the happiest person in all the kingdom.

Chapter 25 Evelyn

T̲he̲ ̲b̲a̲k̲e̲r̲y̲ ̲d̲o̲o̲r̲ ̲s̲h̲u̲t̲s̲ behind us, the air bursting with a sugary farewell. We practically crash into a group of children laughing and wielding wooden swords. Some are fighting imaginary dragons, calling themselves the "dragon slayer."

"They're pretending to be you." Gwen lovingly smirks as she steps into a pretend battle with them. "Roar!" she bellows as she looms over one of the tiny swordsmen. He gives his best little war cry and lunges his sword towards her chest. Her hands cover her "wound" in the most dramatic of theatrics as she gasps for air and falls to a knee. The boy pretends to slice her throat before she falls to the ground, all the other children cheering.

My heart swells.

The way these children look up to me, to what I have done. Paired with the manner of Gwen's playing, it's almost enough to erase the ultimate horrors that are still so fresh in my mind. Swirling blackness could change everything at any moment. *And wouldn't this be the worst kind of nightmare? The beauty of the town, the warmth of the sun on my skin, the feeling of adoration from this child. Then to have it ripped away.*

Still laughing, Gwen gets up and walks back to me. "I'll part ways with you for now, I have an errand to run," she says as she taps her shoulder bag. She kisses my cheek so quickly that she's off before I can react.

"Uh, wait! Where are you going?" I half-stammer, half-shout.

"I have some teas and tonics to drop off at the clinic. You can come with me if you want to! But you do still have more shopping to do. Walk where *you* want to walk. Shop where *you* want to shop. I can't wait to see what you pick out!" She tosses me a pouch of coins, makes eye contact with an absurdly attractive man with a meltable smile, and turns to meander down the street. She looks over her shoulder before she is out of earshot and shouts, "Go! Don't just stand there. We'll meet back at the tavern after!" Before I can ask where, or how long I have, or anything *at all*, she disappears in a crowd of dancing performers, and then she's gone. I weigh the pouch in my hand.

It couldn't hurt to see what this kingdom has to offer.

I'm in and out of three shops quickly. There are so many gorgeous options: floor-length gowns, skin-tight satin, every color rich and glowing. In one shop, I find myself drawn to a rather frilly pink thing, but no sooner than it's on my body do I take it off, having looked like an oversized candy floss flower. *I bet Gwen would have stolen breaths in a gown like that.* A little deflated and discouraged, I move more slowly along the bustling road.

I notice a sparkling necklace and bracelet set in front of a shop window. I move so that my reflection is entwined with the set, and admire the vision for a moment. The shop door bursts open, and a short, rather stocky, elven woman leans against the frame. "You just gonna stare at it, or were you gonna come in?"

"I, uh..."

"I close in fifteen minutes. Fifteen minutes on the dot and not *one* single moment longer."

I still don't know what to say, suddenly overrun with disappointment, both in myself for not finding a dress, and because I have no time left to explore. She must notice the change in my thoughts, because her expression softens. With a gentle eye roll, she says, "Come on, you'd be surprised what you can do with fifteen minutes." And holds her arm out. I tentatively walk toward the door as she ushers me in. "Come on! Come on! Fourteen now!" And she slams the door behind us, flipping the flowery sign to "We'll be back tomorrow!"

Not only is this one of the shops carved into a giant tree, but everything inside screams magick. Her shop seems too large to be contained solely in one tree's trunk, but through the back are more rooms and even more attire. Lights are hanging from the ceiling on little strung-up bulbs. The whole place glows in that same deep sparking light that lines the lampposts on the street. The gowns are lit up like artwork in a gallery, each completely different, and the only one of its kind. In between the gowns are pieces of jewelry or accessory sets that perfectly match the gown next to it. I just stand there with that familiar immovable awe.

"So, do you need a necklace? Dress? Both?" She yells from behind a desk that she is closing up in the corner.

"I, um. I'm Evely—"

"Yes, yes, I know who you are. I'm Nephale. This is my shop. Now enough with the pleasantries, what do you need? Is it for tomorrow? Do you have anything already?"

I just fidget with the end of my tunic.

Under her breath, she mutters, "Haven's Grace, this is like pulling teeth."

"I don't have anything." She stops her flustering and looks right at me, disbelief, and a little shock cause her brows to furrow.

"Shoes even? A hairpiece?" I shake my head. Again, to herself, she says, "The entire town and hours to browse with unlimited money, and this pretty little thing comes to me empty-handed." She looks up to something unseen. "You owe me for this."

I stare at her as she walks back towards the window and grabs the necklace set I had been ogling. I don't see a matching dress near there. She walks back, in and out around the mannequins, behind curtains lining the back walls. Her arms are filled with satins, laces, and jewels. She hurries over to me and throws it all into my arms, draping anything that has fallen over my shoulders and neck. Only when every last jewel is perfectly balanced does she stand with her hands on her hips, staring at me. Her head juts forward, eyes bulging and brows raised. "Well?" I try to move my arm to hold something against me, but a crown falls, and so does a black studded heel. Exasperated, she picks them up and forcefully pushes me towards the back of the shop, straight through a curtain. As soon as I turn back around, the shoe flies through the curtains and lands right on my forehead before falling to the ground.

"Ow!" I duck before the crown flies towards me, bounces off the wall and lands next to the huge pile of clothes.

It's only seconds before I hear Nephale scurry off and shout, "Nine minutes!" Sighing, I lean down and pick up the first item on top of the pile. It's lace, tiny, and held together by string and...I throw it to the corner.

I will NOT be needing that sort of undergarment.

I pick up one of the pretty crowns in my pile of clothes, pointed in symmetrical black diamond spikes, and place it on my head. I'm not sure if it's my messy hair, my lack of makeup, or just my plain attire that makes this crown seem less magnificent when I'm wearing it, but I'm only becoming more discouraged as I go. I sort through the pile and find a dress. The fabric is black with an iridescent silver and purple sparkle that runs throughout. Black silken ribbons tie up the back. It's a different color every time you look at it. It's simple yet elegant, and oozes class without demanding attention through gaudy frills and blatant gems. I quickly take off my clothes and slide it over my body.

It feels like we know each other. *Gods, I have curves? Where have they been hiding all these years?* The fabric cinches down the center of the buttocks, accentuating my natural roundness, before cascading to the floor. The front is low cut—very low cut—but I want to like it. To show off a little, like Gwen said. I search through the pile to find shoes. Although heels would be a stunning addition, slippers seem more practical. These are enhanced with the same gems from the necklace in the window and just feel right when I put them on. I finally feel like I'm getting the hang of this.

Almost embarrassed at how pleased I am with myself, and remembering my time crunch, I peel off the dress and neatly stack it with the shoes and necklace set in the corner of the room. Just as I'm sliding my boots back on, I hear Nephale hurrying over. "Time's up—" I cut her off and burst from the room, smiling. I hand her what I have chosen and make my way to the front. A moment later, she follows. I must be glowing, because she says, "That good, huh?" as she packs my bag. Before I can grab it, she says, "I'll send it to your room, Dragon Slayer."

I swear she slips in something lacey before putting it under the desk. I open my mouth to object, but she is forcefully pushing me again, right towards the front door. "Your time was up five minutes ago!" She says, and smiles at me as I leave the shop and turn to face her. I expect her to slam the door shut, but she doesn't. She is still smiling at me when I open my mouth to speak. She cuts me off. "You're welcome, dear." And she closes the door.

Chapter 26 Evelyn

As I STROLL INTO the dusky center of town, my steps are lighter. It's like a veil has been lifted and the town is even more beautiful than I realized. I can't stop smiling. The lamps begin to flare to life as the day bleeds into evening, casting a red radiance over the streets. It's so welcoming that I don't even miss the warmth of the sun as the cool air caresses my skin. The colors remind me of the mild harvest season that we have at home in Daydream. A flash of the leaves on the trees changing color in the forest behind my cottage starts to form in my mind, but I'm quickly interrupted by a low grumble.

I am starving; it's been hours since I had my treat at the bakery.

Finding the tavern is easy. It's another building carved into the side of a huge tree, perched on the edge of town. Its branches have leaves that are glowing above the door carved into the trunk. And just above is the most intricate sign with whorls of willow tree branches and mugs of ale engraved into it that reads: The Wretched Hollow. Outside, there are tables and chairs, and so many people are drinking, dancing, and laughing. I try not to gape at the blend of hips and limbs tightly woven together.

Inside is buzzing with people too, even louder in the enclosed space. I'm instantly hit with the smell of cedar mixed with that of ale and meats. It wraps around my senses like a blanket, even with all the raucous noise and movements.

There's an empty seat at the long, waxed, butcher block bar, riddled with old liquor stains. I'm instantly greeted by a short, stout man with a long gray beard braided to his belly.

"What'll ye be having, Dragon Slayer? First round's on the house!"

I can't hide the exasperated tone in my voice. "It's Evelyn. And I'm no Dragon Slayer. Whatever happened in the trials was part of the nightmare, nothing more."

He shrugs. "Did ye, or did ye not, slay a dragon?"

Of course I didn't. It was just a nightmare. Right?

He continues, "The name's Piscevens, and Dragon Slayer or not, tell me what yer drinkin'! We've been waitin' fer the last Night Shroud to be picked for some time now, and I want to be the first to serve ye a drink!"

I flinch at the assumption that I will decide to join the Night Shroud over freedom, but I'm too hungry to bicker. "A glass of mead and whatever stew is cooking back there would be great."

Piscevens nods, and not one minute later, he hands me my mead. The first sip is heaven. Sweet and bold, filling my belly with a satisfying burn. I can taste the berries and honey melded together and let out a heavy, satisfied sigh.

My gaze wanders from person to person. Some look back but do their best to look disinterested, and others are lost in their own conversations. The variety of elven people here is astounding. Skin tones that range from the palest white to the richest browns. Hair that spans the entire rainbow of colors. Some people have the same short, stocky appearance as the barkeep. It reminds me of the strong, fierce mountain dwarves in fairy tales.

Others are tall and slender, moving through the crowds like water between rocks. Warriors and commoners alike all mingling and laughing over mead and ale. A sense of longing settles deep in my gut. I want to smile like these folk do at each other. I really don't have any friends, besides Odin.

It's not that I don't have friends, it's that I can't remember them yet, right? Odin is king; we must have hundreds of gatherings and parties and dinners. I just can't seem to recall them.

Suddenly, I feel a prickle run down my back. I swivel around, immediately locking eyes with a tall elven man standing in the back corner of the tavern.

Another completely gorgeous citizen leaning against the wall with a mug in one of his large, tanned hands. His body is unmoving among the chaos in a way that captures my breath. He's like a predator searching for his prey.

I swear everything else in the room slows, like I have an eternity to study him. He's taller than me and built like he has been wielding a sword for the better part of his life. It's almost impossible to guess his age. As far as elves go, he could be thirty or one hundred and thirty, and no one would know the difference. Our stares are tentative, but unwavering, and there's a sharp edge to his curiosity. His chiseled jawline and deep hazel eyes are laced with uncertainty. Deep brown hair hangs to his shoulders with his tipped ears poking through the strands. He looks like he's trying to blend in. But his crisp white tunic, black riding pants, and leather boots are of a higher quality than those of other patrons here.

Eternity comes to a halt when he smirks—those eyes. I can't look away, my heart racing. His grin spreads across his whole face when he sees the effect he has on me.

There's maybe a slight possibility I have been staring for quite some time now.

He starts sauntering towards me. I quickly get up to make my way to the door, but I'm not fast enough.

A smooth leather boot steps directly in front of me. I follow it all the way up his torso until I meet his smirking expression. He is so much taller up close—the glint of something shiny peeks out from his shirt. I have to squint my eyes to make out what looks to be a small silver crossbow with a red gem adorning the center, hanging from a leather cord. The urge to touch it is so strong that my hand starts reaching out for it.

"Stunning," he says. "I-I'm sorry. That was very forward." But he steps even closer, scanning my face. "I'm not sure what came over me. I know this might sound strange, but have we met before?" His grin falters, and his brows crinkle.

All I can think to do is leave. Quickly. His hand reaches for mine, and our fingers brush against each other. I swear I can feel something jolt my senses, which only makes me want to flee faster. But just as soon as I turn to leave, I slam face-first into Gwen.

"Haven's Grace, Evelyn, I thought you ran off on me."

I grab Gwen's hand and pull her out the door, and far away from any possibility that I will embarrass myself further in front of that man.

"What are you doing? I haven't even eaten!" She whines, but follows. She throws a look over her shoulder and sees a person standing in the doorway of the Wretched Hollow. "And why did that excessively hot man chase you out of the tavern?"

"Who?" I say, looking back. "Oh, that guy? I really don't think he was chasing me. It was getting too crowded waiting, so I was just leaving to find you. I'm just not used to being around so many people after being alone for so long." I know my comment is a pointed jab and a lie, but I don't want her to know that a man has gotten under my skin.

Gwen takes one more look over her shoulder before turning back to me.

"Okay, well, I *was* hoping to have a good bowl of stew. It's lamb night..." She looks defeated for all of one second before lighting up again. "I have another idea. Wait here."

She jogs back to the tavern. I refuse to look, afraid that I will see that man standing there staring at me, or laughing at me...or mesmerizing me. Several minutes tick by, and I'm about to suck up my cowardice and go in, when I hear a door shut. Gwen glides out from the tavern doors with a basket on her arm and thankfully, no gorgeous men in sight.

I never thought there would be a day when I would *want* to head back into the castle here in Nightmare, but that is exactly the reprieve I'm looking for.

Gwen skips up to me, links our arms together, and whisks me away down the street. "Where are we going? This isn't the way to the castle."

"It's a surprise." She whisper-giggles with an intoxicating swagger. *Gods, she makes me feel like everything is okay.* I truly hope it isn't all a farce, not with her.

We walk out of the crowded town and down a dark path through an even darker woodland landscape. There is a soft, cool wind rustling the tree branches, and nocturnal animals are just waking up. To my surprise, my soul stills. The magicked lanterns are few and far between now, causing long shadows to dance across the terrain.

I'm still relishing the peace when we come to a grove of wildflowers.

Normally, flowers are but a dark outline in the night. Soft pools of fragrant clouds blanket the forest floor. But these...*these* flowers are glowing. Blues, greens, pinks, and purples illuminate the ground enough that even the air glows and casts colorful light across Gwen's face and hair. *Bioluminescent.* I've read about sea creatures with these properties, but I have never seen any. And I certainly didn't know that there were plants and flowers with them, too. I don't think I have seen anything so beautiful in my life.

Each flower has its own glow. A unique twinkle in the same way people are unique. I run my hand over the petals of a small purple flower. It leaves my fingers coated in a sheen of shimmering sparkles, like it painted me with a piece of its glamour. They seem sentient, pulsing with this magick. I'm desperately scrambling for something to say that will adequately express what I'm feeling. But nothing works.

I don't even notice Gwen nudging my shoulder with hers. She just giggles. "I thought you might like it here."

She reaches for a flower too, playing with the blueish-white sparkle it leaves on her fingers before she reaches over to me and streaks it across my cheeks.

"Some say that the flowers get their color and magick from the raw power that seeps out from the giant roots of the willow tree in the center of town. That the roots of these flowers connect right up to the roots of the tree. I don't know how true that really is, but it does sound romantic, doesn't it?"

I finally find my voice. "Do these flowers have any power of their own? Are they used for any tonics or potions?" Strange that my mind goes there first, when all the awe I feel is still furiously bubbling behind my ribs and in my head.

"Oh no. Well, not that I know of. We consider these flowers sacred, so we protect them. They can grow here untouched, every twinkling bloom free to flourish. And in return, we get to bask in their beauty."

She walks over to a small clearing and opens the basket, pulling out a small blanket and laying it on the ground. Then she's lighting candles, a warm yellow glow against the cool light of the flowers. She beckons me to sit.

"Is it safe out here in the dark?" I ask. It's twilight, and the sky still has hints of color, but soon only the moon will be shining. It's strange because I'm not truly worried about safety here. Gwen is here, and these rich, peaceful flowers are totally unbothered. I just don't think I should be allowed to feel safe after everything that has happened.

"It isn't dark." She gestures towards the glowing field and laughs. "But yes, this is a sacred place. No creature would dare spill blood here."

While I continue to take in the sea of flowers around me, I hear Gwen rummaging through the basket, laying out a jug, a loaf of bread, and cheese on the blanket.

"I know this isn't a proper meal, but since you didn't want to stay in the tavern, I thought this would sustain us until we returned to the castle."

She is so genuine and filled with grace. She looks beautiful, and this place is beautiful. "No, this is perfect." Gwen passes me the jug. The sweet taste of honey mead slides down my throat, and I let out a small moan. "This is so delicious!"

"I would hope so. It's from Piscevens' special cask. It's not cheap either, so don't waste it!" She nudges my shoulder with her own, a teasing grin on her face.

"What did you mean when you said the flowers get their color and magick from the willow tree in town? You mean that dark sparkling tree? How can a tree that far away be connected to these? And even if it is, how does it give flowers power or light?"

"Just like how the people's power is connected to the tree and the life that it gives, so are these flowers," Gwen says with a shrug, like I should just know this information. "You do know where the power of all our people comes from, don't you?"

I must look like a doe caught in the woods because she continues.

"All the magick, the power of the people of Sallix, is filtered into our realm from the depths of the soil, clay, and silt that we reside on. Our main village, Sallows, was built around the large willow tree at its center because it's the source of our magick here in Nightmare. Just like the willow tree in Daydream. Your castle is built near it, isn't it? That was no accident. From every useless thing I learned in my schooling, the one sure thing ingrained in my head was that both trees are the source of our magick, and their roots connect in the center of our realm."

I don't know how much of this story is fact, and how much is mead. But it sounds so fantastical that I want to believe it's real. I think of my willow tree. My refuge. I think about how at ease and at peace I always felt sitting under its iridescent branches. But the thought also brings back one of the last memories I have, the one where my willow tree leaves changed, morphed into the oily hues of the willow tree here in Nightmare. Is that because they're connected? I've never really thought about where the magick of our people comes from. Maybe it's just another memory that will come crashing back at some point. I guess I assumed power was determined and granted by the gods, but that seems more like a fairy tale than Gwen's story.

I shake my head, the mead causing my vision to track slower than usual, and giggle. I tune back into Gwen; her voice is melodical, and it's fun to listen and imagine. It reminds me of listening to my father.

Maybe I should think more about this when I haven't been drinking so much.

So I brush off the hundreds of questions I have and settle in to truly enjoy the view, the food, and the company.

It's been hours of drinking mead and munching on bread and cheese—the sky overhead now the deepest purple speckled with twinkling stars. The world is a colorful swirl, and everything is funnier than it usually is. The more we drink, the more we talk. *I am probably talking too much.*

I tell Gwen about how I grew up on a farm. I spare the details of my parents' death but stick to stories of our livestock. I try to make farm stories sound as riveting as one of my father's stories, and I get her giggling by the end. I tell her that we could never have pigs on the farm again because I cried for days after they were slaughtered for meat. She does her best pig snort impression, and we both lose it.

I tell her about my first and only love. A beautiful boy who became my friend before he became my lover. How we would gallivant through the forest together for hours, months, years. My words are falling clumsily out of my mouth as I become smitten with the memory of loving him. I miss him terribly. Sometimes, I wonder if the power of dreams takes over, because I swear I can feel him, breathe him in... I hold back as I start to say his name. An instinct full of urgency and importance snaps me out of the sweet ramblings.

I cannot say his name.

Gwen notes that I have trailed off, and she pours more mead, her lips curved into a content smile. She hands me a glass, and we clink them together before taking in a delicious fruity sip.

I don't think I have ever had a girl friend before, at least not that I can remember. But being here, laughing and talking, makes me want to stay with her for hours. I want to soak in every bit of fun and contentment. Gwen seems so different from the person she was when I first met her. Or maybe I'm different. Maybe I just need peace and laughter a little more than I've been willing to admit. In the midst of our dizzy, drunken giggling, Gwen suddenly becomes quiet. Her laughs trailing off into the breeze.

"You had such a perfect childhood," she whispers. I think tears begin to pool in her eyes. "I grew up a two-day ride from Sallows." She gestures towards the path we just came from. I briefly think about the similar town outside the Daydream castle, Osieres, still baffled by just how alike both sides of the realm are, but how differently I perceive them.

"My father was a blacksmith, and my mother was a seamstress. I had a younger brother. His name was Zorin."

Gods...was.

"He was six years younger than me. My parents didn't know they could have another child. It had been so many years, and then suddenly there he was. It was such a delightful surprise. When he was two, he came down with a horrible cough. My mother took him to the healer, who assured her it was just a simple illness, that he was strong and would overcome the cough in a few days. They gave her a rub for his chest and sent her on her way. That very night, it got so bad Zorin could barely breathe." Gwen takes a big pull from the jug of mead, not even bothering to pour it into her glass. My heart starts aching.

"Mother and Father were frantic, sitting him up, patting his back, putting the rub on his chest, but none of this helped. The healer was only a few houses away from ours, so they sent me to fetch him. At eight, I knew my way around our village and could have found the healer's house with my eyes closed. I don't think I have ever run so fast in my life, even to this day. I will never forget the desperation in my mother's eyes, the panic. I was running to ease her pain. I slammed my fists into the healer's door and kept slamming until the skin was threatening to shred from my hands. The healer's wife was the one to answer."

Gwen lowers her head.

"Another villager across town needed the healer's help with a childbirth. She barely got out where he was before I was running again." Gwen pauses.

The look on her face makes my own chest tighten. I feel this overwhelming tether to Gwen. I hated her just yesterday and yet...being here... It makes me *want* to be her friend. I want her to finish, to share this with me. I want to hold something of hers and protect it, so that she knows I can be trusted. That, despite my reservations, I like her. We can carry this little piece of her past together.

She lifts her head finally, her slow gaze scanning the field before landing on me. "What is it?" spills out over my lips, the consonants sticking together with mead.

"You don't smell that? It's like..." She breathes in deeply. "I think it's lavender."

I can't smell anything new. "I understand if you don't want to keep reliving this," I say, even though I'm still holding out hope that she'll open up.

An eternity passes before she speaks again. "I was so scared. I knew my village like I knew the beat of my heart. But in my blind whirlwind of fear and urgency, I got turned around. I wound up running down the wrong alley and wasted precious seconds to backtrack. When I finally made it to the healer, he was in the midst of delivering a baby and wouldn't leave. I waited and waited. I could barely see through the sea of tears even as I tried to keep them at bay. I have never needed anything so badly in all my life. And we were just...stalled. My entire family's fate changing with each minute this baby refused to be born. I should have gone back. I should have gotten someone else. Done anything but stand there. But I waited, hating this baby for being more important than my brother. The healer finally agreed to come with me when the babe was born, and the mother was stable. He was exhausted, worn out. But I refused to leave until he came with me. I held onto his robes and threatened never to let go. To follow him home and not let him have a moment of peace to rest until he came with me. By the time we dragged ourselves, pathetically slow, to my home, I could feel it. I could feel it before ever seeing my parents. Just looking at the house, I knew we were too late. I burst through the door to my mother, crying on the floor with Zorin in her arms. He was already a pale, bluish tinge."

I don't know what to say. I can feel the pain emanating from Gwen's body. My mouth parts, but she keeps going.

"I failed them. Nothing was the same after that day. My parents never told me it was my fault, but I knew that was how they saw it. Perhaps they blamed themselves for placing such a burden on their young daughter, but regardless, the responsibility was mine, and I failed. If only I had gotten to the healer sooner, before the birth, Zorin might still be here, apprenticing for my father. Taking care of my mother like a son is supposed to. My father began to drink a lot after Zorin's death, and I can't say I blame him. Our house slowly turned into a silent void. There was no laughter, no family bonding, hardly any words spoken. It was like all our happiness was swept away on Zorin's last breath."

"Oh, Gwen." I take her hand in mine.

"When I turned sixteen, I left that home. I didn't know where I was going or what I would do, but I was dying under the constant, miserable reminder of my failure. Over the next few years, I picked up odd jobs in small towns. When I was eighteen, I came here to Sallows. I met Cane at the tavern, actually. I had been planning on only stopping here on my way to find work in another town, but Cane convinced me to stay. She took a deep breath and offered me a sad smile. "I don't know why I'm telling you all this. It must be the mead. Looks like I take after my dear old father after all."

I feel so much sorrow for her. I want to say it wasn't her fault, that she was brave and did everything she was supposed to. That she was right to leave her home. And that now, all I see when I look at her is this magnetic beauty and grace that lights up entire worlds when she smiles. I'm so grateful she shared this with me. She may never know how badly I needed it.

I scoot closer and put my arm around her shoulder. "Gwen." I steady my words. "You deserve every beautiful thing in your life. You have no reason to carry this guilt any longer. I see the way people look at you, and I can tell your heart is good." She relaxes into my shoulder and softly cries again. I hug her tightly. "Have you ever thought of going back? Seeing what has become of your family?"

She sits up, sniffs, and wipes a tear. "No. It's a part of my life I prefer to leave behind." And just like that, she is back to her jovial demeanor. Her skin glows, and her soft smile accompanies a cleansing sigh. I would never know that she was upset if it weren't for a hint of red left in her eyes. "Enough about me. There is still more cheese to be eaten and mead to drink." Gwen says as she reaches for the jug.

After several beats of silence and a few more sips, I ask a question that has been nagging me since the Nightmare Trials began. "Gwen?" My voice comes out like a whisper. "Why do you keep calling me Little Raven? I don't have black hair, and I certainly can't fly."

Gwen is staring down at her half-filled glass, twirling it in circles before she finally talks.

"When many think of a raven, they think of a bad omen or loss." She pauses. "But really, Evelyn, it's a symbol of bold, unwavering change. I think you will be the change the entire world needs."

She has definitely had too much to drink, but I feel my cheeks blush anyway. "That's ridiculous," My words slur together. "There is nothing that I can do to change anything here. I'm utterly powerless."

"And yet you 'poofed' a dragon!" She makes a swirling gesture with her arm when she speaks. Mead sloshes over the glass, and we both break out into a fit of giggling that makes my sides ache. When we manage to settle down from our joyous fit, she just stares at me. "We will see." She takes another giant gulp.

We finish off the mead and cheese with no more talk of our pasts or futures. We dance through the flowers. We run and run and collapse and run again. The air is glittering with each tousled petal's blessing. Eventually, we stumble toward the castle, fighting with our heavy eyelids the whole way, and even through my exhaustion, all I can feel is the longing to go back to the glowing flowers.

Chapter 27 Evelyn

"Holy Underworld," I groan as a hot, blinding pain slices right through my head.

I lift myself from the bed, which feels less like sitting up and more like swimming in a lake of muck. Clenching my fist to my mouth, I try to push back the bile that is sure to erupt at any moment.

"Fuck," I half-whine, half-moan as I rush to the bathing chambers and expel every ounce of stomach contents into the chamber pot. An ache spread in my chest. Sage would be proud of my word choice.

Much like my amazing tub, the pot empties down a pipe with three taps. When there's nothing else to heave, I sink to the stone floor, relishing in the coolness against my sweaty skin.

What was I thinking, drinking so much last night?

Using the edges of the white porcelain sink vanity, I pull myself up to stand. On the ledge is a tiny bottle of brownish, thick liquid with a note next to it:

This will help your hangover, Little Raven.

-Gwen

I really need to start locking my door...but I smile nonetheless. This is the third time she has come in without permission. To my credit, or to my stupidity, I was pretty inebriated last night and barely recall even getting back to the castle.

I throw back the liquid, my nose scrunching as I swallow the bitter, sticky tonic. The sludge crawls down my throat and pools as a hard mass in my stomach. I feel like I'll be sick all over again, but I hold the liquid down, willing it to stay put. This tonic is nothing like the purple one that I drank when I was dying in the Grimm Lodge.

If she wanted me dead, she's had plenty of other opportunities to kill me.

My thoughts drift back to last night. It was so...*nice* to spend the evening with Gwen. And that man at the tavern? The way we were drawn to each other. Gwen was right, he *was* excessively hot.

What has gotten into me?

I look at myself in the mirror. *What a mess.* My hair is sticking up in all directions, the sparkling dust from the flowers still glittering across my skin, and my clothes are covered in spots of dried mead.

Gods, I need a bath.

I tap three times on the tub's lever and let the warm steam caress my cheeks. There are bottles of different oils on the shelf, and I add my favorite scents to the running water. The entire room is a perfect blend of warm honey and lavender, the smell I now remember as home. The moment my toes dip in, my body relaxes—the heat working its magick on every cramp and ache. I swear I could stay here for an eternity.

After my bath, I write everything about the night in my journal, still working to piece together my missing memories. The brown potion must have worked because as I write, my stomach growls. I'm ravenous. It must be long after breakfast, but I dress quickly to head down to the kitchen anyway.

As soon as I swing open the door, I'm face-to-face with Gwen. I practically slam it shut with the shock. But she puts her hand on it to save herself, "It's just me," she says, in that sing-song voice.

"My gods, you scared the breath from me." I screech.

She starts laughing, and so do I.

I clear my throat. "Well, I'm just heading to the kitchen for a bite to eat. If you just point me in the correct direction, I can be on my way."

Gwen smooths her hands down her dress and composes her laughter. "I was coming to see if you wanted to get food with me! I'm starving." She links her elbow with mine and pulls us off to the kitchen.

⇛ ⇚

Gwen doesn't leave my side the rest of the day. She shows me the entire castle. The pure joy that radiates from her when she shows me her alchemy room is, regretfully, adorable.

"And this over here is where I stock the contraceptive tonic." She winks at me, pointing to a shelf above her work table. "You're welcome to come grab one when you're due for your monthly dose, or I can grab it for you when you need it."

I nearly forgot about taking my tonic, but having sex has been the last thing on my mind since being thrown in the trials. My cheeks blush as I reach up and put one of the small bottles in my pocket.

We end our tour in the gardens, which are delightful to say the very least. It looks like all the colors of the rainbow have been stained with a metallic black sheen. Each shade is vibrant and sparkling with shadows, the whole area alive with a sweet and smoky aroma. A wave of homesickness hits me as I take in the rich beauty. I long to be back in my own garden, to smell the familiar scent of lavender and hear the calming hum of bees as they flit from flower to flower. I miss my willow tree and the calm that it seemed to give me when I was close by. I close my eyes and try to walk myself through the garden paths, picturing where each of the different flowers grow.

"Are you okay?"

I take a deep breath, open my eyes, and turn to Gwen.

"It's just been a long few days. I think I need to lie down for a little while."

Gwen stays with me all the way back to my room and reminds me that we're having dinner with the king tonight, as if I could forget. I watch her leave, her gait light and her expression giddy with excitement. It's impossible not to smile around her.

I haven't seen King Cane since the Nightmare Trials arena. I can only imagine the creatures and debauchery that will be at this dinner. He *is* the King of Nightmares themselves. But, as terrified as I am, it would be a lie to say I'm not intrigued. I have only experienced beauty here and helpful townsfolk. Maybe this dinner will offer the same sweet surprise.

⟫⟫⟩ ⟨⟨⟨

As I pull the sparkling black fabric of my dress over my head, I instantly bubble with excitement. I shift from side to side, marveling in the silvers and purples that move with the gown. The low neckline doesn't intimidate me as much anymore. In fact, if I tug on the fabric just right, you can see the roundness of my breasts.

I don't think I have ever felt so sensual in all my life. My curves shimmer in the mirror as I twirl. The fabric swishes across the ground and wraps around me in a magickal hug.

I put my honey-hued hair up in a twisting braid, swipe rouge on my cheeks, and line my blue and brown speckled eyes with kohl. I must have done this before, because it comes to me naturally.

Gwen comes to get me just in time to help tie up the back of my dress. "You are absolutely stunning, but..." Gwen says as she taps her chin. "It's missing something." Her face brightens as she reaches into her own hair, pulls out a silver comb adorned with intricate flowers and a small opal shaped like a moon, and places it in mine.

"There, now your ensemble is complete."

I give myself one last look in the mirror, a small smile curving my lips. The silver comb sparkles in my hair and really does look perfect. My fingers trace the delicate piece before I glance at Gwen, watching me through the reflection. Warmth hums through me at her thoughtful gesture, and I can't resist running my fingertips over the floral pattern and crescent moon once more. I nod my thanks to Gwen, and she takes my hand, leading me out of the room and towards the dining hall.

"It was my mother's, and her mother's before that. I actually don't know how many women in my family it has passed through," Gwen says softly. "It's one of the only things I took with me when I left home."

"Oh, Gwen, no. You should wear it then." I say, reaching up to remove the comb.

She shakes her head with a small smile. "Honestly, it looks better with your outfit tonight anyway. It's like it was meant for you."

"Thank you. Truly." I say, giving Gwen's hand a gentle squeeze before letting my gaze drift over her dress.

While I may shimmer like the night sky tonight, Gwen glows like firelight. Her dress is red and orange ombre, and scandalously short.

If she bends over even a little, we will all get a show tonight.

The front is cinched, showing off her full hips and breasts, but the back swoops low and hugs tightly around her buttocks.

She tugs my arm before I can open the door. "We're not just going to walk in; they're giving you a grand introduction!"

They call me Evelyn, Champion of the Nightmares, as they open the doors for us. King Cane stands at the head of the table, arms wide and welcoming. There are at least twenty other guests. It seems we're the last to arrive, as there are only two empty seats left. Seats beside the king.

Flashes of memory from the trials are still flickering, but I will them away. Maybe Gwen was right; that was the past, and that's where it should be left.

The expanse of the room is larger than the barn at my family's cottage, with a long, polished wood table in the middle. There's a white runner down the center, with perfectly placed vases of blood-red and black roses. The walls are a deep gray, with large landscaped paintings and thick crimson velvet-draped windows.

I try not to gawk as Gwen and I flank the king. Their hands melt together almost instantly. With King Cane brushing his lips across her knuckles. Then he reaches his other hand towards me.

I'm conveniently just out of reach.

"Evelyn, you look absolutely ravishing," Cane says. I watch his eyes halt on my chest before traveling up to my lips, before meeting my glare. He winks.

"Your Highness," I say through gritted teeth.

The king smiles with unwavering eye contact before he pushes back his elegant chair. I keep a calm, uninterested facade until he snaps his fingers. Just one snap is enough to make the entire room go quiet.

"My court! We are here today not only to enjoy this decadent meal but to praise the completion of the Nightmare Trials by the Dragon Slayer. Let us not only fill our bellies, but feast our eyes upon Evelyn, Champion of the Nightmares!" They all clap, especially Gwen, who almost jumps with enthusiasm.

"Her bravery, strength, and perseverance shone through as she hurtled the wall of terrors and took down the Midnight Skorpios. Her cunning and mental fortitude were forefront when outsmarting the Barghest Maze and breaking through the psychic torment of the Haunted Manor. And last, but not least, her will to survive allowed her to overcome the greatest of nightmares, grief." He pauses, and I can feel every guest lean in as they wait for him to finish. "And in doing so, single-handedly slayed the Nightshade Dragon!" They cheer and clap. He lets them for a moment, but then snaps again. *Silence*. "It is with these traits that she, if she chooses," he pauses as he looks right at me again before turning back to the table, "will serve as the ideal Night Shroud guard. Protecting her king and kingdom."

The room erupts into cheers, the acclamation swelling as it echoes off the walls.

"I hope to see you all back here in seven days for the final ceremony, the Initiation Ball. Here, our dear Evelyn will announce her decision."

My fingers have turned into tense fists at my sides, so tight my nails have started to dig into my flesh. My face remains impassive as my outrage soars. He's wrong for having anyone go through those trials, for having them at all, regardless of the history. And to call him *my* king... The idea itself brings a sour taste to my mouth.

He doesn't ask me to speak, instead motioning for his subjects to begin eating.

How can I eat with these people I don't know, and don't care to know? People who can celebrate after watching the torment. Watching me. *Sage*.

I know I'll be hungry later, but I can't force anything past the knot in my stomach. Across the table, Gwen glares at me. Her gaze dramatically moves from me to the plate to me again before she shakes her head. I just scowl, causing her to roll her eyes and turn her gaze toward Cane.

I've watched the way she looks at people. I've felt her indescribable warmth and vibrance when she looks at me. Always selfless and curious and beautifully loving. But it pales in comparison to the look she gives to Cane. It's like they speak an unspoken language.

They don't tear their stares away from each other until two women burst into the room.

"Catherine, Hilia, you missed dinner!" Gwen says as the women get closer. She jumps up and hugs them each, kissing their cheeks and leading them closer.

Hilia cocks her head to the side with a sly grin on her face, "Gwen, you know we only come to these things for dessert."

Catherine and Hilia approach the table arm in arm. Both wearing floor-length gowns made of chiffon in violet and burgundy jeweled tones. The sight of them almost makes me want to cower in my chair. Before I spot a place for them to sit, I hear Cane's chair scrape against the floor. The women are at his side as he stands, but his hand never leaves Gwen's.

Gwen looks over her shoulder at me. The only person here I can stand, and she's looking at me like she's asking for my permission to leave. So I tilt my head in response, even as my mind demands she stay.

Hilia drapes her body on Cane's free arm, and Catherine trails behind as they all leave the dining room.

Dessert. Here I'm looking forward to the kingdom's dark chocolate truffles, only to realize they didn't mean food.

Chapter 28 Gwen

HAVING CANE ALONE IS an intimate affair that I cherish, but sharing Cane with Hilia and Catherine is like being in an erotic novel. Our bodies writhing and moving as one. I can barely contain the jolts of excitement piercing my core.

Sometimes Cane brings in one of the other men in the castle. He tends to enjoy women's company most, but has a special interest in fucking me while watching Hilia or Catherine being taken by another. I personally like it when Owen joins us. He may not be the sharpest of minds, but that man knows how to use his tongue.

Some people here do end up settling down with their one love, but many in our kingdom decide to share their lives with several. I mean, why limit yourself to one when there are so many?

I beckon Catherine to walk closer and hold my hand, and she does so with her usual shy hesitation, her fingers curling into mine a moment later. I know she doesn't mind that Cane gravitates to me and Hilia, but I want her to feel as euphoric and blissful as I do. She has another lover that she sees regularly, and I often wonder when she'll decide to stop our trysts.

I've heard stories of a place called Haven Falls. A waterfall deep within a forest, shrouded in complete silence. As the legend goes, the only sound that you can hear there is your true love's heartbeat. If your intentions are pure, the magick imbued in the land will bond your soul to that of your love's for all eternity, this life and all lives after. If you travel to this sacred land with nefarious intentions, you will never be able to form a bond with anyone again, cursed to live in solitude forever. It's by Haven's Grace, and Haven's Grace only, that a true soul bond can be formed. Many of our citizens believe in the power of it so fiercely that "Haven's Grace" has become an exclamation of disbelief. As if only the knowledgeable power of the waters would possibly understand their situation.

I have often teased Catherine with the idea that she should go there with her lover, even though we both know it's just a legend. I just want her to know it's okay to leave this lifestyle if she loves someone else.

"Hilia, you are exquisite," Cane murmurs next to me, letting go of my hand to trace his fingers over the side of her body, skimming her breasts.

I fall back with Catherine, letting Hilia have her moment. Gods forbid she doesn't get the praise she expects, then no one will have fun tonight.

Cane pulls Hilia into his bedchambers, and I saunter in after, Catherine giggling like a schoolgirl despite all the times we have done this together.

Watching Cane circle Hilia like a predator homing in on his prey goads my desire, but what will make this night truly unforgettable lies in the decanter by the fireplace. An effervescent pink drink is calling to me—willow root wine. Not only does this taste more delicious than any mead, but it has an aphrodisiac effect on the body. Gods, I could come just thinking of how it makes me feel.

Cane's room drips with masculine decadence, even in the sparse candlelight.I can still make out all the furnishings and fabrics, each one swathed in rich, dark colors that bleed into the accents of gold. His bed is a deep mahogany, draped in black silk sheets and a lush, deep-red blanket.

I make my way over to the willow root, watching Cane stalk Hilia all the way and feeling the heat pooling in my core. Pouring a glass for myself and Catherine, I turn back to hand the cup to her, but she shakes her head. *More for me.* I down my glass in one long gulp, then spend the next few minutes taking small sips of the second glass. Watching Hilia as Cane undresses her, taking in her nipples and listening to her moans. Each pass of his tongue, each groan from their mouths, causing my breath to quicken.

The haze of lust from my own desire and the desire brought on by the willow root wine is so thick I almost forget that Catherine is here, too. Watching, her expression intense, her eyes hooded. She starts to undress herself, running her hand across her bare breasts and nipples as she drags her gown down. Her nipples harden as her hands pass over them, and then Cane's shadowy tendrils take their place. I'm burning up so badly that I don't think I can move, but I ache to be touched.

Cane and Hilia have made their way to his bed. While Cane still has his clothes on, Hilia is in nothing but her high heels, lying on her back with Cane's mouth between her thighs.

I finally make my way to Catherine, taking her hands in mine, preventing her from taking the gown all the way off. Just the feel of her warm skin on mine sends jolts of pleasure through my body, and I moan, drinking it in. I guide her gown to the floor myself. Slowly. As the dress falls, I see Catherine's eyes close, and I trail kisses down her arms before she makes quick work of undressing me. We are both standing in our undergarments, breasts bare, chests heaving, when I hear Cane's commanding voice. "So fucking beautiful. Come here so I can watch."

I can feel the need pulsing off each of us. Like we have been waiting for this moment all night. My whole body is tingling. My need becomes all-consuming. Before Cane can turn back to Hilia, I grab him by the collar of his shirt and slam my mouth against his. It's a clash of lips and teeth and moans, and the sound makes my body feel warm and languid. I rip at his shirt, tearing the buttons free, and then lick a trail from his neck down to the top of his trousers.

He's lean and toned in all the right places with a light trail of hair from his navel and disappearing beneath his trousers. The small patch of hair on his chest has my fingers aching to touch it. On his shoulder is the defined mark of his magick, branding him as Nightmare's king.

"Gwen, let's let Catherine have some fun too, my darling enchantress."

Catherine giggles and steps forward, running her hands down his chest before reaching his waistband.

"Catherine, I'm finding it hard to enjoy myself with my trousers on. Please," he says as he brushes a strand of hair from her cheek, "take them off." As Catherine unties his laces, I crawl onto the bed and kneel behind him, my hands trailing down his back to his tight buttocks before I pull away and prowl over to Hilia. She is still lying on her back on the bed, naked and touching herself, watching Catherine and me. Her fingers dip inside, and I gently cover her hand with mine, feeling the pulse of her movements. The way her palm pushes against the apex of her thighs as her fingers slide deeper. It's not long before I take over for her, her hand moving instead to my breast. Her entire body tense with need, all in my control.

"You and I both know that I can make you come faster." She gives me a wicked grin as her back arches, and she lets out a wild scream as I reach that delicate place inside of her. I pump my fingers faster as I take one of her nipples into my mouth, biting and twirling it with my tongue, relishing in Hilia's mewling. She's unraveling, panting, and screaming in release as I curl my fingers into her.

I hear gasps from behind me, and I see Cane, in all his naked glory, pick Catherine up and toss her onto the bed. It's times like this that worry me, how different my want for him is. It's primal and raw and often all-consuming.

Hilia grabs at my hip and spins me, planting me firmly on her face. I moan and bend over as she licks up my folds. With my legs bracketing her head and my chest planted on the bed above, Cane looms over me and thrusts his hard cock into my mouth. I sit up on my elbows as his velvety soft, engorged tip brushes my lips, causing him to let out a low moan. I can taste his salty need as a bead drips onto my tongue. I can see just enough to watch as Catherine lies on her stomach and positions herself at Hilia's pussy, licking and sucking at her already sensitive area. Hilia is already close to finishing again, her gasps and moans vibrating my core. Cane continues his thrusts. Deep and unforgiving. I try to cry out as Hilia sends me over the edge, but my cries are caught on Cane's cock, tears streaming down my face.

"Look at my women. Look at you all coming with your king." His sultry voice is thick with passion. Just when I think he's about to come down my throat, he pulls out. I hear another moan come from his lips. I look up under lowered lashes and see his eyes roll back as Catherine circles behind him and trails passionate kisses up and down his neck, her fingers grazing his nipples. Cane's eyes flare open and lock in with mine, and as they do, I slowly take in every inch of him until he is rocking his cock against the back of my throat again. I'm gagging, and he loves it. He growls and pushes me off of him to lay me on the bed next to Hillia.

"The sight of you on your knees alone could make me spill into your mouth, but I have other plans for you." He looks like he could burst with need, so tense it hurts. "Gwen, love, you're dripping for me. Catherine, I want you to lie down and touch that pretty pussy while I fuck Gwen. I want to hear you scream by the time I'm done."

The warmth in my core feels like a growing flame getting hotter and brighter. I feel my wetness dripping down my thighs.

Cane flips me over onto my stomach and grabs my hips. My ass is up in the air, and I squirm underneath his touch. With his lips to my neck, he whispers, "Brace yourself, my love." And then I'm consumed by the feel of his very well-endowed cock slamming into me.

"Oh, Gwen, so wet and ready for me. You take my cock so well."

Fucking Underworld.

In one breath, Cane is filling me so gloriously that I see stars. He grabs my hips, pulling out and then slams in again. Over and over, his thrusts are deep and hard. Faster and needier. He reaches around, kneading my breast and flicking my nipple. The sensation inside of me is rapturous. Every thrust into me sends a wave of heat through my body. The ache builds and builds until the feeling is almost torturous. I can feel my wetness covering his cock, feel it dripping out of me with each pull and push in and out. I can feel Cane getting closer, too. His cock, which was already magnificent, seems to grow with each shift inside of me. Reaching around again, Cane begins to rub my swollen clit, and I swear to any gods in existence that I see fucking rainbows explode from my vision. The sounds I'm making are nothing short of carnal.

I see Hilia touching herself and Catherine simultaneously. Watching us. The look on their face tells me that they, too, are almost undone. Watching these women makes the fire coursing through my blood grow hotter. I tear my gaze from them and look over my shoulder at Cane. His glistening abs clenching, his body thrusting into me over and over. He gives me a hooded, sensual look that makes me feel so alive and sexy. That look alone makes my own pussy twitch around him. Without breaking our stare, he licks one lone stripe up my spine, seeming to savor the taste of my sweat.

He feels my muscles fluttering, and I hear him let out a low growl. With the next thrust of his hips, my eyes roll back. I'm just about to come when he pulls out, flips me over, and grabs my hands above my head. I'm slightly frustrated that he didn't give me that euphoria when he bends his head down and consumes my lips with his. A heavy, lustful kiss that will no doubt bruise me.

Cane releases my hands, winks at me, and travels down my body. For one moment, I'm tortured with the emptiness he leaves, but then his head reaches my center. He takes my clit into his mouth and begins sucking and flicking.

"Oh gods. Oh gods," is all I hear myself saying. It's like a chant, a mantra. The pressure builds, and I can feel it about to burst from me—a feeling deep in my core, my chest, even my gods forsaken soul.

He pulls my clit into his mouth one last time and grazes it with his teeth before lapping his tongue around it, then sits back up. He pulls my ankles over his shoulder and thrusts deep enough that it has me seeing stars. The sensation fracturing and causing me to scream out in release, my fluttering walls bringing him over the edge with me.

All four of us are lying on Cane's bed, utterly spent. Breathing heavily, our bodies covered in sweat. Catherine curls into Hilia and closes her eyes before Hilia can avoid it. Cane wraps his arm around me. I close my eyes for a moment and pretend. Pretend that this is *our* room. Pretend that this is *our* bed. Pretend that this is *our* life.

I wonder if I'll ever find my *one* love. The one I would risk finding Haven Falls for, even if it is a fairytale. I know Cane loves this promiscuous lifestyle, but what would it be like if we chose each other and no one else?

I'm probably just drunk on my lust and willow root, but I like to think that I'd go to Haven Falls for him.

Chapter 29 Evelyn

EVERY BITE, EVERY FORCED smile is the epitome of discomfort without Gwen at the table. I reach up and touch the comb she lent me—rubbing a small circle over the moon—the small reminder of her kindness easing the tension in my chest as I sit here without her. My dinner mates carry on while I try to master my facade. Some are talking politics, while others are flirting. Flirting that leads to touching, which then leads to kissing—the type of kissing that you know will lead to *dessert.* I wish I could wipe off the slime of each lustful giggle and actually enjoy my own dessert—a perfectly baked and buttery raspberry tart. I eat it as quickly as I can while still trying to savor it. The one good thing about all these elves enraptured with themselves is that it's easy to slip away. As soon as I get to my room, I peel off my dress, and any lingering awkwardness falls to the floor with it.

I can't even believe I thought that would be a proper dinner.

And not only that, but the king left dinner early and took the only person I can stand in this place with him. I take off the silver hairpiece and place it in the drawer by my bed. Everything I've grown to know about court life and decorum in Daydream has grossly underprepared me for life in Nightmare.

I throw on a plain, white nightgown and head to my table, where my journal sits just begging to be opened. All these strange pieces of an intricate story spilled onto the bone-colored pages. I skim past the memories of lavender and friendship, and land on the day my paradise shattered like glass.

Odin remained so calm then, every bit the anchor I needed to tether me to my sanity. My first glimpse of him as a king, *my* king. He knew exactly what to do when I wasn't even sure what I needed. And he welcomed me to his family that very same day.

It didn't take long for our love to blossom after that. There was so much grief still clinging to me, heavily some days. But I always expected the weight of it to be harder to bear. That I would somehow be fighting within myself to remain stable enough to get out of bed or eat a decent meal. But I never did fight that battle. Not with Odin there as a constant, bursting light. My heart sang when he was around me, and sad as I was, he made me feel weightless. Unburdened. And very much alive.

Still, seeing my parents at the trials, losing them again, it was as if all the years of healing were washed away. And it had a different kind of sadness—a dark, infinite well of hopelessness with no light in sight. My longing for Odin and his closeness consumes me. Now more than ever before. I'm sure the Nightmare King intended to erase any lingering love I had, to drive me to madness, to make me forget. But it's done just the opposite. Odin is my world, the only place I truly belong. I ache for him, and I just want to go home.

Bright light slowly creeps into my sleepy vision. The first thing I see when I open my eyes is green. Filtered light paints my body, and tall pines creak with the wind. *It's my forest.* The wind carries a man's voice to me, Odin's voice, and I find him sitting on a large log with a woman beside him.

Gods, that's me!

I'm dreaming again, walking through this place like I'm really here.

I can feel the earth beneath my feet and the smell of the sweet forest air.

Please don't be a nightmare.

I wince at the knowledge of what's coming. I know this scene well, and I don't want it to keep playing.

I shake my head over and over. I try to scream. I bash my head against the harsh tree bark. But there is no sound, no pain. I run up to my younger self and try to grab onto Odin's shirt, but I just pass through every damn thing. The scene is relentlessly progressing, in even more detail than before.

All I can do is watch as the image of myself wraps her arms around Odin's neck. I know the warm tingling feeling in my belly when he kisses me. The ache is unbearable. But that feeling is wrenched away as I anticipate the screams that I know are coming. My emotions are so strong that I feel as though I could throw up.

I sink to my knees, pleading and urging them to stay away.

Why couldn't I dream of my father's bedtime stories or watch my mother cook dinner? Or Odin's lips pressing against my neck as I slept. I can't bear more torture like this.

I try to run away, but no matter where I go, I end up by the tree line, looking over my farmhouse.

Something seems different, though.

I watch as my younger self emerges from the forest. Then, I see men dressed in hooded black robes dragging two bodies away from my home. Bodies that are...alive. Alive! They are kicking, trying to free themselves from their captors. They vanish into the forest on the other side of the road just as I see my younger self make it to the house.

"They were alive," I say this aloud to myself, to solidify its importance. "They were alive."

I try to run to where they were just dragged away, but every time I step into the field, I'm pulled back to this one spot in the trees. The frustration of it all makes time creep by, though I'm sure it's only been minutes. The scene has played out, identical to my memories in every way but one: my parents were alive.

Everything is vacant and dark after everyone is gone. But I'm still here watching. *Why would Cane do this now? Why torture me if I'm to protect him in the shroud? It doesn't make sense. But this can't be a real memory. Can it?*

Can't I just wake up now? I start pinching my arm. So hard I begin to wonder if I could peel my skin clean off and not feel a thing.

I'm about to try just that when suddenly I'm tossed into the throne room in the Daydream castle.

Odin is sitting on the throne, a gold crown donned, and a lazy grin on his face. He has a tray with wine, cheese, and fruits next to him and a servant at attention standing to his left.

I see myself walking in. The trust and innocence in my eyes are captivating. There isn't a hint of doubt in my smooth brow.

I've let the Nightmare Kingdom destroy that side of me.

I never noticed before how I, too, was a beacon of light. I'd give anything to go back. I don't want Odin to see the changes in my face now—the darkness. There will be time spent weeping over the loss of this version of myself, but I tuck it away for another journaling session.

I watch this timid, doe-eyed girl tuck a loose strand of hair behind her ear as Odin makes eye contact with her. He doesn't break his stare as he tilts his head to the side and says, "Dismissed." The servant leaves without a word.

Gods, do I love the way he gives me his undivided attention so freely.

I watch as I run to Odin and jump into his lap. He holds me with all his strength, and yet caresses my waist with the softest touch. So full of intention and love. I wish I had reveled in it more. I had no idea how precious it was. My heart is aching. I need to feel Odin's warmth and feel his arms wrapped around me.

I walk close enough to hear what we're talking about.

Odin tugs my chin up to look into my eyes.

I smile at my younger self's face. I'm drinking him in, my expression a portrait of total devotion. And he's just as enamored with me.

"My dearest love, it's time. If we don't find the rune stone now, if we don't stop the king..." He trails off, his lust-filled expression turning worried. "The Kingdom of Daydream is stronger than it has been in years. We must make bold moves to ensure our safety before the citizens are consumed with fear and doubt. The longer we are stagnant, the easier it will be for the Nightmare Kingdom to overrun our people. This rune stone is said to bring power, longevity, and strength. We can use these blessings to protect our people and unite the realm. Imagine what the King of Nightmares could do with that kind of power." I tuck in closer, and Odin wraps his arms all the way around me. "We won't let that happen. Just imagine what *we* could do. Imagine if we destroyed that awful wall once and for all. Imagine if we were able to rule over Daydream *and* Nightmare, bringing us all together. It would be just like one of your father's stories."

My expression hardens, and I pull away a little. "I'm not nearly ready. I've been training with the knights for what, a month? Two? I need more time. *We* need more time. And in the meantime, we can try and reason with King Cane. We haven't received any threats. Why not simply arrange a peaceful meeting between our kingdoms?" Odin kisses my neck causing my eyes to flutter closed.

"You're too kind, my love, too trusting."

I pull back a little. "But this won't be what Cane expects. If anything, it would give me more time to train. What's the worst that could happen?" I soften again and whisper, "I don't want to leave you."

Odin looks as though he was about to say so much more, but all he says is, "I cannot bear the thought of you not being by my side. I can't even imagine waking up without you next to me." His expression hardens, but I can still see the pain in his tightening jawline. "But we both knew this day was coming. Marshall says you are excelling beyond expectations in your training, like you were born for the dance of battle. He knew you would be a fast study after watching all your morning sessions. It's just one more way that you are exceptional, darling. You can do this. And know that I am never actually gone. I will always find you in our dreams."

Tears stream down my cheeks, and Odin brushes them away one by one before kissing me softly, gently.

"Tell me again. Tell me how this plan works."

"Once we get you to the border, you'll need to scale the wall and cross over. From there, it should be easy to find a guard and pledge yourself to the Nightmare Trials. You'll say you're a lost soul, looking for redemption, looking for a place in society. Just saying it out loud is grounds to be taken to their prison, the Grimm Lodge. As soon as they take you in, you will take this." He holds up a vial of pearly swirling liquid. "It's the key to keeping you safe in Nightmare. I will infuse this potion with memory-erasing magick, tailored specifically to your mind. You can even help me write the story. I can weave the details into this bottle, making new, temporary memories. It will feel so real that even you will believe it." He smiles cheerfully. "You are so captivating, Evelyn. I think you will impress yourself."

But even my younger self can't be distracted from the weight of what I must do. "How do I do this without you?"

He pulls me in tighter, rubbing circles over my back, soothing not only my tense muscles but my heart and soul as well.

"The second you are out of the trials, I'll be there with you. I'll find you in your dreams. I know your dreams better than I know my own," he says through a dazzling smile. "You are the most genuine and charming person I have ever met. There is no doubt in my mind that they'll trust you. Enough for you to find the stone, maybe find every last secret they're keeping. Think of it as the biggest, most elaborate story you have ever told, a grand tale that we can tell our children. And they can tell their children. Once we are wed, you will be known as the legendary queen who mastered her craft and brought peace to her kingdom. How could anyone not love you as much as I do?"

I still look grim, deflated in his arms.

"And gods, Evelyn, every fucking day from the moment you leave until I can reconnect with you in our dreams, I will reach out to you. I will go to sleep every night trying to find you. You won't have to wait; I will always be reaching for you, waiting for the connection. However long it takes, I will be there."

I simply can't help but sit a little straighter.

"As soon as you find what we're looking for, you get out of there. Swear it."

"I swear it, Odin." I pause before asking, "How do you know the rune stone is there?"

"I have scoured all of Daydream. There is not one rock that has not been overturned. If it's truly in this realm, it must be in Nightmare. I don't trust anyone to do this but you. "

The ache in my chest swells at how much I miss him. How lost I feel right now knowing he is still not by my side in the waking world. We have been together for so long that the distance between us now is a physical pain. We had no idea the magnitude of this plan. The way the trials would torture me. How could we, when all we knew were stories passed down over the decades?

"And you're sure that tonic will work? King Cane won't be able to see into my memories?"

"We've been testing this tonic on others over the last year, and the results are promising. You'll be okay, my darling, I know you will be. No one has ever lost their memories forever, but there can be a...delay...in getting them back, and things may feel muddled and confusing until you do. But you're the strongest person I know. You *will* be okay."

I strain to hear more, to stay in this memory, but blackness creeps in from the side of my vision. I desperately try to hold on, but I'm overtaken by darkness.

My eyes fly open. I'm panting, barely able to catch my breath. Flashes of my life play before my eyes. I remember. *I remember all of it.*

Chapter 30 Evelyn

I CAN'T BREATHE. I plant my feet on the floor, press my palms to the bed, trying to ground myself, trying to stop my freefall. My head splits open with pressure as if a dam has burst inside my mind. My heart hammers against my ribs like it's trying to escape.

It's too much.

For ten years, I've carried the image of returning to my farm to find only blood, only certain death. I remember the silence, the stillness. But never bodies. Never anyone dragging them away. Not once. *Why didn't I see it then? If I had looked harder, could I have saved them? Who were those hooded figures?*

A fragile seed of hope begins to grow amidst the wreckage of my torment—a deceitful, painful bloom. And yet, I feed it. I have to know. *Are my parents alive?*

I know that even if they were, there won't be a happy ending to this part of my story. Still, hope is screaming in my mind. *What if I could see them again? If they're not dead, who took them? And why?*

I force it down. Smother it. It feels unnatural, almost cruel, but I crush that fragile hope until it's barely more than a whisper. I can't risk unraveling completely.

The pieces of this puzzle just aren't fitting together. Even with my memories restored, many areas remain hazy. *Odin said that would happen.* All I know for sure is that my purpose is clear: infiltrate Nightmare, find this rune stone, and unite the kingdoms.

My sweet Odin. I didn't think I had any space left in my heart, but my love for him keeps breaking through, overwhelming everything. Saying I miss him doesn't begin to describe the void his absence leaves. I *need* him.

Why hasn't he been able to find me in my dreams? Where is he?

Then, like a blade, a new thought slices through me. Something must be wrong. Something terrible. Panic chokes me—my heart fractures. I just need to see his face. Hear his voice. Just once.

A knock sounds on my door, breaking my spiraling thoughts, but before I can get up to answer it, Gwen steps in.

She pauses when she sees me.

"What's got your knickers in a twist?"

I burst out of bed, tripping over my discarded slippers on the floor. I can't stop the pacing that takes over. Back and forth, from my bathing chamber back to my bed. Over and over before Gwen grabs me by the shoulders to steady me.

I twist my fingers together, nails digging into my skin. I want so desperately to tell her everything clawing at my insides, but the truth lodges in my throat. And with that truth, any hope I had of being Gwen's friend shatters like glass. My eyes drift to the table, where her silver hairpiece rests in the drawer. My chest tightens, sinking with the weight of knowing that the fragile trust we'd built can no longer hold.

My mind flashes back to the night in the bioluminescent field. What did I say? Did I slip up? Was I too relaxed? Too drunk? Too stupid? Odin would be ashamed of me. *I'm* ashamed of myself.

I force myself to breathe. Slowly. Deeply. Then, finally, I speak. "I-I had a nightmare. It felt so real. I forgot I wasn't still locked in that dungeon."

The lie tastes like ash in my mouth. All I want is to go home to Odin. Gods, why hasn't he dream-walked to me? He promised he'd be waiting.

"Oh, hun." Gwen pulls me into a tight hug, wrapping me up in warmth. "You're not there anymore. You will *never* be there again." She steps back, holding my gaze. I look away quickly, terrified she might see too much. "I can't imagine what you went through," she says softly. "I wish I could have done more."

I pull away from Gwen and turn toward the tall, glass doors. Beyond them, the view is stretched out—breathtaking and surreal, a sharp contrast to the grim and broken landscape I once believed Nightmare had to offer.

"Cane tried to help too, you know," Gwen says gently.

A scoff escapes before I can stop it. I bite down hard, forcing down the rest of my vitriol.

"I know he comes off as brash and arrogant," she continues, "Imagine it were you in his shoes, with an entire kingdom to look after. Not to mention he doesn't know you."

I turn slightly, just enough to look at her from the corner of my eye. "But you don't know me either, Gwen," I snap, more sharply than I intended. "We went shopping once. That doesn't make us friends. It doesn't make me any less confused about what's happening to me." I soften my tone, remembering what I've already told her, what I *need* her to believe. She still thinks I don't have all my memories, that there are pieces of myself that I can't grasp.

"I woke up in the trials with no memory, and I left the trials still unsure of my past. I don't know why I entered them. I don't know where I belong. I don't know Cane. I don't know you." I pause and add, "I don't know *myself*."

Gwen doesn't flinch. Instead, she steps closer, touching her hand to her chest, right over her heart. "You have no reason to trust anything," she says, her voice calm and sure. "But I can *feel* something, right here. You're different, Evelyn. I've felt it since the first movement I saw you in the trials. Your soul...it speaks to mine. Like a sister I didn't know I had. I know you're meant for something great—for this kingdom, for this realm."

She steps into my line of sight, cutting off the sprawling landscape outside the window like she is physically placing herself between me and my need to escape.

"I don't have magick," she continues, "not like the others at court. But I've never been wrong about people." I want to laugh. Loudly. She's never been more wrong about *anything*.

"I would like to be alone, please, Gwen."

She opens her mouth as if to offer more of her warm, sugar-coated comfort, but then thinks better of it. With a slight nod, she turns and quietly leaves me alone with my thoughts once more.

Chapter 31 Gwen

I LEAVE EVELYN'S ROOM in a hurry. Something's wrong. Her rising panic changed the colors I see in her. She's usually bursts of white, but after tonight, I see hints of red, screaming with anger and fear.

I have to find Cane. I search everywhere: the dining room, the throne room, his bedchambers. Of course, when I need him most, Cane is nowhere to be found.

I can't stop thinking about how strange Evelyn seemed. Maybe she's angry with me for leaving her at dinner last night. I wouldn't have walked away if I thought it would upset her. Or maybe it has to do with Daydream. What if she decides to return?

I finally find Cane in the gardens, tucked away in the trees, just like the day after we first met Evelyn.

"Gods, Cane, I've searched the entire castle for you."

I sink onto the stone bench beside him, resting my head on his shoulder. His fingers gently brush back strands of hair that had come free. When his lips graze the top of my head, I melt into him, the simple tenderness nearly making me forget why I was looking for him in the first place.

I let the silence linger for a few moments longer, savoring what feels like the calm before the storm. Something is coming. I can't explain it, but I'm not ready to face the dread that's been building since I left Evelyn's room.

Cane removes the clip holding up half my hair, letting the curls fall free. His fingers drift through the strands again and again, soothing me. The gentle rhythm against my scalp nearly lulls me to sleep.

"You saw something, didn't you?" I whisper, my voice barely audible. "In her dreams, you saw something." This time it's not a question. I already know the answer.

I keep my head on Cane's shoulder, unwilling to meet his eyes. As if the gods themselves are watching, a raven flutters down onto a nearby deep purple rosebush. Its head tilts, studying me in eerie silence. We stare at one another—the raven and I—like we share some unspoken understanding.

"I was able to repair most of her memories." Cane finally says. "She entered the trial to get into our kingdom. She wasn't fleeing. She's here on a mission. A mission from King Odin."

The breath leaves my lungs.

No. That can't be right.

I'm never wrong about people. I *feel* their essence. My intuition has never failed me. So why now?

"Odin sent her here for a rune stone. The self-centered coward couldn't do it himself, so he sent his betrothed to do it for him. And all for a godsdamn legend. The rune stone is as much a fairytale as Haven Falls."

I sit upright, startling the raven into flight.

"But no one really believes there is a rune stone. It's just a campfire tale." Cane nods in agreement. "The rune stone is said to give its wielder the power to bend another's will—to control them completely. That's basically mind control. Do you really think Odin believes it's real?"

"I don't know what to think, love," Cane admits, rubbing a hand down his face. He looks utterly spent. "But I know we need Evelyn gone, now. It's too much of a risk keeping her here."

The thought of Evelyn being cast out, or worse, killed, sends acid through my veins. The raven returns, settling on the same branch, cawing sharply as if echoing my resistance.

"No, Cane. She stays." My voice is steel, my conviction unshakable. "I was getting through to her; I know I was. We keep her here. We watch her. If she betrays us, we act. She deserves this chance."

Cane's jaw tightens. "How can you still believe that? This is my kingdom. My people. I swore to protect them. The Night Terror Golems are appearing in record numbers, Kyustos continues to harbor every degenerate in the kingdom, and now this." He drags a hand through his hair, I'm listening to him but that perfectly tousled look that makes me want to crawl into his lap despite this crisis.

"If you get rid of her now," I argue, "people will ask questions. Why didn't she choose the bounty or the Shroud? What was her reason for being here? And gods forbid someone sees her return to Daydream, there'd be an uproar." I reach for his large, calloused hand, threading our fingers together and squeezing tightly.

"How do you do it?" He murmurs. "How do you keep seeing the good in people?"

"I told you before. Right here. On this very bench. I feel something different about her." The irony doesn't escape me. "Just give me a little more time. Let us see how the initiation ball goes."

Cane pulls me into a sudden, deep kiss. He tastes like warm sugar, and I moan into his mouth at the contact. Just as quickly, he pulls away, leaving me breathless and entirely flustered.

"You are infuriating, Gwen," he growls softly. "She stays—until after the ball." With one final kiss, he turns and disappears into the garden. I look back at the raven still perched on the branch.

"Gods, I really hope I'm right," I whisper.

Chapter 32 Evelyn

DESPITE MY COLD DISMISSAL, Gwen shows up at my door later that afternoon, all bright smiles and unbothered charm. She hands me a detailed list of what's expected of me this week. Training with the Night Shroud and shadowing their duties, as well as attending the morning council meetings. All to prepare for the ball and the choice I'm expected to make—to take the bounty or pledge myself to the Shroud. Apparently, all of it begins tomorrow.

I have seven days.

Seven days to find the rune stone.

Seven days to escape the castle and the Kingdom without raising suspicion.

Seven days until I'm back with Odin.

I let Gwen lead me around the castle for the rest of the day. You catch more bees with honey, after all.

I do my best to keep my guard up, to stay detached. These people, people like Gwen, they're what make up Daydream's nightmares. And no matter how kind or warm they seem, I have to remember, I'm not here to be charmed. I'm here to protect my people from them.

We end our day in Sallows. There is a life here that pulses through the streets and buildings alike—like the very stones are infused with energy. Even after nightfall, with the stars dusting the sky like glitter on velvet, there's a warmth to the town that I haven't felt anywhere else in this kingdom.

It reminds me so much of Osieres. The main town just beyond the castle walls in Daydream has the same vibrancy, just tinted in pastels and sunlight. The people aren't all that different either. Except for the public displays of affection. Not just affection—*intimacy*. Full-on, unapologetic intimacy.

The warm air even smells lovely, like burnt sugar and nutmeg. But I just know there is evil here. It's hidden well—it's here.

We are just about to go into a bakery for a tart before they close, when I pause and tug on Gwen's shirt. I try my best to look at ease and curious. "This part of town is beautiful. But if I'm going to choose to stay here, I want to see more than just the beautiful parts. I'm not well-traveled, and I want to be sure I can manage, should I choose to stay."

Gwen just smiles and ushers me inside. "Are you talking about Kyustos? There are definitely some seedy elves there. Nothing you can't handle, though." This is the second time she's mentioned Kyustos to me. Right before I ask more about this supposed "dark town," Tabby greats us, and the choice of sweets almost entirely distracts me. It's much easier to pretend I'm content with a strawberry tart in front of me.

⇢⇢⇢⇛ ⇚⇚⇚⇠

I close my eyes and pray that Odin will find me while I dream. But when I wake, I'm only met with bleak despair. Another night where he hasn't found me. Another night alone. So I do the only thing I can, and I get out of bed and get ready for my first council meeting in Nightmare.

I've never sat in on a full meeting in Daydream; that right was only granted to the king and his immediate council members. One day, when I'm queen, I'll be able to sit alongside Odin, but until then, I will help him in other ways. *Like this crazy mission.*

The one day I wish Gwen had barged into my room to walk with me to the meeting, I'm left on my own. I think I may have taken three wrong turns, and by the time I finally make it, I'm the last to arrive. Not only that, but I come wearing gear for training, and everyone else looks like they just rolled out of bed. Gwen's hair is a mess, she's barefoot, and I'm pretty sure she's wearing the king's shirt that is hanging like a tunic paired with her leggings.

I don't know what I was expecting, but it wasn't a full council meeting in the dining room surrounded by casual attire and a spread of breakfast food. *Daydream would never hold important meetings over eggs and coffee.*

The meeting is quick and uneventful. More like a brunch than a meeting at all. Afterwards I go with the king and the other Shroud to Sallows. The citizens cheer and line the streets as we get to the main road. We stop at shop after shop, meeting the townsfolk and mingling with the merchants. I'm shocked that Cane knows each person by name. He holds their gaze, asking things like, "Did you end up mending that tunic?" Or "How is your brother holding out in his training?" He treats every person as his friend, and he seems genuinely interested in how they are doing.

Odin never had many friends, at least not outside of me, and he has never been comfortable being so close to the townsfolk. That was where I would come in. I loved my weekly meetings with the people of Osieres, walking the gardens with Freyr, and sneaking cookies to Timothy, the stable boy.

After the trip to Sallows, I'm set to train with the Shroud.

Returning to regimented training comes easily to me. There is one other female in the Shroud, Isla, and three males, Aidan, Jamic, and Theo. With my memories fully restored, I can recall the hours, days, and weeks of training in my own kingdom that prepared me for this mission. The stretches, obstacle courses, and sparring are like second nature. I can hold my own with a sword, but I am exceptionally good with daggers, favoring a set of haladie knives—beautiful, double-sided daggers, lethal and fast. When my fingers wrap around them, it's like the blades and I are one.

When I pick them up, each of the Shroud members grins. All except Theo, who rolls his eyes, reaches into his pocket and places a small piece of gold into each of the others' opened palms. When they notice me staring back, he says, "My money was on the crossbow." A little bloom of pride swells for a moment before I shove it down.

These are not your friends.

I thought I would have to work to win over the Shroud, but we mesh with ease. It seems like winning the trials has also earned me their respect. A pang of guilt gnaws at me when we are together. The more I'm with them, the more they treat me like I'm one of them.

What if these guards are good, genuine people and they just don't know what I know?

Gwen meets me for a late afternoon lunch, and we walk to the nearby garden where we sit under dark, sparkling birch trees. The spires from the castle peek out from the branches in the distance. Glittering leaves fall beneath a dusk-colored sun, casting a cascade of rainbow over everything. It takes my breath away time and time again.

Isla joins us and tells me of her own journey into the Night Shroud. She won her spot when she was only twenty. She's the youngest of five siblings and the only girl. I can picture her now: A small auburn-haired girl with freckles and hand-me-down boys' clothes, absolutely dominating fights with her brothers. If Sage were still alive, I know they would become fast friends.

She decided to enter the Nightmare Trials on a dare from her oldest brother.

A dare!

"Little prick was always picking on me. Making bets that I couldn't beat him in a race, let alone the trials. I was fifteen when I decided to say 'fuck you'. I started training to win and never looked back."

"My gods, I bet he felt horrible."

"Oh, he did. He begged me, over and over, not to go through with the trials. Tears and everything. He practically groveled in the mud to get me to stay." Gwen jumps in, "But you didn't!"

"Nope, and I remind him every chance I get who's faster now." Isla's green eyes sparkle and there is a small gap between her two front teeth behind full red lips. You can never tell if she is blushing because her cheeks are always pink and dusted with freckles. She is every bit the feisty little sister I pictured.

It's only when she talks about her time in the trials that her demeanor changes. Her cheeks lose some of that rosy glow, and her eyes are distant. She doesn't mention any specifics, and I don't ask.

There is an unspoken bond between us. Between myself and the people I will ultimately have to betray. But I need to protect my kingdom. *I won't let anyone else in.*

Chapter 33 Evelyn

My second morning meeting unfolds like the last, Cane combing through correspondence from throughout the kingdom: Infrastructure, farming, petty thieves.

After just a few days, I've gained a general understanding of the political structure, which bears a resemblance to Daydream. King Cane holds the final authority and makes the ultimate decisions on all matters, but he relies on counsel for guidance. This council is composed of the other Shroud members, Gwen, and six of the kingdom's nobles, each with knowledge about a different aspect of the realm.

The Shroud members' primary focus is on issues of security within the castle, as well as the safety and well-being of the other towns and smaller cities. Gwen, on the other hand, is outspoken on nearly every topic; her main contribution regarding alchemy, serving as a representative for the healers in town and their needs. As for the nobles, they mostly sit in silence, muttering under their breath and shaking their heads, offering little helpful input.

I find my thoughts drifting. I have always had a hard time keeping my attention on one thing at a time, and the droning on about the local stocks, water supply, and the upcoming lunar festival is making it hard for my mind not to wander. Today my attention is on memorizing the details of the flowers outside the dining room window. Watching the insects flit from one flower to another. The roses in particular are magnificent, their deep red and purple petals shimmering with the faintest glimmer of sparkles in the amber light of morning. I'm trying to come up with the name of such a deep purple—plum?—when something new cuts through the air, Night Terror Golems.

That's different. How long have they been talking about this? Who reported it?

I swallow my mouthful of eggs and give my full attention to the conversation. Apparently, there are multiple reports of these creatures, and they sound dangerous.

No one else, including Cane and Gwen, seems surprised by this topic. The conversation has moved on from those golems in an instant.

Should I ask about them? I can do that if I'm going to be on the Shroud, right?

Before I can muster the nerve to speak up, the meeting concludes. Chairs are scraping, people are flirting. *Dammit.* If I'm going to get the answers Odin needs, I need to get out of my own head and act. I need to do better tomorrow.

⇝⇛⇛ ⇚⇚⇜

Somewhere in all my training for the day, I made a mental note to find the castle library. I have already wasted too much time trying to fit in and not enough time looking for the rune stone. I bet there's information there about those golems, too. It would be much easier to read a book than try to speak at a meeting.

The library in the Daydream castle is one of my kingdom's hidden gems. The ivory walls are lined floor to ceiling with every bit of knowledge you can imagine—history, adventure, art. I've lost myself so many times in the grandest of ways on gold gilding and glittering windowsills. I've never entertained the possibility that anything equal to its beauty even existed. I didn't need to. And yet, the grandeur of this building is only second to the scene through the doors. I step into the sprawling room. It's warm and buzzing with magick. And the smell. All cloves and pine and that glorious old paper scent. Beyond the doors is a room that looks impossibly larger on the inside than the outside. Where most libraries exude a dim, cozy quiet as thick as fog, this library is buzzing, bright, and loud. Vibrant glowing orbs are floating toward the ceiling, casting bursts of reds, purples, greens, and even lighting the darkest corners with a soft ambient glow.

There are rows and rows of new and old tomes alike. The shelves go up as high as a four-story building. I can't even see the top. There are rolling ladders attached to the shelves, allowing access to every book, and spiraling staircases leading to each level. There are so many other elves here, too. Some are reading, others are filing, and some appear to be swinging on the ladders just for the fun of it.

And then there is the window. Or is it the ceiling? I can't tell where one ends and the other begins. The landscape beyond is a soft blanket that blends from emerald to crimson to plum, stretching to waves of snow-capped mountains. It doesn't look real. I must have been staring for longer than I realized, as someone nudges at my back, urging me to move. *Not someone, a book!*

Small leather-bound books float and twirl around me, gently nudging me toward a nearby table. They look like butterflies, their pages fluttering like wings, a little blue shimmering wisp of magic illuminating their path. Every time I lift a hand to touch one, it flutters just out of reach. And they're everywhere! I can see some so high up, they are nothing but stars.

There are tables scattered in the center of the room with a few people sitting, and stacks and stacks of books.

Daydream would never allow for such disorganization.

The fluttering books usher me to a particular table with so many stacks that I can't even rest my hands on the table top. Through the scattered bindings, I see an older-looking elven man seated in the opposite corner from me. He must be over two-hundred years old to show that level of aging. His face is buried in the book he is reading.

I clear my throat. Nothing. I clear it louder and scooch a stack of tomes, trying to see him better.

At the touch of the books, he lifts his head. A kind, wrinkled face meets mine through thick, tarnished glasses. He wears his auburn hair up in a messy knot, and I can see the white and silver streaks shine in the room's glow. He certainly appears to be the academic type. His simple emerald robes are brimming with quills and papers. And a few other glasses, or pieces of glasses, are stuffed into the many, *many* pockets.

"Ah, Dragon Slayer, I was wondering when I would make your official acquaintance," he says as he rises from the chair.

I want to tell him that he doesn't need to get up on my account, but he is by my side before I can even speak the words.

"My name is Gerald, and I am the keeper of this library. May I help you with anything?" As he speaks, his face lights up like he has been waiting his whole, long life to help me.

"You really don't need to call me Dragon Slayer." I say with a slight blush forming on my cheeks, "Evelyn will do just fine." I don't want to bring attention to myself by asking about the rune stone right away, so I go with my other topic, "I'm looking for more information about Night Terror Golems."

He happily stands there like he is waiting for more. Maybe I'm supposed to say something else? His face sinks a little when I remain silent. "Oh, that's all then?" He's so sweetly hopeful, I wish I had something else to research. "Well, that's easy enough. Come, find a better seat, and I'll bring the books over."

I watch as book after book floats into the air, forming a balanced stack right out in the open. In Daydream, the librarians don't use magick, so I'd need to make three trips to get all these books in one place. He uses the same magick to clear a spot at a nearby table.

"Thank you," I say with a smile and pray he knows I mean it.

"You're welcome, Evelyn, always. Please let me know if there is anything else you need." A fluttery book starts to buzz around his head, and he swats it away, unsuccessfully, as he makes his way back to his own reading.

With my purpose set and no one left to talk to, I pick up the first book. *Night Terrors: The Dream or The Beast.*

I read book after book about magick and the Night Terror Golems. I don't even stop when a little book flutters down onto the table, as if it's watching me, its amber glow illuminating the pages.

I only notice it's well into the night hours when Gerald kindly brings me a fresh cup of tea and some biscuits.

I guess I missed dinner. I take a bite and continue.

There was a time hundreds of years ago when these things weren't a violent problem. The very first recording of a golem is fading on the pages of an old book, but I can still make out the words. It's written that they appeared as a result of some dreaded "sundering." Many books have referenced this, or something similar. And for all the times I read about "the Sundering," there is nothing about what it is or what came before.

The creatures are utterly grotesque and heinous. They feed off of the other forest creatures, leaving a trail of bloodied limbs, heads, and shredded bodies. So far, the kingdom has been successful in keeping them at bay. Now, though, they are growing in number. And seemingly with an element of stealth. For such large and vile creatures, the farmers don't see them coming until it's too late. They're smarter now, too, going after defenseless civilians. The forest isn't enough anymore.

A shiver washes over my skin as I recall stories of such beasts from my childhood. I barely paid any attention to them, assuming they were just scare tactics to get children to stay safely at home and away from the Nightmare border.

There is a long period of time where there are no recorded sightings here in Nightmare. They don't start again until just the last few decades.

My mind is reeling, trying to organize all this new information. The more I read, the more interested I become. There is so much about what the creatures look like, how to kill a golem, but nothing about their origin. Some speculate that they are born from our deepest fears, from our very nightmares, but others say they spawn from nothing. There were even accounts from individuals who claimed to have seen a person transform *into* a golem.

In Daydream, we are not without our own eerie creatures. We have mist sprites, similar to the golems in that they cause havoc and destruction in their wake, but nowhere near as savage. They are fae creatures about the size of a five-year-old child with shimmering wings. They thrive in the forests that border the Nightmare and Daydream Kingdoms. Some of my people, including my family, thought they were actually Nightmare Kingdom creatures, sent to terrorize our people.

The mist sprites get their name from the haze they materialize out of. No one knows for sure what it's made from, but it's said to appear fast and thick right before a monster forms.

As children, we all learn the same rhyme to warn us of the creatures that can lurk in the forest:

Run, skip, jump, in the forest you play.

But if you see the mist, you'd better not stay.

From a twisted haze, a monster will rise.

Caught in its clutches, you'll meet your demise.

I can still hear my mother singing to me as she braided my hair as a young girl. I was more intrigued than alarmed. I wanted to meet a sprite for myself.

I've never seen one, but I've heard that their haunting smile sports two lines of razor-sharp teeth. Odin came face-to-face with them once. He was out on a trip to the coast to meet with one of the noble houses, one of the only times I had stayed back at the castle. A group of three vicious mist sprites were closing in on a small farming town. He was able to take one down all on his own with one swipe of his short sword, and immediately skewered another with an arrow. I remember shaking when he told me the details. So scared for his life and so grateful he was still there with me. We spent that night making love, cherishing the life we almost didn't have together.

I keep thinking of that night with Odin. Of the roses that he laid on my pillow the next morning before he left for his meetings. I miss our bed, the way he smells, the feel of his skin. I start to lose myself in the memory when Gwen unceremoniously plops down beside me with a stack of books.

"Hi! I've been looking for you since you missed dinner. What are you reading about? Don't tell me, let me guess. I bet this is a very spicy shifter romance. I love those the most."

"No! No. That is not what I'm reading."

"You've been ignoring me, Little Raven. Why?" She's not wrong. What started as a friendship with Gwen was tainted when my memories returned. Now I struggle with a desperate need to spend time with this bubbly woman, while also needing to keep myself on track.

"I've been busy. Training has been difficult. I really appreciate seeing you at lunch." I smile over at her and hope this is enough of an answer for her.

"Ah, well, I guess that's as good a reason as any. You have such a big choice to make. Have Isla and the other Shroud won you over yet?" Gwen begins pulling the books away from me and stacking them at the end of the table. As if on cue, they flutter away and nestle back onto the shelves.

Amazing.

"I don't know yet what I'm going to do. I'm still trying to piece so many things together. I just wish I had more time." All of what I say is the truth, even though she has no idea what I really mean.

Chapter 34 Evelyn

I CAN'T STAY AWAY from the library. I'm like a sponge, soaking up all the knowledge of the kingdom's creatures and magick. I still haven't found the right moment to visit Kyustos, but the well of information I'm gathering in this library quells my urgency.

Some days, Gwen keeps me company, reading from one of the spicy books she's picked up in Sallows. Other times, she shares the latest court gossip, and I try to keep a straight face as she recounts her nighttime activities. It's hard not to feel a connection with her, but I just make sure I'm buried in a book. What she does with her time is her own choice, and if she wants to sit here and watch me read books, so be it.

Gerald usually has stacks of books waiting for me, and somehow he always knows whether I'm in the mood for coffee or tea. As often as I can, I search the shelves on my own in hopes of finding even one mention of the rune stone, but so far, nothing of value has turned up. There is a mention of an "enchanted gem" in an old children's picture book. *How Father would have loved to read these.*

In this tale, there's an old crone tasked with making five jewels for the gods. Alone, they were nothing but pretty trinkets, but when used together, they bound an evil god to the Underworld. With the help of a gallant prince and a beautiful princess, the crone banished the evil, and they all lived happily ever after. A sweet story, but not what I'm looking for.

The steamy clove and ginger tea wafts over the pages. I let the scene from the window clear my mind as the warm herbs coat my belly. *What would this realm even look like with no ominous onyx wall? How will these people adjust to the ways of Daydream?*

I return my focus to reading, this time about magick. I have always been drawn to it, even though I, my parents, and about half of Daydream were born magickless. My exposure to it mainly comes from Odin. His powers are as much a part of his irresistible charm as his blue eyes and natural charisma. As king and a member of the royal Beckett bloodline, Odin can walk into someone's dreams, see their memories. And he was never short on new and beautiful ways to impress me.

Almost all Daydream magick wielders can manifest these beautiful illusions. The size and level of detail depend on the person's magickal power. The smaller, most common ones are what they call *wifts*. Just little puffs of magickal essence, gone as quickly as they came. But some more powerful users can project a corporeal form for a period of time. All magick wielders can do basic magick, too. Lighting fires, heating water, flipping pages of a book with a small burst of air. I love it all.

I can't help comparing the kingdoms as I learn more about the magick in Nightmare. Since Cane is the king, he can dream-walk too, but only if the dream is a nightmare. A trait that has been passed down in the Callidora bloodline. Once he is there, he can forage for memories at will. To make matters more terrifying, anyone with Nightmare magick can control a black, fog-like cloud that changes into creatures like shadows, fiends, and goblins. The creatures and how long they last depend on the amount of power the wielder holds. For someone with lesser power, the creatures are purely an illusion, one that you can pass through. But for those with greater power, the creatures can take true form for a short period and do as the wielder wishes.

This is what I've been afraid of. This is the power that threatens my people in Daydream. *But why have I not seen the chaos they are capable of? Why are they restraining it?*

I wonder what type of magick Cane infused into the trials. He was able to implement both nightmare illusions and power for the participants to use. I was even able to wield it by the end, even if I was horrible at it. And it felt *so* real. All of this points to Cane being far more powerful than I thought, more powerful than Odin even, and capable of so much destruction.

My journal is always with me, always open. Every new bit of information I scribble into the pages, furiously trying to piece the puzzle together. Tonight, I fear my hand is permanently cramped in the position of the quill before I take my last sip of lukewarm tea and head to bed.

⤞⤞⤞ ⫷⫷⫷

I only have one more night until the ball. I don't want to be part of the Shroud, but there's no way I can leave yet, with no stone and hardly any information except messy journal notes. And Odin still hasn't found me in my dreams. *Do I go to him? What if he's hurt?*

He would want me to stay. I know it. He would never value his life more than the kingdom's. And if I go back now, I could ruin everything when we are so close to unity. I can't assume the worst. If he were dead, I'd feel it. *Wouldn't I?*

All these thoughts and theories only give me one conclusion: I'm going to join the Shroud. I could be Odin's only hope.

⟫⟫⟫ ⟪⟪⟪

Warmth envelops me. When I open my eyes, I'm wrapped in a cloud, soaked in sunlight, drifting down towards a lush green field blanketed in wildflowers, surrounded by an enchanting waterfall and a warm, welcoming forest. The sky above is a deep cerulean blue with more plush white clouds floating overhead.

My cloud lands on velvet emerald grass, every blade bursting through rich earth and dank moisture. I walk off easily, spinning in circles. Everything is coated in a rainbow of colors, like a bright oily blanket.

A figure appears dressed in sunlight.

My hand raises against the light, but it's still so hard to make out the shape. Until-

We sprint to each other.

"Odin," I breathe into his neck. "You're here."

I knew it. I knew if I just thought harder, urged our souls to find one another, that we would.

He doesn't say anything, but he doesn't have to. I can feel his love in the way his heart quickens, the way he breathes me in, his grip in the strands of my hair. It feels like ages pass before I let go and look into his eyes. My body shakes as I cry and laugh at the same time. My fingertips trace every single strand of hair, every contour of his perfect face. I gaze upon him and see the sun—a radiant beacon illuminating my existence. He is the light that dispels the shadows and nightmares lurking in the recesses of my mind.

"Are you real? Tell me this is real. Tell me. Say it, Odin. Say it's real, and we never have to do that again. I can't bear to lose you again."

A small chuckle escaped his lips, the only confirmation I needed. I crash my lips into his and whimper at the feel of it. Odin pulls me closer, consuming me. His fingers travel up and down my arms, through my hair, around my waist. My spine is tingling, my heart exploding, and I can barely contain myself.

He's here.

Odin breaks our connection before I want him to. I notice now that behind the joy, his eyes are tired and weary. "It worked. I have tried to reach you every single night. Every unending, torturous night. It's been months, Evelyn. Where have you been? Did you just get out of your trial? How could it have lasted so long?" His eyes survey every inch of my body like he's looking for wounds or scars. Like he already knows I must be broken, but he can't find where.

"There is so much I need to tell you. I don't even know where to start."

Odin waves his hand, and a giant white fur blanket appears on the ground with oversized pillows and a knitted pale-yellow quilt.

I look down to see that I'm wearing a beautiful white off-the-shoulder sundress. Odin's blue eyes sparkle with longing. With a snap of his fingers, a floral crown appears. Blue petals and light green vines twining together. He places it atop my head, and neither of us can stop smiling.

As we sit on the blanket, he pulls me to his chest. It's like we're floating. We just lay like that for minutes, hours, eternity, just together. Suddenly, and without remorse, my words spill out of my mouth.

It feels so good to share this with someone I can trust, who will believe me.

I tell Odin everything from the second I woke up on the wall in the Nightmare Trials to the moment I went to bed this very night. Between every detail, my mouth is full of his lips, kissing and kissing and kissing.

Odin doesn't say anything as the last detail falls from my mouth. He just firmly holds my head and kisses my face. And then he finally speaks.

"I am so sorry, my love. I am so sorry for what you went through, and for what you are going through now. I am here. It isn't your fault. How could I have been so naive to think that this would have been easier? I should have found someone else. Anyone else. It has been miserable without you by my side. The castle is a shell of a home without you in it. Freyr asks about you every day. He says the flowers do not bloom as vibrantly without you. And he's right. The stable boy, the one that you insist on bringing treats to, is more than grumpy without your gifts. He says he misses the sweets, but I know he misses you. We all do..." Odin chuckles, and I swear I smile a genuine, joyous smile for the first time in longer than I can remember.

I miss them, too. I miss it so much. My home. My people. *Our* people.

"Have you heard anything about Nightmare since I have been gone? Does anyone suspect us?"

"Nothing, the borders have been quiet. I was beginning to think that something went horribly wrong. I couldn't get to you. I tried to push into your dreams every night, but I couldn't feel you. There was no warmth waiting for me on the other side. It was cold and dark, like a foggy barrier was preventing me from finding you. If it weren't for the castle servants, I would have wasted away to nothing, my appetite diminished to ashes. Tonight, I went to sleep, and I was met with the most blissful feeling I have felt since you left. I could feel the energy flowing clearly again, and hope blossomed. It was like you were right next to me. But something was still wrong. It was much more difficult to penetrate your dream barrier. Like something was actively fighting against me all the while. Even now, it's a constant battle to stay here with you."

I tilt my head up and brush my lips across Odin's cheek. "We are here together. It's all that matters. Everything since has been a blur of new memories, old memories, and lavish parties—a strange combination, I know. I'm trying to learn what I can with the little time I have."

I stare up at the blue sky that looks so much like the sky back home. I pretend that we are back in my garden, safe and carefree.

"Three months. You have been away from me for three whole months. I would stay here and live an eternity with you, safe in my arms, love. But our time is coming to an end; I can't hold it. Your energy feels restless, like it's already waking up. But I need you to know this: something doesn't feel right at home. The people are quiet, not as charismatic and energetic as usual. Like a light went out, I thought it was because you haven't been home, but it's something more than that. Nightmare is doing something, I just have no idea what. I feel out of place, a stranger in my own kingdom." His face is gaunt, unreachable. I just want to fix it, but he's right, something is different.

"You must find the stone, Evelyn. The future of our kingdom depends on it. You are every bit the queen Daydream deserves. I'll search for you here every single day until you come home, because you will come home, I have no doubt in my mind about that."

"I love you," I whisper into his lips as I kiss him one last time because I'm floating away on a cloud of warmth.

Chapter 35 Evelyn

CANE HAS MADE MY initiation ball day excessively grand. There are more people than usual gallivanting around the castle, going to brunch, and walking the gardens. But despite all the grand affairs, I spend much of the day locked in my bedroom. I just want to fall asleep and bring Odin back. Last night was the first semblance of hope I've felt since my memories returned.

I can't let him down. He still believes in me.

I need fresh air; skulking around all day isn't helping Odin. I sneak off to the gardens to be alone and let the flowers soothe my soul. Maybe it's from seeing Odin again, but I feel lighter.

When I make it back to my bedchambers the floral scents still clinging to my hair, there is the loveliest honey wine waiting on my reading table. Complete with piles of fruits and pastries—a note in scrolling letters resting beside it.

Don't forget to eat!

-Gwen

P.S. Check the bathing chambers.

I let out a squeal when I see that there's honey lavender soap waiting for me, just like the one I made with my mother.

Mama, if you are out there, I'll find you. I'll draw you the biggest bath there ever was and fill it with lavender soap and flower petals.

When the ball approaches, Gwen brings her things into my room, and we get ready together. In expected fashion, she's here without being invited. Somehow, she has turned this intrusive trait into something charming. Just tonight, I put aside that she is my enemy and I pretend that we're just two friends getting ready for a party together.

I chose a deep purple gown with stars and moons embroidered in silver across the waistline. In true Nightmare Kingdom fashion, the neckline is scandalously low. The gown shimmers with silver as I walk, and a matching pair of silver slippers hug my feet, teardrop silver diamond earrings dangling from my ears. Gwen helps me arrange my golden hair with loose curls and holds it off my face with silver diamond-encrusted combs. The lilac purple eye powder swept over my eyelids brings out the light blue and honey colored speckles of my eyes, while the black kohl makes them pop like the sea's horizon at dusk. I barely recognize myself when I look in the mirror. I want to hate it. I want to feel disgusted with the skin I show and the tight hug of my dress. I swear it shows off curves that weren't there before. But all I feel is profound confidence.

It feels... I feel sexy.

Much like our first formal dinner together, I am the twilight sky, and Gwen is the golden dawn—her gown changes from reds to oranges and yellows in between. The colors are so perfect, my breath catches as I watch her. If these were different circumstances, if I were a different person, I would think that Gwen has been an unrelenting beam of light and warmth. I would think that she is someone worth getting to know, worth befriending. Someone to spend nights with in a flower grove, drinking mead to the point of delirious laughter.

But I will one day be *Queen* of Daydream. Guilt begins to take over at the thought of lying to her. I know it's coming. I'll need to leave her behind.

"Where are you, Little Raven? I can see you traveling somewhere behind those eyes."

I smile, "I'm just happy to have you here. Helping me, keeping me from being alone. Thank you, truly."

I add a new task to my ever-growing list: prove to Gwen that she's being deceived by those in power in her kingdom. That it isn't her fault. And I will offer her as much time as she needs to accept it, even if she hates me at first. I will be patient with her, and I will repay her as she has cared for me. I vow it to myself.

As resolute as I am about why I'm here, I still feel the buzzing pressure of anxiety starting to spike. The unknown outcome of this night haunts the periphery of my mind, and my heart rate uncontrollably quickens. I turn from Gwen and walk toward the mirror for one last look at myself before we leave. My hand grazes the fabric of my dress, steadying myself. I remember that small scar on my leg, and my hand lingers on that spot for a few long moments before I move on.

"This is for us. For our kingdom," I whisper to myself.

I spin back to Gwen, the hem of my dress making a satisfying swish as I turn, and take her hand. With a warm smile and a gentle squeeze of her fingers, we're off to a ball.

There are no introductions tonight. Gwen and I just waltz in hand in hand. Servers are walking around with trays of flutes containing a bubbly, pink, effervescent wine, and others with trays of small finger foods.

It smells divine.

Through the crowd of people, I can see a table filled with enough meat and vegetables to feed the whole kingdom. In the other corner of the room, musicians play an unending stream of melodies while countless attendees dance away the evening.

Gwen grabs two wine flutes and passes one to me. With a clink of our glasses, she downs hers in one gulp. I gasp. "Gwen, that isn't regular mead like in the tavern. It's actual willow root wine. Much stronger and I heard it's said to…" A blush creeps up my cheeks—I can't say it.

"What are you trying to say, Evelyn?" She puts her hand to her chest and drops her mouth open, mockingly appalled. "Are you trying to tell me that this little glass of bubbly, delicious wine will make me feel euphoric, warm? That this intoxicating liquid will slide down my throat, like a gentle caress, until it reaches my stomach, where it will explode throughout my body?"

She gets closer to me so that her voice is now a whisper in my ear, and her warm breath tickles my nape. She isn't mocking anymore.

"It's said to make you feel on the brink of orgasm, readying you for that final ecstasy. Driving you mad with want. Look around you. How many of these elves do you think have been drinking this wine? Can you tell?"

Oh gods. Yes…Yes, I can tell.

Many people are eating and drinking from smaller cups, clearly not containing *the* wine. Some are dancing. But then there are others, the majority of the crowd, who are up against the walls in various stages of debauchery. There are elven women with men, women with women, and men with men. There are small groups of people taking turns touching and kissing each other. If I concentrate, I can hear flirtatious giggles and breathy moans. The elves that are dancing are doing so with skirts hiked and shirts unbuttoned. There are some on their knees with their heads buried under a woman's dress, while some are sprawled on the scattered settees, stroking, licking, sucking.

King Cane is sitting atop his dais with a glass of clear liquid in his hand. Gwen drags me towards him.

"Does the king not partake in willow root wine?" I whisper.

"Little Raven," Cane coos. "I don't need wine for my pleasure." My cheeks heat. How did he hear me? Gwen straddles the king on his dais and begins nibbling and sucking on his lips as he runs his hands up and down the open back of her dress. Hilia is behind him, sucking on his pointed ears and trailing kisses down his neck. She sees me staring and glares. Gwen told me that she was harmless, but the hostility she exudes has not tapered.

Willow root wine is scarce in the Kingdom of Daydream. At least, we make it appear so. There, it's a sacred symbol of intimacy. One carafe is given only to a bride and groom on their wedding night and never again. Our people would never display this crude sexuality in front of anyone. It's savage. It's so far from purity and royalty.

If Odin only knew...

I turn away and stand in the middle of the room. I try to smooth my dress down and smile at guests. But I'm really not sure what to do.

A server passes with another tray of the wine, and I put mine back, wiping my hands as if I had been tainted with poison. Someday I will know the flavor of it. I will feel the warmth it brings, like Gwen said. And I will do it with Odin on our wedding night.

It's impossible to find anywhere to hide or look less uncomfortable. *I need to fit in, but how?* I can feel the annoyance dripping off my expression. Then I remember the feast.

Food. Perfect.

As I make my way to the table, between delirious, sweaty bodies, I see the man that I met at the Wretched Hollow is among the crowd.

Our eyes lock and he lifts a goblet—*full to the brim with pink bubbling sex juice I'm sure*—as if to toast me. And he winks! The wine clearly gives confidence as well, since I'm positive that I'm scowling.

A stout elderly woman bumps into my side, and suddenly a tray of the most delectable cream-filled croissants is pushed up toward my face. "Excuse me!" She says as she clearly struggles with the tray. Her frazzled gray hair is just about as frustrated as she is. I grab two croissants before she violently moves the tray and sees who I am. "I'm so glad you're here, Tabby," I say through a mouthful of pastry. We're both about to laugh as King Cane snaps his fingers. All the revelers stop their dancing and go silent.

"My kingdom. Many of you have traveled far to take part in our feast and to lay eyes on your Dragon Slayer. Today, she is tasked with giving us her final word. As you know, my Night Shroud is an elite group of elves. To become one, you must prove your worth in the Nightmare Trials. Our Shroud has had only four total members for five years. For five years, many have entered, and everyone has failed." He pauses and looks at me, the crowd hanging on his every word. "Evelyn must decide. She is worthy of a Night Shroud, but must choose between joining or returning to her home with a lifetime's worth of riches, never to want for anything again."

Everyone has turned to stare at me. I swallow—too loudly. Tabby snatches my croissants and brushes off the crumbs from my dress.

How very royal of me to be caught stuffing my face.

"Evelyn, my Little Raven, please join me."

I glide past the other attendants, careful not to touch anyone's bare skin or sweat. I can't imagine I look graceful, but I'd rather not touch anyone just the same. I walk all the way to the dais where the king stands. Gwen is still beside him, but has moved off to the side with Hilia.

Do I bow to him? Offer my hand?

I begin to lower to my knees, but before my legs touch the marble floor, King Cane reaches out his hand. To me, and not to the crowd, he says, "There is no need to bow, Evelyn. Am I not elven like you? Does my heart not beat like yours?" He's staring so intently, my belly heats even without the wine. "Do we both not crave pleasure and the heat of another's body?" And then he addresses the crowd again. *Thank the gods.*

"I may be the King of the Kingdom of Nightmare, but respect is shown in actions and fealty. I am not any more important than you are."

My mouth must be agape because the king chuckles as he touches under my chin and closes it for me. His emerald-green eyes meet mine again, alive with life and excitement that make this all feel...*fun.*

He looks back at the crowd, but speaks to me.

"Evelyn. Tell us now. Will you do our kingdom the honor of joining my Night Shroud?"

I hesitate for just a moment. Enough that the king raises his brow at me as if he is surprised that I don't have an immediate answer to this life-altering question.

But it's not really life-altering for me, is it? This is what I'm here for; this is exactly what Odin and I planned. The option of leaving without the rune stone is not really an option at all. I swore to *my* king that I would do everything in my power to find the stone, so that is what I'll do.

I lower my head slightly. "King Cane, I accept the position on your Night Shroud, and in so doing, vow to protect you and your people." It's silent for just one second, but it feels like an eternity.

Quietly and intently, he says, "They are *our* people now, Evelyn. Welcome." The way he says this feels deeper than just a king speaking to his guardsman. It feels like a hidden message that I don't have the code to decipher. Cane just gives me a little smirk.

He directs his attention back to the attendants, and an uproar explodes from the room. I turn to the crowd and soak it all in. I may be the quiet ruin in their midst, but this attention still feels earned. I'm grateful that these people trust me. I will always put Odin first, but I also want to help them. The rune stone is the key to doing both; I just have to lie for a little longer.

When the cheers calm, and everyone is looking upon us, he continues. "My fellow people, welcome Evelyn as I have welcomed her. In the coming days, you will see her often, at the castle, in town, by my side. Take tonight and be your true selves. We are safe, we are serendipitous, we are family, and we know how to throw a ball! Now go, dance, drink, fuck. Today is a day five years in the making!" He holds his glass up before drinking the entire thing. The audience copies his motion before continuing the ruckus.

Gwen runs to my side, hugging me. "I knew that you'd join. I knew it, I knew it!"

I panic a little at her joy but conceal my fear by embracing her back and smiling along. As Gwen pulls back, I see her look up to Cane, where Hilia is still perched next to him, no smile in her eyes, whispering to Cane in a desperate attempt to get his attention. But his eyes are on Gwen.

"I'll be back. Enjoy yourself, I'll find you soon." She flashes me another smile and then goes back to Cane. The closer she gets, though, the more Hilia talks, her mouth moving frantically as she pours whatever she's saying into Cane's ear. The king looks out at the ballroom impassively, but I can tell that something is bothering him from his clenched jaw and tight grasp on the throne. Without looking at her, he waves his hand, dismissing her before Gwen is next to him. Hilia straightens abruptly, her face contorting as if it had just been slapped. Before she regains her composure, she shoots me another look of pure disdain.

Why does she hate me?

Cane takes Gwen's hand in his, and she pulls him up, angling them to the dance floor, all concern washed away from his expression. As he passes me, he brushes his knuckles across my cheek and whispers, "Save a dance for me," and then he is swept up in the heat and passion of the dance floor.

How much time is an acceptable amount before you can leave your own party?

With all the movement and undulating, the only safe place to look is up. I make my way towards the entry doors, picking up the pace as the crowd thins out, and then clash with a hard, firm body. I throw my hands up in an instant, silent surrender, still trying to avoid looking at whatever I have disrupted in my desire to flee. But a hand reaches for my chin, and tilts my head upwards until our eyes meet—extraordinary hazel eyes, like the color of the woods from home.

"Oh. It's you."

The man from the tavern releases my chin and grabs my elbow, guiding me to the dance floor. I clumsily follow. I can't see a way out of this without looking suspicious. I just want to be away from this party.

"I didn't get to introduce myself the last time we met. I'm Gabriel."

"Do you make it your prerogative to encroach on a woman's space every chance you get?" I try not to sound spiteful, but I know my smile looks more like a sneer. He just smiles to himself, one of those genuine understanding smiles that everyone dons in this insufferable kingdom. I almost ask him what he's still smiling about, when I'm suddenly aware of his warm hand on my elbow. How long has it been since a man really touched me? Since Odin touched me.

I shake my head like I'm trying to dislodge thoughts from the bookshelf of my brain. His grin spreads, revealing a row of perfectly white teeth, stark against his pink, full lips.

"What was that look for? Did you see something you like?"

My annoyance with him is instantly shattered by embarrassment. I didn't realize I had been thinking of Odin so strongly.

It's so hot in here.

I feel redness creeping down my throat and across my chest.

Gods I'm undeniably blotchy now.

I have the urge to scratch my chest. The gown is suddenly too tight and my breathing too shallow.

"You know nothing about me..."

He spins me and brings me back tightly to his body. My hand goes up to his chest as I finish the move, and *sweet gods,* the muscles on this man. As I move my hands away, I feel the shape of a pendant under his shirt. I trace the lines with my fingers, entranced by the warm hum emanating from it. Without missing a beat, he takes my fingers in his, like he didn't want me to touch the necklace.

Why am I still touching him? Was there willow root in the food?

"I know that there is something different about you. You have this...pull, that I can't make sense of."

"Excuse me?" I try to cut him off, but he doesn't stop talking.

"I know that you are not like the other people here. I know that you have been wandering around this ballroom, keeping your eyes down because the sight of all these people dancing, being *together,* is too much for you." He spins me again, and when our chests brush back together, he leans in closer. "I'm here looking for something *very* important, and every instinct in my body is telling me that *you* are the one who can help me."

I feel the color draining from my face. *Does he know about the rune stone?* I try to keep calm. "It seems you may have had too much to drink tonight, Gabriel. It was nice to meet you, but I think our dance is over."

He pulls me in so close and firm that I can smell hints of cinnamon and oak. He isn't breaking eye contact, as if he's searching my face for something. "Very well then, Evelyn," he says, just barely a whisper. He raises my hand to his mouth and brushes his lips across my knuckles before he spins me away and walks off through the crowd.

And here I am, smack dab in the middle of the chaos again with nothing to do but smooth my dress and smile.

I need a drink.

I grab a glass of mead as a servant walks by, and without thinking, I down it in one gulp. *Wait. That wasn't mead.*

I hold up my flute to the candlelight, the sides still sparkling with pink dew. *Willow root wine.*

Gwen was right. It feels like the flower petals from the garden are a part of my insides. Trailing warm caresses down my throat. The second it hits my stomach, a gush of warmth floods my body. I feel my cheeks redden, my pulse quicken. I can feel someone watching me, and my head snaps up to find Cane staring, a smile spreading on his face. He whispers something to Gwen, who smiles as they saunter over.

The effects are settling much faster than regular libations. I feel a pool of warmth growing in my core and the feeling of butterflies fluttering through my chest. The rub of my dress causes my nipples to harden, and the brush of the fabric across my taut peaks leaves me gasping for breath.

"Ah, Little Raven, it looks like you are finally ready to play."

The sound of his voice makes me clench my legs together, seeking friction. His nose flares, smelling the lust seeping off me as my pulse races and my body aches. It's like I'm fighting an uphill battle. My skin is alight with need and want.

"I do not want to play anything; I'm simply enjoying the refreshments," I say as heat blooms on my cheeks.

Fucking willow root wine.

Gwen smiles at me sweetly, clearly intoxicated. "I warned you, Evelyn." She says in a sing-song voice.

"It's not even that different from regular wine. It just tastes a little rosier. Honestly, I was expecting more." I fight the words out as I push past Cane and Gwen to head for the doors. I don't care who sees me. I need to get out of here. Now. Every person I run into, every graze of my shoulder is like fire shooting to my core. Every part of my body is oversensitive.

I stop to take a breath in the hallway, the aching want consuming me. I trudge on because that is precisely what this is, a hike through a lust-filled haze that I can't find the end to. Every door I pass, every hall I turn down, I hear the moans of ecstasy, the slapping of skin on skin, the erotic sounds driving me crazy.

I'm only a hall, maybe two from my bedchambers, when I hear a scream, "Cane!"

Oh gods, is that Gwen? Is she hurt?

I turn around, rush towards the sitting area and halt. And Gwen is most definitely *not* hurt.

Chapter 36 Evelyn

I'm standing mere feet from Gwen's sweat-slickened skin on full display while she's writhing on Cane's lap. Thick brown curls fall down her back, and she tilts her head up, letting out a sultry moan.

I can't watch this. But my body is frozen to the spot.

I shouldn't be looking at Gwen's pert breasts bouncing. I shouldn't watch as Canes's fingers graze over her taut nipples. And I shouldn't listen as needy moans fill the space between us.

But I do.

Cane's pants are pushed down around his ankles, and his white shirt is unbuttoned, allowing Gwen to slide her hands over his bare chest.

"That's it, my love, my enchantress, take what you want from me." I hear Cane groan as Gwen continues thrusting her hips, grinding into him. She tears a low growl from his mouth when she rises nearly to his tip and sinks back down, slowly, deliberately.

Candles light the sitting area, but much of the room remains shrouded in shadow. My insides war, and my feet remain leaden. *It's the damn willow root wine.*

I reach out for the entryway, my arm feeling less like an elven limb and more like a drunken eel. Somewhere between fumbling for the anchor of the entryway and shuffling my clumsy feet, I slip, just barely catching my fall on the wall.

Oh gods.

Cane and Gwen pause, the rhythm of their bodies replaced with an unbearable silence. Cane looks up at me and grins while Gwen turns her head and looks over her shoulder, latching her eyes on mine—and holds them there as she starts moving again.

Cane tilts his head back and lets out a chuckle. "So the Little Raven likes to watch?" he grabs Gwen by her hips and pulls her down harder, moving her over his lap faster while moans wail from her sweat-silken body.

The stone wall beneath my hand is cool, steadying. I don't want to move. And something deep in my belly starts to ache. Gwen closes her eyes, and her head hangs back. I focus on Cane's hands, the way they press into her hips and guide her over his hard length. Both of them dangling over the edge of ecstasy.

My breaths begin to pick up, my nipples grazing the fabric of my dress as I lean against the wall. A small mewling noise passes my lips. As if it has a mind of its own, my hand begins to trail down my body, over my abdomen, down to that writhing ache. I've never wished I were wearing less clothing more than I do now. I need the friction, the pressure over my most sensitive areas.

No! No. No. This can't be happening. What in the Underworld am I doing?

Another, more sensible part of me takes control. It's like entering into some dark private room in my mind and turning the lights on. *Thank the gods, the willow root wine must finally be wearing off.*

I stand and straighten my dress, and while the room is decidedly still spinning, I quietly walk away. Even once I'm far out of sight, I can hear Gwen's loud moan as she reaches ecstasy and Cane's growl as he finishes with her.

❧ ❧

I fumble down the hall, mortified at what I just saw, that they saw me, and worse—at how turned on I am.

As if this night can't get any worse, Hilia is walking straight towards me. Her porcelain skin on full display, only covered by swatches of red laced fabric on her breasts and *other* areas. Her dark hair hangs in long, loose curls down her back. The ensemble is complete in its seduction with a pair of black strappy heels. She is the picture of sultry pleasure. *Too bad she's nothing but venom and vanity.*

She raises her brows and shakes her head slightly, almost laughing to herself. I can't read the expression on her face fully as she starts to back away. "Isn't this just completely adorable?" She says just low enough for me to hear, and glances in the direction I just came from.

I keep my mouth shut, but her gaze digs in, demanding something. Something I can't give because I don't even know what it is.

It feels like an eternity before she turns to go, and even then, she doesn't take those hateful eyes off me. She struts away with her long legs and black heels, and slinks into the darkness like she was never even here.

Anxious tears are burning behind my eyes, but I finally make it to my bedchambers. As I close my bedroom door, remembering to lock it this time, the images of the night flood back to me. I want so badly to lie to myself. It has to be the wine. I refuse to believe that I could ever feel anything close to this unless I was enchanted somehow. Not unless I was with Odin. But my whole body *needs* release. How long has it been? I just want it to stop. I need it to stop. I need Odin. Sleep. I need to sleep.

Chapter 37 Gwen

I COULD FEEL EVELYN'S gaze before I saw it. Burning into us, her eyes locked on every movement, every breathless moan. She didn't look away—was barely able to hide her hunger. I wonder what she would have said if I'd asked her to join? But she drank the willow root wine...and no matter the heat in her eyes and the pure *want* emanating from her, I could never cross that line. Not like that. Not when I can't be sure she won't regret it.

Cane's hands treat the delicate fabric of my dress like precious rose petals as he drapes the silk onto my still glistening skin. Even once I'm fully dressed, a warm caress trails down the curve of my hips and lower back. He makes me feel like a work of art. He doesn't move until our eyes meet and we share that smile that speaks more than words ever could. I want to stay and do this a million times over, but I take his hand and lead him upstairs to his room.

While I fill my glass with cool water, Cane pours himself a deep amber spirit, the liquid catching the firelight as he swirls it in steady, slow circles. He moves toward me as he takes a sip. My own glass leaves beads of condensation trailing over my skin. I press it to the hollow of my throat. The fluttering embers of my lust still burn there, and even this icy glass can't put them out.

Cane breaks the silence.

"My enchantress, seeing your bare skin, your scent and mine clinging to your curves," he whispers into my ear as his lips start to press into the sensitive skin on my neck, "It's euphoric. No wonder Evelyn was watching. Even she couldn't take her eyes off your perfect body."

Gods, this man knows exactly what to say to make the embers inside me turn to furious flames. I reach down and take off my strappy shoes, sighing as they fall to the floor. Wiggling my toes, I brush them across the lush rug as Cane sits next to me. Swiftly, he grabs my thighs and turns my body so that my feet are right in his lap. His hands are so big that they almost envelop my foot. He starts kneading and rubbing up and down the arch. The moan I let out rivals the sounds I was making earlier.

"What do we do now, love?" His low, breathy tenor sinks into me. My body sinks deeper into the couch as his hands continue their slow, perfect work on my feet. "We gave her the week. What now?"

"Haven's Grace," I sigh, "if you keep rubbing my feet like that, I'd say we can just stay here forever and let the kingdom figure itself out."

Cane's deep chuckle rumbles through me, low and effortless. So carefree, so rich with warmth, even as it brushes up against the tension of the situation.

"We let her stay," I say evenly. "Let her keep training with The Shroud. Let her visit Sallows. I see her falling in love with our people. We have nothing to hide, so let's just not hide. We're not the monsters she was raised to believe we are." I pause, my voice softer. "And we hope that, in time, she opens up. Tells us the truth on her own. I know she will, Cane. Just a little longer."

Cane sits forward, and dark shadows billow from his hands. I can feel them rubbing my feet as if his hands never left, but he stands to face the fireplace. "And what if she doesn't tell us? What if I'm harming our people with every second she stays here?"

I brush the shadows away. I know they aren't alive, but they look sad. "One more week. One more Cane, and if she doesn't change, I will take her back to Daydream myself."

"What about the repercussions of that? The people's questions? Are we really prepared to send her back with such insight into our kingdom?"

"I'll figure it out—"

"You're not the king, Gwen, I am. And as much as I trust you, it will be me who bears the consequences of this decision." There is a long silence. I don't have his answers, and it's true, I wouldn't know what to do. I just have this feeling that I won't have to.

"I know I'm not the king. Or a queen. I don't even have magick. But I have never been wrong about a person, and I would never do anything to hurt you. You have to know that."

He turns to face me. "You're an awful adviser to the king, you know." He says with a soft grin. I sit up on the edge of the couch and clasp my hands together over my mouth so I don't squeal in relief and delight. "With any luck, Evelyn will come clean and maybe—just maybe—we can finally work *with* her—"

I barrel into him with such force that he almost tips over. "Thank you," I whisper and start to nibble at his ear.

Without warning, Cane's shadows lift my legs and wrap them around his waist. "Come on, love," he murmurs, fingers already tugging at my dress. "The night's not over yet." In one smooth motion, he peels the fabric away from my body and lays me in the center of the bed. I love being alone with him, like we belong to each other.

I watch him undress before sliding in beside me. I revel in the flurry of silk sheets and tangled limbs and Cane's sweet scent. I climb on top of him and we stare at each other for a moment. Our unspoken words dancing across the fire now raging inside us both. I don't ever want him to stop looking at me like this. I slowly raise my hips so that the velvet tip of his cock brushes against me, both of us dripping with desire, and slide down for another unforgettable ride.

Chapter 38 Evelyn

I CAN'T CLOSE MY eyes without seeing them. The sight of my intrusion seemed to spark their lust even more. The way they were moaning... Even with my palms pressed painfully to my ears, I can't block out the sounds. The worst part is I enjoyed it. Watching them together was like watching a sensual dance. Their bodies moved like they were made for each other. It planted this relentless, aching need that still lingers. There's no way I can sleep like this, even though all I really want to do is find Odin.

A nice bath will help, *has* to help.

I watch the tub fill, adding a generous amount of lavender oil and soap. Inching my toe into the hot water, I allow my body to adjust to the temperature before sliding into the bubbly bliss. *Gods, it's so soothing.* My eyes are already heavy, and my head rolls back to the rim of the tub. It smells so much like home that I don't remember falling asleep.

It's the soft chorus of chirping birds that stirs me, and my mind wakes up before my body. Eyes still closed, I stretch out with a groan, limbs heavy and slow. "How long have I been asleep?" I murmur to myself.

"You've been asleep for quite some time, my darling," a voice replies—smooth, elegant, familiar. "So peaceful… I didn't want to wake you."

His voice washes over me like a chorus of warmth.

Odin.

My Odin.

He stands above me, serene and radiant. I'm still unsure if I'm dreaming or not, but my hand meets his face—warm, soft, real. Drops of water slide down his cheek beneath my touch, trailing from where my fingers rest.

"You're here," I whisper. "You came for me."

I move closer, my body aching for his and that's when I realize this isn't my bathing chamber. I'm lying in the shallows of a waterfall, the one we dream-walked to the last time he found me. The same white dress clings to me, soaked and translucent, molding to my every curve.

Odin is wearing his full regal attire this time, all sharp lines and polished grandeur—so much like a king, and so unlike a lover.

A flush rises to my cheeks as I glance down at myself again. The soaked dress leaves nothing to the imagination. I cross my arms over my chest and begin to rise, the water growing colder by the second, biting into my skin. A sharp clinking sound breaks the silence: My teeth chattering.

"It's much colder than last time," I murmur, reaching for him still. Why hasn't he reached out for me? Warmed me with his body heat? In fact, he steps back. Straightens. His expression shifts. Gone are the soft eyes I know so well. In their place, something cold and unreadable. Almost…cruel.

"What's wrong?" I ask, voice cracking. Something must be wrong with Daydream. Odin may have been at battle while I was taking a luxurious bath. Oh gods— "What's happened?" I practically cry out.

My foot slips on the slick, algae-covered rock beneath me, and I stagger as I reach for him again. Somehow the tables have turned and it is I who desperately wants to comfort him. My hand catches only air, and I collapse onto the cold, mossy ground, the impact jolting through my knees and palms.

He looks down, so unconcerned, like I'm nothing but a rodent scrambling beneath his boots. "I tried to convince myself that I was wrong." He says, more to himself than me. "I tried to change the facts, twist them into something that I could accept. I had to be missing something." He squats, his head closer to mine, but his eyes elsewhere, like he can't bear to look at me. "And then I thought, maybe she doesn't think I'll find out. Did you think that, Evelyn?"

I want him to look at me. "Tell me what you're talking about, Odin. Whatever happened, I can fix it," I say as my breath catches. But he doesn't respond. It's like he's somewhere else and I can't reach him.

"I can hear you now," he spits. "Mocking me to that woman—Gwen." His voice is slick with venom. "You've been mocking me since the beginning, haven't you?"

"No—Odin—my love," I say quickly, rising to my feet, heart pounding. "I don't know what you think you heard, but it's not what you—just please, sit with me. Let's talk. Whatever is hurting you, I can fix it."

I take a step towards him, desperate to close the distance. *If he just looks at me, sees me, he will understand.*

"I love you, Odin," I say, voice trembling. "We can figure this out. Whatever happened—" Before I can finish, a sharp sting explodes across my cheek. I gasp, staggering backwards.

He struck me.

I press my hand to my face, the skin already throbbing. My mind can't catch up with what just happened. I stare at him in shock, barely able to breathe.

"You fucked them, Evelyn! Say it!" His voice is loud, desperate. "I can't even believe I need to have this conversation with you at all," He's trembling with fury.

"What are you talking about? Who told you-"

"I saw it! I trusted you—our people trusted you." His eyes blaze with such wild anger, I shrink back. "Did you honestly think this would go well for you? That I'd let you crawl back into my bed after you *fucked* the King of the Nightmare Kingdom?"

"Whatever it is you think you saw, I didn't sleep with them Odin—"

"So you didn't leave a party, drink willow root without me, and walk straight toward the depraved sounds of King Cane and that woman fucking each other? What part of that was for our kingdom, the wine, or the cock? How should I explain this to our people? 'Your brave and courageous queen who united our kingdom by fucking the nightmare king.'"

"That's not how it—"

"How long have you enjoyed yourself in this kingdom? The enemy's kingdom? *Our* enemies!" He screams. I can't hold back my tears. "Only since winning the trials? Or your entire life? Maybe I was blind when I fell in love with you in those woods. A foolish boy with a foolish dream. You were meant to be *my* wife. *My* queen. We were going to rule together—the power we would have wielded, what we would have conquered." He steps closer now, voice dripping with contempt.

"Maybe you never loved me at all." He shakes his head, jaw clenched. "I should kill you now for what you've done, for the sake of our Kingdom. Consider your banishment the one last act of love I can offer you."

"Odin, stop!" My voice shreds with the weight of desperation. My insides feel like they are made of sand, contained by a sieve, every spilling grain a piece of myself that will never be the same. I fall to my knees, my cheek still burning. He just needs to feel how much I love him. "Please," I whimper. "I did not sleep with anyone, Odin. Look at me. I swear it on my life. You have to believe me."

His chest heaves like he can barely deign to talk to me. "Did you forget that I can see all of you in your dreams? I'm fairly certain you knew that, considering the mind work we did to get you here. The memory practically jumped out at me when I came to meet you. When I came to meet you because I was longing for you, Evelyn, praying to the gods above that you were okay, aching to feel you in my arms. Imagine my surprise when all I found waiting for me in that pretty mind of yours was a blazing memory of you *with them*. I felt the lust that you felt, the pull that you had to join them. I watched as another man's cock slid into you. Not just any man, the Nightmare King!" He is screaming again.

"Please!" I sob, the words torn from my throat. "You're wrong, Odin. Look again, look now! You'll see you are the only one who has ever been inside me. The only one I want inside me. My body and heart are yours. I swear it."

Odin's gaze softens for a moment. For just one moment, he is the boy in the woods. My boy, my home. This whole thing was a mistake. But as I reach towards him, his expression hardens. Something in me changes, and I know this is the last time I will ever be this close to him.

His eyes are glassy, but still concise, sharp, final. His voice is so low. "When Cane learns who you truly are, I hope he throws you straight back into the Grimm Lodge where you belong."

Chapter 39 Evelyn

I WAKE UP SCREAMING through my tears.

This isn't real. It was just a dream. A *nightmare.* But when I leap from bed and rush to the washroom, I see the fingerprints blooming across my cheek in the mirror.

Pulling at my hair, I scream—a raw, guttural wail that echoes through my chamber, maybe even through the entire kingdom.

"No," I whisper, then louder and firmer. "No. You do not let this stop you, Evelyn." I can fix it. He was angry. I didn't have enough time. He'll calm down and feel our love again—*gods, my head pounds.* My heart aches. My soul feels split in two. I need to find Odin. Make him understand that what he saw wasn't real. I didn't betray him.

Fucking willow root wine. Why does he think I had sex with them? Could he feel what I was feeling?

If I made it into Nightmare on my own, I can cross the border again. I can return to Daydream. Return to Odin. I may not have found the stone yet, but he'll understand. We'll do it some other way, without being apart ever again.

I grab a worn leather satchel, shove a few essentials inside, and dress quickly. My haladie daggers are strapped to my sides in seconds.

I have no idea what hour it is, but the castle is dark. I creep down the hallways, the leather of my boots creaking with every step. Muffled moans and the slap of bodies rise behind closed doors as I pass, curling in the silence like smoke. The sounds conjure those damned memories. Images I don't want—Cane and Gwen, tangled together—and I shake my head hard, cursing them.

Most people are either lost in a lustful stupor or drunk on mead, which makes slipping out of the castle almost too easy. No one stops me. No one notices the tears. I walk through the gates without so much as a glance back at the castle. Once I'm beyond the walls, I break into a slow jog, desperate to put as much distance between King Cane and myself as possible.

The ominous wall that divides the two kingdoms cuts through the forest past Sallows, but I've never gone far enough myself to see it—not since arriving here. Still, I know it's out there, looming. Waiting.

Before I reach the town, I veer off the road and into the woods. The trees rise high above me like sentinels, ancient and indifferent. The canopy is thick—so dense that barely a sliver of moonlight reaches the forest floor. I trip often, stumble over roots and rocks, half -blind, half-lost, with no sense of direction. I pray—desperately, silently—for the gods to guide me. Gods that I don't even know if I believe in.

The further I go, the more doubt creeps in.

Should I have stayed long enough to find the rune stone—prove my loyalty to Odin that way?

No. I need to get to him. *Now.* The rune stone can wait.

The deeper I go, the colder it gets. The unforgiving forest floor is full of gnarled roots and sharp thorns. I just keep pushing. And I can feel it now—eyes, watching me from the shadows. There must be hundreds of animals out here. At one point, I think I catch a glint of metal flicker in the trees. I freeze, breath caught in my throat. But nothing moves again. Maybe it was nothing. Maybe.

The sounds in the forest fade the farther I walk. I can't hear insects; all the birds have gone silent. There's nothing at all but a suffocating stillness all around me. Something's out there, just beyond the trees—and every step I take feels like a trespass.

Panic threatens to crush me. *What was I thinking?* I had no idea how big these woods were. I was so loud. I'm going to die before I ever make it to Odin.

Suddenly, a loud crunch of leaves and the snap of breaking twigs shatter the stillness. The ground beneath me trembles. I spin in frantic circles, but it's just an endless dark cage of pines. Another crunch, closer this time. My heart is slamming into my chest. The vibrations echo in my bones, and instinct takes over. I run.

But the forest has other plans. A root, black as death, curves just enough that my boot snags on the bark. My body crashes to the ground, but I scramble back to my feet. The night is so thick I can barely see my own hand in front of my face. Then, *crack*, I slam into a tree. My ears hum. The impact ricochets through my body. I hit the ground hard, landing on my tailbone, and my head snaps back, striking a rock. Stars explode behind my eyes. My vision spins. Dizziness washes over me, dragging nausea in its wake. I roll to the side and retch, the sweet pastries from the ball coming up in bitter heaves.

Panting, I reach back and press trembling fingers to my scalp. It's sticky with what can only be blood.

Another crunch—louder, closer—splinters the air. Branches snap, the ground trembles beneath my feet.

I force myself upright, clutching my throbbing head. I try to run, but my balance is gone. My legs move sluggishly, unresponsive to my commands. I stumble and sway, blindly reaching for tree trunks to steady myself as I push through the dense vegetation.

The sound is gaining. Whatever's behind me is closing in fast. I can't outrun it.

A low grumble rises into a growl, deep and guttural. The moment I feel its breath hot and damp on the back of my neck, I know I've lost this chase.

The buttons on my holster snap open as I draw my haladie daggers. I spin to face whatever's hunting me. The world tilts, vision swimming, and my skull pulses with searing pain. I feel the blood running down my neck, thick and steady, clouding my senses with every drop.

I strike with one dagger and drop into a fighting stance. The creature lets out a grating roar as my blade slices across its taut, purple flesh. It stands just a breath away, towering over me, an immense and monstrous figure. As I stare up at it, only one thought comes to mind: *this must be what the giants in my father's stories looked like.*

The beast is massive and menacing, its body sheathed in deep-purple, leathery skin. Red eyes burn with a fierce glare. It opens its mouth to bellow again, revealing row upon row of razor-sharp teeth. I slash out once more, aiming for its abdomen, but it rears back and strikes. Talons sprout from its hands, and as it swipes, they rake down the sides of my body and tear into my abdomen. But it's not just the pain in my abdomen that clouds my senses. There's also a sharper, burning pain in both my shoulders that races down to my hands. I must have hit that tree harder than I thought.

I collapse to the ground, the fresh lacerations and pounding injury to my head making it impossible to stay upright. The world spins and blurs around me, but my mind suddenly focuses on one sure fact: This isn't just any creature, it's a Night Terror Golem. I swear I see a cruel smile curl across its face as it raises a massive arm to strike again. Before it lands its final blow, its eyes widen, and thick black blood starts to ooze from its mouth. Protruding from the golem's chest is a bolt from an arrow, and another in its throat.

I didn't even hear the twang of the bowstring.

The golem slams down beside me, the impact shaking the ground like a falling tree. From the corner of my eye, I catch movement, the crunch of sticks and leaves drawing closer. I have no fight left in me. Just before I close my eyes, I see my fingertips glowing. It's gone in less than a second, but I saw it. *Gods, I hit my head hard.* I take one last steadying breath and surrender to whatever fate awaits me.

A figure appears closer, and with the snap of their fingers, a small torch flickers to life. I can't make out their features—covered head to toe in black, a hood pulled low, hiding their face.

They step closer and kneel beside me. "Shh, I've got you. It's going to be okay." Gentle fingers brush the hair from my face, and I feel my body lift from the ground.

I whimper as the jagged wounds across my abdomen stretch painfully.

"This might hurt, but you'll be alright, Evelyn." The hooded figure rises, cradling me in his arms. "We need to get you somewhere safer." Their hood falls as they move, and I can see their familiar face.

I can't help but gasp, "What are you doing here?" But it's all I can say before darkness swallows me.

Epilogue

I jolt upright.

My mind is a churning pool of mush, and my stomach is a vicious sea of liquid. I can't even stand before I stumble back to my knees. A bone-deep weakness holding me down. My raven sits on a branch beside me.

"It's good to know you were watching over me, old friend."

I can still see the remnants of grime and blood where I touched her hand. *I touched her hand.* I see flashes of brambled walls and dragons.

I wanted to stay. I *needed* to stay, but my gods-forsaken mind would not allow it. It's been too long since I walked in a dream, since I answered a prayer. I'm a fool to think that I could maintain my power after so much time spent forgetting. *Being forgotten.*

The people think that it's the gods who hear their prayers and create the miracles. But it hasn't been the gods in centuries. And me? My mind has been nothing but a murky husk of what it once was. I haven't heard anything besides my own self-pity in years.

Until tonight. But that can't be. There was too much that I encountered. Too much that I walked through. I look around and find a coating of leaves covering my body; when I move, all my joints ache. I reach up to rub my eyes, and when my hand reaches my face, I feel my beard has grown longer than it's ever been.

How long was I asleep?

I think back to my dream-walk. That elven woman seemed so familiar but so broken. It's no wonder her voice reached me. She had gone beyond desperation, beyond fear or pain. She became something more in that moment, something I can't describe. And she called to me.

Even when I was able to hear many prayers, even at the height of my power, I could rarely materialize in a dream.

And yet, she faced no problem. She stormed into my mind, screaming and begging. There was something different about it. Something that made me feel connected. And it made it easy to find her in an instant.

Her face is permanently etched into the front of my mind. I will never forget the striking similarity to my love. My *one*. It was enough to make me hesitate, to make whatever pieces of a heart I have left crack into a thousand more pieces. A few parts of her were unmistakably her own, but the blue in her eyes. I've only ever seen it before in Serabeth's.

I've learned, with all this time, that tears do nothing to soothe the pain, and yet I fight to keep them down anyway. Without her, every moment is a fresh wound. She was the color in everything I saw, and now, even the vibrant sun at dawn is the same painful gray.

What have I amounted to? I ruined everything. *Everything.* I had forgotten that I had power at all. We had forgotten each other, my power and I. But somehow it reached me. It called to me in that dream.

She called to me.

To Be Continued...

Acknowledgements

This book has been nearly three years in the making. What began as a series of unhinged text messages slowly grew into late-night writing sessions, and we could not be happier with how far this story has come.

We would never have made it this far without the support of our families. From our husbands, who patiently listened as we talked through plot holes, to our littles, who were just as excited as we were to see our first proof copy arrive in the mail, they have cheered us on through every step of this whirlwind journey. We can't forget Becca's dad! And yes he did read EVERY chapter. His crass and colorful comments kept the editing process interesting to say the least. Thank you for keeping us laughing.

Writing this book was a steep learning curve, and we are endlessly grateful for the support of the incredible author and bookish creator community. Jenessa was the very first person to read our truly awful first draft, and we cannot thank you enough for your guidance and encouragement as we refined ATOD into what it is today. Jenessa, along with Shelia, have endured many very long voice messages filled with panic over navigating the indie author world and we honestly would not be here without either of you. Gina! thank you for championing us and believing in this story from the beginning.

We would also like to thank the people who helped bring this book to life. Peter, thank you for creating a cover that so perfectly captures the essence of the story, we could not imagine ATOD without your vision. And to our incredible editors, Kelly and Tabby, thank you for your patience, expertise, and for making this book stronger in every possible way. We are endlessly grateful for your care and attention to detail.

To our amazing beta readers -Jenn, Teressa, Jenny, and Alyssa- thank you for helping two slightly unhinged women chase the dream of publishing a fantasy romance. Your feedback was invaluable, and we are so grateful for each of you.

And last, but certainly not least, our ARC readers. We were blown away by the number of readers who asked to early-read ATOD, and we have cried more times than we can count over your outpouring of support. From emails and DMs to social media posts and reviews, your encouragement has meant the world to us. We truly could not do this without you.

Thank you!

~Remy Steross (Becca and Amy)

About the authors

Becca and Amy make up Remy Steross. They have been best friends since 7th grade. Becca was always a sports star, and Amy leaned more towards theater and music. But there was never a shortage of late nights, mischief, and imagination. Now, years later, they have poured their magic together to write epic tales, bringing to life unforgettable characters full of romance, passion, and a touch of the girlhood that built their friendship. Their partnership weaves together richly imagined worlds, exciting characters, and steamy romance. Every part of the story is a true collaboration of friendship and imagination.